Afsaneh Knight was born in December 1978. She lives in London with her husband and two children.

# *Slaughterhouse* HEART

## Afsaneh Knight

**BLACK SWAN**

TRANSWORLD PUBLISHERS
61–63 Uxbridge Road, London W5 5SA
A Random House Group Company
www.rbooks.co.uk

**SLAUGHTERHOUSE HEART**
**A BLACK SWAN BOOK: 9780552774659**

First published in Great Britain
in 2008 by Doubleday
a division of Transworld Publishers
Black Swan edition published 2009

Addresses for Random House Group Ltd companies outside the UK
can be found at: www.randomhouse.co.uk
The Random House Group Ltd Reg. No. 954009

The Random House Group Limited supports The Forest Stewardship
Council (FSC), the leading international forest certification organisation.
All our titles that are printed on Greenpeace approved FSC certified paper
carry the FSC logo. Our paper procurement policy can be found at
www.rbooks.co.uk/environment

Typeset in 11/16pt Giovanni Book by
Falcon Oast Graphic Art Ltd.
Printed in the UK by CPI Cox & Wyman, Reading, RG1 8EX.

2 4 6 8 10 9 7 5 3 1

for my parents
Sabiha Rumani Malik    Andrew Stephen Bower Knight
who are my heroes

(for a book is a song)

From the Author's Preface to *Kaas* by Willem Elsschot

# Slaughterhouse HEART

# PART ONE

PART ONE

# James

# 1

In London it's raining mulch, and James Hallow is being moved from St Dympna's Hospital to St Margaret's Hospice. He lies in a nervous no man's land between the two places, not sure of anything but the drizzle on the ambulance windows. He sees ghosts outside the glass, suspended in a purgatory of rain, like dead rats pickled in laboratory jars. Like gobstoppers in jars on shelves.

It's dark, five p.m. winter dark, dark as the middle of the night. Streetlights pus pools of neon yellow; the evening is lit by cheap institutional light, is one big hospital.

James expects his breath to form a cloud above him, but it doesn't, and he remembers in a small voice that he is not outside. He is inside – an ambulance – strapped – to a bed on wheels – covered – in blankets. He pulls at a blanket, to be sure of it.

Oh. Oh. Something is coming for him, he knows it. There's a stranger's hand pressed into the small of his back, he can feel it. Darklings in the night, shadows in the day, waiting for him, wanting him.

This is the thing: James's brain is determinedly dying. His body resists, clutching at blankets at life in an unthinking panic. But his brain? – great clods of it are breaking away and squashing themselves against the inside of his skull.

The jigsaw of his brain has for some time been loose like this, faulty, jangling like a bunch of caretaker's keys. But in days past this only showed itself behind the closed doors of home, only pressed its angry thumbs into the flesh of those who stood inside, wife and child. Outside, for the most part, nobody could tell, nobody would know. There were bills paid, waste cans emptied, a job done. Only in the corridors of home did the loose brain lash out, and wound, and pull, and tyrannise.

For this James, the landscape has largely been a fog. There was the rare clear day, when eyes opened to the unexpected and blinding brilliance of the sun, to the filigree of leaves on branches, teeth in smiles, glistening like pearls, fresh from the water in the mouth of his son. Then the world pushed its glory in on him, every mote, every gravel of it, each song of the ice cream van, each whisper as a fingertip brushed over the gossamer pages of a bible. Good God, it was a spectacle of incense and heather those days, a riot of retina, a carousel of loud, shouted life.

But then the mists would spectral back over the gorse, tendril back through the damp Edwardian walls of the suburbs, and the party was over, the shapes receded back into their coffins, and life was, largely, a fog.

Why was this mould creeping up James's soul? Where did this damp rot start? After all, nobody's born this way.

Well. Here is a fat paramedic, a sorry advertisement for the health industry. Beside him is a folder, closed, and a clipboard, the clip of which holds down a form, all about James. We can read: TRANSFER FROM: *St Dympna's Hospital*. TRANSFER TO: *St Margaret's Hospice*. PATIENT DETAILS: SURNAME: *Hallow*. GIVEN NAMES: *James Meredith*.

Then times, dates, smudges of glob from the biro. OCCUPATION: *Retired*.

Retired.

Retired how? Retired from what?

A retired butcher is a different man from a retired baker or candlestick-maker. A retired tinker will not be the same person as a retired tailor, or soldier, or sailor.

*Retired* tells us nothing, and the fat paramedic's paper tells us nothing worth more. But the face tells. It's evident when you look at this face, dented and scuffed, what it has retired from. It is pummelled, poleaxed –

James Hallow has in his history taken some smacks. Bones broken many times over, bones almost flattened. His muscles have taken mashings, punches, splittings, and inflammations. His nose has been pressed hither, thither, sideways, and into its cavity.

James was, for too long, a boxer. Even though it's not, as they say, *rocket science*, no one official has yet put their finger on it – that this is what started the brain bawling and falling apart: the thumps to the head. From the guy in the other corner, with the gloves, the fists. Those cranial smashes – merciless – ding-ding-ding. Howling knuckles, crunching through the air. It seems obvious – Disney could not have drawn a cartoonishly clearer boxer's face than James's – and yet no doctor has thought to question the reasons for his craziness, to take a good look at the battered mug of him and do some sums.

A fine boxer James Hallow was, but a soft skull, a skull of soft, smashable bone. Crumbly, crashable cranium. His was a human head, made by God. And so, once, twice – three, four times – punches shaved skin away from his brain's surface, scuddering brainskin irretrievably into the puddle of his neck.

Nope, the doctors at St Dympna's, a hospital for the mad where, up until the moment of this ambulance journey, James has been a resident for three, almost four years, didn't think to go deducing. Didn't think to poke in the cracked, scuffed head. They are not as curious as us. Nor need they be – one well-behaved lunatic is much the same as another, in terms of tax-payers' money. And now James is going to die, anyway. So.

*Parkinson's*, the doctors said, and then *Alzheimer's*, and then a few words were scribbled in the margin, like *paranoid* and *delusional*. When they saw the word *retired*, saw the lopsided, put 'em up face, they didn't think to ask, retired from what?

Were they to have done so, they would have done away with spectator sicknesses, and found that James's is a fighting disease:

Boxer's Dementia, *Dementia pugilistica*. They would have found that James is Punch Drunk.

Thirty-six years ago, before mental hospitals and medication or any such things were a part of his life, James's left foot flops behind him like dead wood as he walks back to the pub table. He sits, with a thump, drinks from his dark beer, and takes his tobacco pouch from his pocket. He must concentrate, now. He places a cigarette paper in his left hand, which is not steady, which is swaying from side to side like a scythe. This will take some attention. He pulls a small wad from the tobacco cluster, and holds it above the waiting, wobbling paper. He focuses, trying to slow the move-ment of his hand, and lets go of the tobacco pinch. It floats down into his palm and lands a neat centimetre

19

away from the paper, remaining in the shape pressed by his thumb and index finger. At the touch of it his left hand jumps like a frog, as if it has been scorched. The tobacco and paper drift to the table.

'Fuck it,' says James.

'You're pissed, mate,' says one of his companions. 'Yeah, and after one pint,' says the other. 'The middle-weight's more of a lightweight,' says the first one, and then they laugh.

James feels heat rushing to his face. 'Fuck off, both of you,' he says. 'I may have had a drink, but I'm not drunk.'

'Mate, you can barely walk straight,' says one. 'Yeah, do you want some help with that, mate?' says the other, motioning with his chin towards the unrolled cigarette, the paper and the tobacco resting humiliatingly on the table. And then they laugh.

James doses himself with beer. This shambling of the hand, and shimbling of the foot, it will pass, as it has passed before. It comes, this shameful dragging and quivering, and then it passes. He will cramp his fingers against the pub stool until it does, as it will, it will pass.

The mortification, though, may not pass with it. James's shame is a thing that sticks.

The trembling and bobbing of the left hand and dead wood no good left foot have happened too often now. They are a regularity, every other day. It makes no sense. He's not sick. And although not a boy, he's nonetheless not yet left his prime – thirty-three and still winning fights. Maybe it's a trapped nerve, like before, when the nerve got pinched on the right side of his back. But that was a whole rage of pain, even into his toes, whereas there's no pain with this.

It will pass. He knows it will pass.

It will pass like urine into the water of his life. Already it has begun to seep.

*Dear God,*

says James before each match, in the dressing room,

*I believe in you. Let me win this fight.*

This simple prayer has been said for seven years, and so the words are robotically gibbered. But now there is an add-on. A postscript which James prays more passionately than he has ever prayed anything:

*Dear God,*

says James, Prayer Mark 2,

*Make my hand stop shaking, and my foot stop dragging.*

This is a hard prayer. A fearful, confused prayer.

*Amen.*

Well, the hand didn't stop. The foot didn't stop. Say what you may about prayers prayed hard, but the hand and the foot got worse.

Everything got worse.

Until one morning the second hand finds James alone in the house, as he always is these days, because his wife is dead.

21

When he wakes, when his eyes open, there seems to be an indentation in the bed next to him, from where Hannah has just got up. There seems to be a curve down into the mattress, which must have held Hannah's body this night past, and now she must be downstairs making the tea and making the toast and opening up the curtains and windows, to get the air in.

Except, no. Because the curtains were never shut – the light comes in unfiltered, on to James's eyes. If Hannah were still here, she would have closed the curtains last night, so as to open them this morning.

But, no. The curtains are open, as they will be throughout the house.

And these days, now that Hannah is not here, the house feels sticky. The tabletop tacks to your fingers, and to plates and glasses. A few days ago, whenever it was, a glass with a stem stuck to the table, and when James tried to tug it free it snapped – snap! – like that. His fingers closed around the bulb, and it crushed itself. There were bits of the glass on the table, and bits sticking to his palm, although they didn't break his skin. They were just peppered there, like honeycomb.

Today is the same. The sheets feel fatty. The hollow is in the bed next to him, but no one was ever in it.

James goes out on to the street, in his coat. He walks slowly, because he believes that if he walks slowly the breakdown is less likely to come. He will walk to the

22

corner shop, where there is a nice man with dark skin and a moustache who helps him find his money. What James does is hold out the coins he's got, and the man takes what he needs, and James takes home juice and bread and sometimes a packet of ham.

He walks, sure at least of the steps in front of him, left, right, left, right, and of the fridge in the corner shop that has inside it ham, and cheese, and milk. But then, unexpected and perplexing, a football comes falling, and lands just to James's right, wedged between the pavement and the wheel of a car. James looks at it, and feels slightly afraid.

'Oi,' says a voice. 'Mate. Can you throw us our ball back?'

James sees a head and hands and body of a boy through the mesh of a fence.

The boy has stripes of facial hair streaked across his cheeks. The tip of his nose is raw and pinkish. The rest of his skin is fluorescent, chicken nugget white.

James looks at him, and then further back to the two other boys. One is in a cap. The other is in a football shirt, with vertical black and white stripes.

'Mate,' says the first boy, 'our ball. It's right there by your foot. Next to the car.'

This boy is nothing like his son. This boy is nothing like his Jamie.

'Bloody hell,' he says under his breath. 'Old nutter.' The other two laugh. He puts his hands around his mouth like a loudspeaker. 'Could – you – throw – our ball – back—'

How different it is, the inside to the out.

James's inside: collects the ball in dread, a hostage to the fits and tremors that come as unpredictably as wasps. The inside wonders how – *how* – it will strike the ball over the fence, that is higher than a man. The inside with desperation chants, *God is beside me, God is beside me*, and thankfully does not stop to count the unanswered prayers of the past.

The outside: picks the ball up slowly, in one arm. Turns to the fence, and looks over it. Pitches the ball into the air, and watches it sail over.

'Nice one, granddad,' says the boy behind, in the cap.

They turn away from James, and begin their game again. Kicking the ball between them, heading it, knocking it with their chests.

James watches this gentle game, that does not seem competitive, even though the boys look so hard.

They are not at all like Jamie.

Why isn't Jamie playing this game?

Why doesn't James's head contain a single memory of his Jamie, playing, kicking, chasing, catching a ball?

James takes his two hands and places them, his fingers spread, on either side of his skull. He presses into his hard head.

One of the boys has noticed, and motions to the others. They look around, until the one with the loudspeaker hands shrugs. They go back to their game.

James knows he must get home. He can no longer be outside. He cannot make it to the juice ham bread shop.

His hands shake unlocking the front door, but not with the palsy this time – with something closer to his central string. He drops the keys, twice, smatter, on to the ground.

Finally inside, he sits, on the left-hand side of the sofa, where he has always sat, although not always so alone, and the days take on the whitish wash of weeks and months, and everywhere James looks, these days weeks months, he sees flashes of his son.

For his son was in this house, once. Touched everything within it, watching, sitting, quietly, thinking, looking up at James with those eyes, hooded by lashes, but never playing.

He did all those things, but he never plays. Why?

James knows the answer, and he sees his Jamie everywhere.

# 2

When James was a boxer they called him The Sidewinder. But unlike other boxers and their nicknames, he never took it up. He never allowed it into his dressing room, on to his robe, or into the ring. Of course, he couldn't stop people from calling him Sidewinder – indeed, he didn't try to – and as aliases went it was a good one. The punches that got him knockouts were the punches that came in slamming hard from the side. He would make a rapid diagonal lunge, feel his fist on the side of his opponent's head, and then spring backwards, fast. In some ways, it was a counterintuitive movement, a foolhardy one that went against conventions of footwork and made him vulnerable. But with his speed it won him fights, it racked up KOs, and it was his signature. It came instinctively to him, and couldn't be trained out; he'd started fighting too old to be trained out of his way.

When James started ratching up the rankings and the press started writing up his fights, he learnt that a sidewinder was also an American rattlesnake:

> *Hallow, aptly named The Sidewinder, snaked across the ring in diagonal bursts, seeming almost to slide on his feet . . . planted the knockout punch on the right side of Rabid Roy's head . . . Taylor must have wished that Hallow had a rattle at the end of his tail, so he might at least have heard him coming . . . slithering up the rankings towards the title shot that must be on its way.*

Bang. Smack. Wallop.

Hiss.

In truth, James was flattered by the name. It wasn't part of the crude streetspeak that British boxers normally got tarred with – *Catcall, Welter, Rabid Roy* – but had instead an international cadence to it, a higher class sound, a ring of the open plains and goldmines of the United States, perhaps? A promise of great things to come? It was a nickname for the history books. It spoke with that kind of sound.

Still, though, he wouldn't take it on.

James was well liked: an Englishman of the educated working class, who drank at the local, but only to jollity, not to excess. He wasn't flash. He laughed loudly. Didn't wash with nonsense. But his refusal to assume his Sidewinder tag may have crimped his

27

popularity a little. It smacked of the high and mighty, and as a fighter this dented his support.

When the man comes out on his side of the arena, and your heart is with him, and you cheer, and he punches his gloves and shrugs his shoulders, it's a true and full feeling. His name is sewn across his back, and it is the name you have given him in the pub and in the pit. The name on his back makes him yours, brings your heart into your mouth with pride and right-feeling, you can almost taste the metal. He is yours, and you carry him on your shoulders.

James liked Sidewinder, it was a cut above. But, still, he wouldn't take it. He was James Hallow, his full name James Meredith Hallow, that's who he was. If his own clean name mottled his popularity, so be it. He was James Hallow, stubborn with destiny, and he would swing his arm under no other name.

For two and a half years, his star was on the ascendant. James won fights, and fights, and bigger fights, and soon was in the race for going international. He won the British title in early 1969, and began to fight in Europe. America, full of riches, was in sight. America! Big cars and blondes. Hamburgers and cowboys. Money spilling, swilling, rivering into oceans.

Late the same year Hannah gave birth to a son, christened James, called Jamie. The best boy ever born. James celebrated with champagne and cigars. Life was bursting in all directions.

Until a few months later, early 1970, when aged thirty-three James lost as challenger to the European title. In mid 1970, he lost the British title. He fought for two more years, retiring after a white-hot humiliation at the hands of a mediocre opponent.

James had come to professional fighting a few years too late – in boxing years, he was an old man, and slowing down. But the poisonous fact bubbling underneath his age was that his brain was not holding up. For nearly a year already James's leg had had bouts of losing feeling and dragging behind him, and his hand had already had small tantrums of jiggery-pokery-juddering. But until this last fight the episodes had been controllable, James had thought, not serious.

Twenty seconds into the second round, James lost control of his hand, saw it in front of him trembling, swinging like a jack-in-the-box. It would not respond. He felt like a mute. He could not raise his fist to shield himself. One side of his head was open.

He took four punches, uh, uh, uh, uh, fell to the floor, rolling on to the dead arm and twisting his forearm backwards.

He had to submit. It was the first resignation of his career, a career which was now plainly over.

They all crowed *Age*, and a few years later the doctors boomed *Parkinson's*.

Except in addition, unsaid but there regardless, were the early stages of Boxer's Dementia – which would condemn James to life in a distending and contracting smog. It would seep in to the corner of his vision, so that the edges of things were often cloudy. He would begin to find that when people spoke (normally his son) their mouths would move silently, and the sound would follow after: out of synch, like a badly dubbed movie, like Concorde's famous sonic boom. There were sounds inside him crawling to get out. Sounds as ugly as worms and money-blonde rivers.

All boxers got hit, and most survived with flattened noses and slow speech. But James's brain was chalkier, damper, more unlucky than most, and by 1970 was neatly butchered. It warped and frayed and flipped itself over like a pancake. It would get stuck to the ceiling and then land soggily on James's face: that's how it felt. Then the shame would set in, and the fury would set out, and the wife and son would shrink into corners.

Undiagnosed Boxer's Dementia, secret Punch Drunkenness, was a life of eggshells on which Hannah and Jamie had lived, electrified by anxiety. When the eggshells cracked, as they had to, punishment came as an elbow in the ribs or head, threats, belittling, shoves, and the constant dread of James's malign and powerful God. Hannah wished – she no longer prayed – for the onset of the reeling, alcoholic-seeming wobbling fits, as at least no petty violence was possible when James was suffering from one of these.

They had some days – one day, say, out of thirty –

when things were different. Maybe James had slept at an unusual angle those nights, and a chunk of his brain that had been hanging scrawny on a thread fell back into its designated place, long enough for the fog to lift.

Then slices of happiness were offered, that Jamie, still a child, was confused and exhilarated by, and Hannah was grief-struck and exhausted by. They reminded her, as if she were a very old lady, of what her life had once been. But how could it last? when during the next night, another clod of James's brain would wriggle from its place and fall irrevocably into the pea soup.

Prayer had started off self-serving for James. He had recited his prayer-poems as a child recites wish lists to Father Christmas. Dear God, Let me win this fight. Dear God, Make my hand stop shaking.

But one day, in syncopated beat with an uncontrollable bout of shuddering and gimbolling, the God-talk became something more. James felt it rumbling within him like a great truth. He knew it was real.

Here's what happened.

A week after he lost his last fight, a week after it was made luridly clear to him that he could not fight any longer, James saw a monster at the edge of his bed.

It was a small, ragged thing, covered in a film of what looked like plaster dust. Underneath the plaster dust there was a transparent yellow mucus, covering skin so raw it must have been burnt. Three layers to this creature, dust, and slime, and burnt meat. There was a smell about it, too – it was the smell that had actually woken James – of something terrifying and black beyond description.

As James's lower legs and hands began to shake, waking Hannah from her mouse-like sleep, snuffle snuffle, he knew, with immediate clarity, that this thing was a Devil. One of God's devils. And it was here with him for a reason.

As the minutes passed and the shaking subsided and the small deformed thing remained in the room, with a bloody expression that suggested it was waiting for something, James let out of his mouth words he remembered from the Bible: *their land shall be soaked with blood, and their dust made fat with fatness.*

These words came from nowhere.

James prayed, certainly, he believed, certainly: but he was no Bible scholar. He had no Bible in his head, great tracts or small verses. He had never, before this moment, been able to quote any of either Testament. So he could only presume that these colossal words just uttered had come from somewhere greater.

It was so. These dusty, bloody, devilish words had come from somewhere greater. They had come from a secret place that had descended into James's soul like God's terrible angels. Like The Host.

He said the words again, feeling gigantic as he did.

*Their land shall be soaked with blood, and their dust made fat with fatness.* He was ringing with the weight of them, the urgency of them. Hannah was sitting up in her nightdress, too amazed to be afraid.

God had arrived.

And from then on, God, James's God, grew larger and larger in the Bolan Street house, like a bulging mushroom. God was taking over the lampshades and festooning out a murky God-light of menace and irrationality. God was baking himself into biscuits, so that the jar reeked of him and his warnings when it was opened. God was ballooning in the toothpaste tube, rancid peppermint; peeling up the wallpaper like damp, glutinous snot; the taste and smell of him spread its threat everywhere.

– James,
  says Michael Antrim, the doctor,
– this is not something I can fix.
  James leans forward in his chair, resting his elbows on his wide-apart knees, his hands knitted together in their centre. He stares at the floor.
– I have an idea of what it could be, and I need to refer you to a specialist.
  James is flexing his hands now, extending and balling his fingers, as if preparing punches. But he gives no word. No response.
  Dr Antrim sighs,

- James, I'm sorry.

  James looks up from the floor.

- What exactly are you sorry for, Michael?

  Dr Antrim has known James Hallow for ten years, and knows how to choose his words.

- Sorry that I can't give you the All Clear.

- Why do I need to see a specialist? Tell me what this is, and what I need to do to get rid of it. I don't need to see some specialist. Waste of fucking time.

  There's a small ball of fear growing in James's hands. They are starting to feel clammy.

- It sounds like you've fought your symptoms brilliantly already, James. But you said it yourself, they're getting worse.

- Symptoms? So they're suddenly symptoms?

- I can't diagnose this, James. That's why I need to refer you.

- To someone who *can* diagnose this.

- Yes.

- And what will they diagnose?

- I've only an idea, James, an inkling. I can't give you anything with certainty.

- Don't fuck me around, Michael.

  James has sat back in his chair. His heart is thundering.

- James, I'm going to ask you to see a consultant, and he can take a look at everything, and be clearer with you.

- Don't fuck me *around*, Michael. What specialist? Who are you going to send me to?
- A doctor. A professor – Charles Hammle is his name, if you want it.
- And what is Charles a professor of?
- He is a professor of neuromuscular disease.
- Don't fucking waste my time, Michael, for fuck's sake. You're telling me I have a fucking *disease*?
- James, listen to me. Disease is just a term. But what's happening with you, the shaking, the fits you describe, is happening because of some,
*pause*,
miscommunication between your nerves and your muscles. It may well simply be that there is some nerve damage, that needs to be identified and con- tained, if possible. In which case we're worrying for nothing. But I cannot tell you one way or the other. I can't diagnose this. I'm a GP, James. All I can do is send you to see Professor Hammle.
- Nerve damage.
- That would be what to hope for.
- From the fights.
- If it *is* nerve damage, then that would be the logical cause. If it's something else, then the consultant will be able to diagnose with certainty.
James listens.
Alright. He feels soothed. *Nerve damage*. Okay.
Alright. Okay.

So Dr Antrim writes a letter, writing longhand the words *deterioration*, *possible*, and *Parkinson's*. He only has half the story, though – half the symptoms – for James has no way José told him of the trembling visits he has been receiving from the small satan with the long arms, or of the prodigious Testament words that fly into him from above. No one knows of those outside number 24 Bolan Street.

Michael Antrim's letter arrives on the desk of Charles Hammle, an appointment is made, and James goes to the hospital in Queen Square, storming and sneering and fearful; yet suddenly subdued and reverent once in front of the professor, who wears a waistcoat, and ministers from a dark, impressive office. The professor asks questions. James answers what he can honestly. What he can't, he answers evasively. He can't give the truth that God has entrusted to him. That Truth is his own.

James, according to his answers, shows no signs of dementia. Certainly no inklings of schizophrenia, and not even a whiff of a personality disorder. So there is no referral to a psychiatrist. It's not even thought of. Not one of James's answers or hesitations betrays the fact that the punches he had taken for eight years had been working evil in this spongy human skull, stirring and snarling up the fragile mental jigsaw.

James only gives evidence on: wobbling hands, dead

legs, can't even light cigarettes at times. Body won't listen to command centre. Body in revolt. Wasn't passed to fight anymore. Professor Hammle writes everything down.

Obligingly, twenty minutes into the meeting, James's left arm starts quivering and increases its quivering until it insurrects into a full convulsion. Degrading and panic-inducing in this hushed, learned place. But handy for the professor.

Professor tells James, not without kindness, but fore-mostly in a matter-of-fact way, that he suspects with virtual certainty that James is suffering from Parkinson's Disease.

There are more tests to run. Professor will need to see Mr Hallow again, but Mr Hallow must prepare himself for the likely reality.

James leaves Queen Square, his fate sealed, his eyes bulging, his chapter closed.

He could have told Dr Antrim or Professor Hammle of the God-monster, black like burnt wood and quick as a dart, that now visited him regularly. He could see it sometimes in the corner of his eye, peering around the door, when he was at the table eating, or watching tele with Hannah. 'Psssht,' he'd say to it, out of the crook of his mouth, signalling for it to leave when there were others in the room.

But he told no one. Those around him knew of the growing presence of GOD in his life (hard to miss,

37

especially as it came with capital letters and rough handling) but nothing of God's fetid wee visitor. The small, slimy devil was a secret.

Doctors' forms, notes, letters, and conclusions remained free from hallucinations, apparitions, delusions, and deliriums. James Hallow told them nothing. It was his secret. His Truth. They only had the shaking, the fits, and the loss of coordination to go on. Of course they had noted that James had been a professional boxer – of course they had – these men were *eminent*, for God's sake – and that frequent bludgeoning of the skull may well have contributed to the onset of the disease, and may well have caused independent damage.

But the gargoyles pitching tents in the folds of James's brain, the neural beasties, bivouacked onward undetected. God had shown them to James and James alone, and no one else must know. Professor Hammle would have to make his diagnosis without them.

Had James described his devil to his son, Jamie, he might have discovered with some surprise that his monster bore uncanny resemblance to Jamie's monsters – childhood bogeymen that haunted and tormented the small, lonely boy, lived in the wall outside his bedroom. And looked much like his father's misshapen friend.

It is as if the monsters had first visited the son, and

receiving no succour from him had fingernailed themselves down the hallway into the father's room. Jamie wouldn't let them in – would rather wet his bed and grow tough and angry than open his mind to them – so they weevilled their way into his father's soggier head. And there they grew, like maggots. There they stayed, somehow to be confused with God. God comes a'singin' with his terrible Truth. With a headachey drum around his neck like a tin soldier. Rat-a-tat-tat.

James went to church once, and was unmoved, the words were just words. But he started reading the Bible, right from page 1. He even read the introductions, actually, with all those xxxivs. The television would be firmly switched off, and James would read in the silence, body taut, eyes gleaming.

For the first few days of this, Hannah sat in her opposite corner of the sofa, twitching nervously, watching her husband while trying to look like she wasn't watching him. When it was clear that his plan of action was to sit slowly turning pages of the Bible, nothing more, and that she may as well be anywhere else, feeling less nervous, she moved to the kitchen, and sat at the table reading the *Radio Times*, or sipping with small bubbles at a cup of tea, or just looking down at the shiny tablecloth and thinking nothing much. Once, she found herself unexpectedly crying, and a single fat tear fell from her bowed head into her teacup with enough force to cause tea to splash up in droplets on to her chin. Hannah wiped the tea away with her hand. Crying wouldn't do.

There is a woman pressed up against James's chest, and it's not his wife.

This woman has sat in a ringside seat throughout the fight, watching and gasping and titillated as every punch fell.

Hannah, who *is* James's wife, was not at the fight. Hannah was at home, as always, imagining the fury that may be falling on her husband's body. And imagining was bad enough. She couldn't be there to see.

'Don't you want to see me fight?' asks James.

Hannah shakes her head, looks at the floor.

'Why not?'

'I couldn't.' She closes her eyes. Her naked husband is on her eyelids, fragile and bare, his jaw being pounded to powder.

James doesn't understand. His brow is dense.

'Don't you want to see me win?' he asks.

All James knows is what it would mean to him, to have his wife there. When his hand is pulled up into the air – *triumph*. And more – when his breathing goes, and he has to shake his head from side to side, so hard he almost breaks his neck, to keep oxygen going in and out, to keep from suffocating. At a moment like this, James has found himself scanning behind and down, to the pew at the front, to find his wife. To look at her and drink her in, to see her so small and so full of everything, with her hair tied back. She would blow the air back into him.

But he looked and she wasn't there. Only other women were there, a row or two behind, ready to lock eyes with him. Yellow hair over their shoulders.

'No, James!' Hannah says. 'What if you lose? What if you get hurt?'

'I don't lose,' James says, and armours into silence.

'But what if you do? What if you get hurt?'

James looks at his wife, and shrugs. Her words are falling into the wrong pockets of his thought, and he feels wounded, angry. The world calls him a champion, a champion-in-the-making, and his wife says – he'll lose. Fuck, what's it all for?

'The thought of those men,' says Hannah, 'beating you up.'

She puts her hand on to James's shoulder, as if her fingers, white and dimpled like flowers and bread rolls, were strong enough to protect him. If only! If only they could keep him here, safe from bloody noses and black eyes, an eye one time pushed so far back into the socket, caked and hidden like a tortoise, that Hannah had bad dreams for weeks.

James shakes her hand away by standing up. He is a head and a half taller.

'Beating me up?' he says.

Hannah looks at him, quizzical, several moods away from where he has suddenly landed.

'You think I get beaten up? By who? Who do you reckon beats me up, Hannah?'

Hannah is lost, engulfed by the charisma of James's hurt; hurt, that for the first time is bleeding into fury.

'James, please, I don't know why you're angry.'

'Ptth,' says James. 'Fuck you.'

Hannah's hands both rise to cover her mouth, as if it is her who has said these words, not him.

James looks at her. A harpy of stench and loveliness she is to him. So lovely – appalled white hands, wild hair controlled back from her face. And a stinking fuck off witch. Not a woman in the world says he'll lose, but his wife.

These are the days when Hannah still burns bold, when her instinct is still uncut, and she says, from behind her hands,

'Don't speak to me like that.'

She almost whispers, but not quite: there is a voice there.

To save himself, James walks from the room. He walks out into the street and grabs great tractfuls of air and stuffs them to the pit of his lungs.

He fights tonight, and he will win, as he always does. He will not wait for the car, he will walk the miles to the boxing hall, his vessels expanding with the hurt that has alchemised to rage. His bitch wife might say he loses, but he'll win, of course he'll fucking win, like every time before.

Even before the match begins James is sweating, and as the referee steps back, he is murderous.

*Fuck me!* says one popcorn-muncher to a peanut-cruncher beside. *Reckon he must've caught his wife cheating!*

And the man is right. Hannah, with her hands up against her face like white gloves, has betrayed him. She said he would lose. She said he would be beaten up. She told him he would fall. A million, a thousand, a hundred thousand voices from around the ring bay for him to win. They all know that he will win. But the one voice that he hears like a bell, over the din of everything else – that one and only voice, so quiet and so clear – tells him he will lose.

James leaves the ring this night to a muted blend of cheers and boos; the men are disappointed. Their main attraction was over in six minutes. They will have to go into the streets and find fights of their own, in order to rid themselves of the dissatisfaction of a massacre too swift.

In the dressing room James can hear them still stamping their feet. He doesn't care.

He sits on the physio table. His manager Bill and trainer Steve are with him.

'Fucking hell, James,' says Bill, 'you could've given 'em a bit of a show. You pulverised him in two seconds flat. The great fighters, James – and you *are* a great fighter, believe you me, or I wouldn't be here – you know, the Cassius Clays, Muhammad Ali, they all put on a show. Even if they're fighting minnows. They know they need to entertain, as well . . .' Bill stops, swills the unspoken words in his mouth, and swallows them. James is looking at him with shining eyes, eyes full to the cornea of terrifying things. Bill is not a brave man.

So, instead, they discuss the coming schedule, and the negotiations around the European title fight that is approaching. James nods, half listens, looks down at the concrete floor, at his boots, still on, black and red. Steve checks his hands over, unwraps them.

'Had any more stiffness in the fingers?'

James frowns dismissively. Shakes his head.

Business over, Bill smiles. 'How's Hannah?' he asks.

James looks up. 'Fine.'

'Shame she's never made it to a fight. She'd make a great little cheerleader.'

James glares, the hard light flares metallic into his eyes. Bill takes a step back. 'Coming for a drink?' he says.

James shakes his head. 'I'm getting an early night.'

'Good,' says Steve, a soft, economical man, with none of Bill's toothiness. 'You need as many early nights as you can get. Heavy workload coming up. Well done tonight, James,' he is putting a hat on. 'Regards to Hannah. No place for a woman, anyway. She'd be a distraction.'

44

James nods. 'She can't take it,' he says.

Steve looks at him from the door.

'She doesn't want to see me get hurt.'

'Fair enough,' says Steve, and raises a hand in farewell.

Bill pats James on the back. 'You don't get hurt, mate,' he says, smiling. 'I'd like to see the fighter who could take you down right now! I'd sign him up no questions!' He titters. James doesn't respond. 'Night night, then, James. Good work.'

The door closes, and James is alone. He looks back at his boots, at his feet. Above him he can hear the chomps and rustles of the last dribs of crowd dispersing. Going out to eat curry and drink beer.

Hannah has never seen James like this, and she never will. If she were here, they could sit shoulder to shoulder, both looking at his boots. But Hannah has never seen him in his boots, his gloves, his shorts, and she never will. She will never see him snorting with nerves and certainty as he walks to his entrance, followed by his men, chalk in the air, his shadow thrown in front of him like the shadow of a god.

She will never see him as he enters the arena, the roof lifting with his name, a king in that hot, sticky, blood-rich world – a hero. She will never know how his name sounds, spoken by a thousand people, like a name called out from the earth. She will never see him in his corner, a man ten times his normal size, with providence on his side. She will never see how he moves in the ring, a snake god; inimitable, dangerous. She will never see his hand lifted into the air: *triumph*.

She will never see him fight. A fighter is what he is.

And although he knows, he does know, that the reason for Hannah's absence is caught up with her love of him, her absence will nonetheless fester. In times fast coming, as the plump loaf of his brain corrodes and turns in on itself, Hannah's absence from James's ringside will become a cancer. She will be punished for it. Punished, yet again, for loving a man with biceps and a temper, with a dear, delicate head, so delicate that the punches turn it to oats and make him the worst of himself.

There is a knock at the door, and James looks up defensively. Sideways, a woman steps in.

'Hello, James,' she says.

This woman is unreal. She was not expected here, and James does not know her. He narrows his eyes at her, as if he can't quite make her out.

She is wearing an electric-blue dress, and James can see her body in it. It pushes at the edges of the material, bosom softly pressed above the neckline, thighs outlined against the skirt. It is as if the dress makes her naked.

'D'you mind if I come in?' the woman asks.

But she already is in, holding her coat, and smiling.

It is the coat that James notices, that cuts through the

46

apparition of the woman and makes her exist. A beige raincoat, unglamorous, domestic, that James can imagine hanging on a peg by a front door, that of course she would need for the outside. A naked blue dress on an outside street – would not work.

The woman is walking towards James, and still he has said nothing. He looks at her face. Her skin is painted and James can't see how old she is, she could be twenty-five, forty-five, thirty, fifty. She is in front of him now, her breasts are level with his eyes. They are the kind of breasts you see on posters, round and forward and separated. James can see their edges and their shape, he can see their weight.

'Aren't you going to stand up for me?' she asks, this woman naked in the dress, in front of James's face.

And James, stuck in stupid surprise, speechless, does as he is told. He stands up, like a trained dog. In her high heels, she is almost his height.

She takes half a step towards him, and protrudes into his chest.

'Haven't even had a shower yet?' she asks, smiling. 'You're still in all your gear.'

She presses harder against him, and as she does she puts her coat on the table. James notices the coat, again. Feels it in an ordinary, household heap next to him.

But he doesn't look away from her. She holds his look, eyes large with inevitability. Her hand touches his chest and it is cold, and something is running through

47

James, causing his breath to come fast through his nose.

'Don't you want to know what my name is?' she asks. She is smiling. Her hand moves down, and even through his protection he feels her touch.

Involuntarily, like a rush of water, James feels repulsed.

His hands, so recently a boxer's hands that they still have the marks of the gauze indented, close around her upper arms, and push her without gentleness away. James feels saliva in his mouth, and wants to gag.

'Get the fuck away from me,' he says, before turning around, hocking and spitting into the sink. Mucus always comes churning up after a fight, from deep in his lungs, but this, is different. It is something he has never felt before. He feels revolted.

The woman takes another step towards him.

'Come on . . .' she begins to say, her voice creamy at half-speed. But James turns towards her mid-sentence.

'Get the fuck out,' he says again. She is still smiling, but she hesitates.

'Get the fuck out,' James's voice has raised, 'or I will break your fucking face.'

The woman in the blue dress takes her beige coat from the table, and moves to the door. It slams behind her.

The newspaper the next day writes James's headline: *Sidewinder Missile Attack: Hallow ballistic, destroys Lawrence in two rounds.*

Hannah brings the paper to him in bed, along with tea. He kisses the hand that holds the mug. She, in turn, puts it on the side of his face, stubble, warm, that scratching sound of her skin against his bristles, that belongs to her. She grins.

James puts the mug on the mattress next to him, and waits for his wife's reaction. It is a game they have – her baited nervousness that the tea might spill over the bed, his provocative movements of leg and arm, jogging the liquid towards the rim. Sometimes Hannah can't bear it, yelps and picks the mug up, sometimes James relents, laughs and picks it up himself.

This morning, Hannah simply shakes her head and smiles, before going back down to the kitchen. 'You can't tease me today,' she says.

James looks at the newspaper, turned to the right page and folded in half for him already. He reads his headline.

The journalist, who James knows, notes that his opponent was a sacrifice, a young boy who was never going to be a threat. A show rung on the way to a title fight. James sees the boy's name in print, but he can't remember his face.

The journalist notes that James last night lost his trademark technique. He notes that the sidewinder sideways loopings that set James apart, did not appear. There was no grace. James simply, in a straight line, pummelled.

But a sidewinder, the paper teaches James, is not only a punch, and a snake. Also, it is a missile. Now being used in Vietnam; a faraway war in a faraway world. *Hallow*, says the newspaper, *bombed Lawrence back into the Stone Age*.

So, they say, he is a Sidewinder still.

# 3

Somebody is looking for him, he knows it, he knows it. He can feel that person hovering, like a UFO, hovering uncomfortably in midair. *SHOW YOURSELF!*, he wants to say, in loud tones: it would be a command. But commands seem not to work anymore. His days of commanding are over.

A nurse comes in carrying a food tray. She puts it down on a moveable table that can be wheeled back and forth, lowered up and down. It is a table for the ill and elderly, of which James is both.

She mechanically raises the head of the bed with a slow buzz, and rearranges the pillows, drawing her hands around the back of James's shoulders, and pulling him with experience and strength up the mattress.

'How are you feeling, Mr Hallow?' she asks, cheerfully. Her accent is not English. James's eyelids are pushing kilo weights, they winch themselves open, they falter, they open, they grind themselves up. 'It's a beautiful day outside today. The sun's out.'

James doesn't remember this girl. He doesn't know who she is. He looks at her.

She is a nurse. Okay.

She is a nurse called Felicity and she does her job with evenness and goodwill. She has a family outside this compound. A boyfriend, maybe even a husband, although she wears no ring. She has friends, and eats sandwiches, and pays rent, and goes to the cinema, and drinks vodka lemon and limes on a Friday night. She comes to work every day to deal soft blows to dying men, and she does so with clear eyes and kindness. Only once or twice in the passing years has it all got a bit much for her.

She pulls the table so that it floats over James's bedclothed knees. He can see the food on the tray – it all looks so multi coloured and childlike. He could reach out and rub his fingers into all of it. Putty.

'Do you fancy a little bit of breakfast? I've got some weetabix here for you, or a bit of banana?'

She puts a doll-sized mouthful of mushy weetabix on a teaspoon, and holds it towards James's mouth. He shakes his head, 'No,' it comes out as a thirsty growl.

'If you could just have this one mouthful for me, and then a couple of sips of drink, and I won't hassle you anymore, I promise.'

She's so nice, this girl. James allows the weetabix into his mouth, and chews as best he can. He rolls it around his mouth with his tongue. He swallows with difficulty. It immediately starts a nausea churning in his stomach.

'Now, can you have one more for me?' The nurse is offering another fairy-small spoonful. James doesn't open his mouth. 'I know I said only one mouthful, but I think you can manage two today. Go on. It's a very small bite.'

He parts his lips, and again moves the food around his mouth with his tongue, it feels like paste. Sickness invades, and James struggles to swallow. When a third mouthful is offered, James says 'No' again, and the nurse Felicity, whose nickname is Flop, recognises his limit.

James Hallow never went in for nicknames. Had he known that this Felicity was a Flop, he would have called her Felicity regardless. Nicknames were a depreciation: he found them contemptible. *Names* were the thing, *names*. A man has his name, if that's all he has. James Hallow was his name, and he had it. James Meredith Hallow.

No monikers for him in the ring. He was always embroidered JAMES HALLOW, and late in his career JAMES M. HALLOW. He fought, and won, and ultimately lost, under his own name. That was the only way.

But this nurse is so nice to him that James, even if he knew she had a nickname and was Flop, would continue to find her wonderful. He likes her. He likes her, and especially he likes her kindness. Kindness, kindness, kindness is the thing. It hits him so profoundly when he can see it from a gap in the cloud. He wishes he had been kind in return. He wishes he could throw kindness all about.

The nurse is shaking a small carton of high-protein milk drink, 'Strawberry flavour, is that alright?'

James lowers his chin in assent, and raises his right arm. It comes, shuddering horribly, towards Felicity the Nurse and the drink she holds. She waits for him to place his hand, trembling violently, on the carton, steadies it with her own, and then moves it with him to his mouth. He sucks a pink beesip up through the thin straw. He rests, with the straw still in his mouth. He tries another sip.

No, it's no good. There are kilo weights on his head, pushing him down. He is exhausted and beginning to shake.

Felicity takes the straw from his lip, and moves James's hand back from the carton down to the bedsheets. She leans across him and puts the drink on the bedside cabinet.

'I'm going to leave your milkshake just here on the stand, and hopefully you can have a few more glugs of it a bit later.'

James is too tired to respond. Felicity lowers the bed-head down. Bzzzzz. As she does, she says, 'It looks like you could do with a shave, Mr Hallow. Now, I'm just going to turn you on your side, so you don't get sore. Here we go. Then why don't I come back to see you in an hour or so and we can give you a nice, clean shave? Have you feeling a bit fresher.'

Moving the table on wheels away, and walking around the bed, Felicity again scoops her arms behind James, her fingers spread firmly, and lifts him towards her. It is like an embrace. She manoeuvres him in one swift movement and lowers him on to his right side. She pulls her arms away in a way that should be awkward but isn't, and as she does her fingers trail along his shoulder blades in light massage. It feels to James like having wings.

'Thank you,' he says, and it sounds like a croak, from a small frog.

James can hear his son Jamie playing next door. He is in the kitchen, making car noises, vroom vroom, and occasionally he says something, which Hannah answers in a voice too soft for James to hear. They are in there together, those two.

James has not seen his son yet today, he has been up late. He remembers his wife getting out of bed in the early morning, and dressing in the dark. She does this so as not to wake him, fat lot of fucking good he was awake already. It seems the quieter she tries to be, the more deafening her movements are. She shifts in her sleep, and James hears it like a juggernaut turning.

Now he sits downstairs on the sofa, in his dressing gown. The television shimmers, but he doesn't see. Instead he watches the carpet, and the carpet looks back, into him. His feet, flat and long and elegant, are bare.

Sitting there, behind a front door and windows and brickwork identical to the forty-nine other front doors and windows and brickwork the length of the street, James feels cursed. The lid has been lifted on this house, none other, and a black finger has pointed in, marking James with its ill will. He cannot move but he is broken. He gave up his fists, that was suffering enough, and now whatever has come for him wants the rest too.

Yesterday evening, you see, the shaking spread through his whole body. His head remained helpless, stiff and locked at the top of the jelly. He ended lying on the floor, on his side, like a slug, his breath sounding to him like a jet engine; he couldn't see or think or move, for the unmanageable loudness of his own lungs.

And now, here he is. Sitting. Wishing – he had died in the ring. A clean snap of the neck from a punch.

He should not be here, to see this television glowing. He is alive where he should be dead.

Hannah has rushed to the room, and stands in the doorway. Jamie is behind her, one hand holds on to the back of his mother's knee. They see broken glass in an arc around the television, which has been pulled face forward on to the floor. James stands, dressing gown and bare feet, still alive. He looks up at his spectators, his crowd of two, his family.

Even a year ago, Hannah would have said, *James, what happened?* She would have said, *Are you alright?* She would have tried to ascertain, in some way, what was going on. Why the television was in smithereens on the floor, why her husband stood over it, his jaw set. But, now, he is a different version of himself. She will not speak. Her hand protectively touches the top of her son's head, fluffy curls.

Frame by frame, James watches them.

He sees first: Jamie holding on. Touching Hannah in a delicate spot, the crook behind her knee. The small boy touches Hannah as if she is his to touch.

It is strange that he exists at all, this child, in their house. With large eyes and with hair like Hannah's. James looks at him, and – yes, he's sure of it – the boy in response holds on tighter to Hannah.

This boy, James feels, does not belong. He is here like a changeling, a foreigner, with memories in his tiny face of other people. With looks about him that James recognises, but can't quite pinpoint. It is jarring, and eerie, that this child is in the house. It used to be just him and Hannah.

Next James sees: Hannah. She is allowed here. She can see this, arc of glass, smithereens, and she can see worse.

Then he sees: Hannah's hand impulse out, and touch the top of Jamie's head.

James strides to the boy, picks him up from under his arms.

'James,' Hannah says, suddenly panicked.

James holds his son out in front of him, as if he is a thing contagious. His face is stretched wide with something unnatural, pathological, wired.

'I don't want him in the house,' James says.

Hannah follows at a run, watching Jamie scrabbling up his father's grasp, for all the good it does him. James's arms are strong, even now he no longer fights. They are too full of muscle, as Hannah has always known.

Jamie is looking at her, over his father's shoulder, trying to fly to her. *Muma*, he says, over over again, his arms frantically out.

As James opens the door to the garden, Hannah tries to make it past him, to take Jamie back. But with one arm, the other still holding his wriggling son, James stops her; he puts his left hand against her chest. The movement is light, he doesn't even push her, but to Hannah it is a body blow. She feels his handprint through her dress, on her skin, and she cannot resist. She stops where she is. Her arms stop reaching. They hang beside her.

It is the sight of this, his mother's defeat, that terrifies Jamie totally. The wriggling becomes kicking, and the cries of muma become incoherent shrieks.

James walks, unaffected, to the end of the garden. He puts Jamie on the grass, by the back fence. He returns to the house, into the kitchen, and locks the door behind him.

He walks past Hannah, and for one hot second she considers pulling him back and plunging her nails into his flesh and drawing blood. She imagines herself running to Jamie, scooping him, taking him back into her as he once was. But these thoughts call inside her for only a moment, and then – pouf! – they are gone forever.

Through the glass panes in the kitchen door she watches her son. Jamie can see her – he is pointing at her with both his small hands. His voice is broken, and he sounds as he did when he was newborn, like a kitten. He was her baby.

And now, there he is, alone. She had dressed him that morning in a white t-shirt, with a hot-air balloon on the tummy, and a rainbow. It is one of his favourites. He had touched his tummy throughout the morning and said, *my br-loon*.

He is screaming.

She will have to think of something to tell the neighbours.

Jamie, two and a half years old, watches the outline of his mother, through the glass, turn away from him.


James's catheter tube had got twisted, and it caused in him the discomfiting feeling of needing to pee, but not being able to. It was nobody's fault. These things happened. They were noticed soon enough. A nurse would come in and iron out the kink.

Pain and tiredness didn't bother James, he knew how to cope with them. When he was fighting they were part of the job description, and he had learnt to remove himself from them early on.

It was not the pain or the tiredness or the twisted tubes, but the sickness that racked him. The sleeping-waking feeling of his body being melted down, of there being something far beyond physical pain and exhaustion that was wrong with him. A terrible melting feeling. The strangeness of everything.

It was a dark room, because it was night time. There was not much in it. There was a big window with more dark night time outside it. There was an open door, which James wanted to shut. He waved his arm towards it, but it did not move. No magic left. It stayed open. Someone would come through it.

Who was that person? Who was walking past and not

seeing to come in? Hovering like a moth? Like a UFO?

Who are you? You are coming for me.

James knew it. She was coming.

Come fast, dark lady, come fast, because something, everything, is melting.

*Margaret*

# 1

Margaret smooths the front of her dress with her palms, a gesture she hasn't lost in her thousand years of being. She is watching an arrival being wheeled from an ambulance, on his back, through the rain, and through the automatic sliding doors into the foyer of her hospice.

She moves to the desk, and looks at the papers that are being handed over. *Hallow; James Meredith.* TRANSFER FROM: *St Dympna's Hospital.* TRANSFER TO: *St Margaret's Hospice.* She looks up from the forms and down at the new man, into his face. He's muzzled with a pepper-white stubble of a day or so, and his eyes are closed.

'One of Dympna's,' thinks Margaret. She walks to the head of the stretcher bed, bends like a bulrush to the sweat-licked forehead of the man, kisses it. This is one of her rituals.

James Hallow grunts at the lucent pressure on his skin.

Margaret skims away, like a ripple over water.

Margaret is the patron of this hospice, and she watches over her dying with indiscriminate poise, and gentleness. Each one she kisses as they enter, each one she blesses as they leave. They are all her charges, although they not one know she's there. She is invisible to them – not a ghost, not an angel, perhaps a strange combination of the two.

She died in 1093, as Scotland's queen. Her husband, the king, had died three days before.

She was canonised in 1251, after one hundred and fifty years of forgetfulness.

And then, in 1967, a hospice bearing her name opened in north-west London, and Margaret let herself into its waters, became its patron and protector. She has been here since.

The statue outside the sliding doors resembles her not at all. It is placid-faced and round-cheeked, like a milkmaid. But the stonemasons had no accurate physical information, and so, fair enough, went for the usual chocolate-box template. The statue wears a generic kind of nativity play robe, tied with a rope. Margaret cannot see the statue full-frontally from her boundary at the foyer door, but she sees enough of it to know that she doesn't remember wearing a robe like that. She knows she never wore rope.

And the robust butter-churning face of the statue is far from Margaret's cool loveliness – Margaret is long-boned, like winter. There has always been a magnificent frigidity about her beauty, a sexless glitter that spreads before and after her as she walks. But the stonemasons weren't to know.

A small tumbling child of about five or six brings his grandfather a card he has made. It is a carbon rubbing of a manhole cover, made, the boy explains, by placing a thin piece of card over the metal – it has to be thin or it won't work – and rubbing with a crayon. He had learnt to do it at school, but there they had done different barks from different trees for Science. But he wanted to do this manhole cover for Grampa because he thought it was better patterns.

'Aren't you clever,' says his grandfather, who dies two nights later, alone but for Margaret. The manhole card perches next to him in those quiet hours, as his body grows cold and all life leaves the room. Margaret watches it all.

Later that night, as James on another floor sleeps his first sleep in this last home of his, Margaret sits on a swivel chair in the administration office. She sits in the dark, another outline among the outlines of desks and filing cabinets and spiderplants. How different this room is now, without the whirring of hard drive, the chapping of fingers on keyboards.

There is a photograph on the desk in front of her. It is not in a frame, but the shiny surface of the photographic paper reflects the yellow spot of the desk lamp. The picture is of a man, a little plump and in a loose blue checked shirt, holding a smiling toddler with wispy white hair on her head and red jam on her face and a pink plastic spoon in her fist.

Margaret strokes the edges of the picture – how she would love one of these, to press against her heart these endless wakeful nights. A photograph of her husband, to remind her of the shadows in his face, of his bones and tones and his eyes when he loved her. The look she sometimes caught him in, a mix of awe and amusement.

Tonight Margaret feels pained by something. She feels ancient tears inside her, pushing against each other like tadpoles, rushing to out. Surrounded by all this dying, alone, unseen, and with everything that she loved so irrevocably faded.

Margaret cannot envisage exactly – precisely, that is, in minutiae – the small scar of her husband Malcolm's top lip, that runs from about a centimetre above into the left corner. She cannot picture the beard hairs on either side, she can't see whether they brush it, or whether the scar is isolated in a virgin ruck of skin. What she would give, for a moment, to have him walk in and just let her glut herself on the facts of his scar. Burn it into her memory, in all its precision, so that she could remember. Or what she would give for a photograph.

Margaret never in life knew how many eyelashes Malcolm had, but they were there in definite number had she chosen to count them. Now, even if she squeezes the present shut and forces herself into the past, she cannot know how many there are. She would have to invent a number. One thousand? One thousand four hundred? One thousand four hundred and fifty-two? When she stood for those years beside him, when she could have counted, when she could have spent so much more time *looking* at him. She thought she knew his face, but she realises now that she didn't. Not entirely, not its every pore and line. She wants it here, please, just for the briefest moment, she wouldn't even touch him, she would just look.

No can do.

He is gone, gone, gone for ever, and the loneliness, the horror of this, crushes the will from Margaret's soul, as she sits as beautiful as a reed beside filing cabinets and hard drives and spiderplants.

To think of his body, gone for ever.

Or the last of it rotting in the dun of Scotland, nothing soft left, every scrap of muscle and fat eaten.

Or maybe they found him long ago, and dug him from his chalk and cocooned his rusted armour in a museum case, and placed his remaining femur in a drawer for study. Her Malcolm, her husband, her king.

The years of shyness; why did she have to be so shy? Why didn't she just love him as she wanted to? Instead of feeling bare, exposed as a white light. Instead of retreating nervously like a small, scared bird. His little bird, his little English princess.

Why was she so shy at night? Shy of his smell – earth, and antlers, and honey – too shy to reach over for his body and study it, the backs of his thighs, his neck and elbows and thumbs. And now he is gone, and she will never be able to go towards him and look at him. When for all those years she could have. Had she known that this feeling would come – the annihilating grief of being without him – without even the possibility of him – never able to hope for just a glimpse of him – she would have clung to him like lichen like death like iron, and never would have allowed him from her grip.

Margaret's heart starts, and gathers itself up.

'Hello,' says a voice behind her.

She knows whose voice this is, without turning. She has been expecting it.

'Hello, Dympna,' says Margaret.

She swivels around in the swivelling chair, which immediately makes her feel ridiculous. She wishes she had just stood up and turned on her own heels. And as she walks towards Dympna in greeting, she realises that she still holds the photograph of the man with the baby and the pink spoon.

'Oh,' she says, and turns to prop it back to its place on the desk.

Margaret's inside is fluttering with confusion, having had to snap up too fast the Pandora of feeling for her dead husband, for her dead self. But her outside appears only gently furrowed, and her movements, although inelegant in her own mind, appear as they always do, balletic, and balanced.

'I have caught you thinking,' says Dympna in apology, taking both Margaret's hands in her own. 'I wish I'd had the time to warn you that I would be coming.'

'No, no, I knew you'd come. I hoped you'd come.'

'It is a joy to be here, with you, Margaret. Even though I haven't long.'

'Yes,' says Margaret, still lost, a little. 'Yes.'

Dympna's visits, so rarely possible, are always a respite: it feels as though they are huddling around a hurricane lamp together, the two of them, taking comfort in the other face in the glow, not alone anymore; even if merely, just and only for a few minutes.

They walk together to the chapel downstairs. It is empty. Three candles are lit – prayers for an easy death, or for an impossible recovery. This is a hospice. There are no recoveries. Margaret is the only miracle.

'I envy your candles,' says Dympna, moving in sideways to the centre of a pew.

'Yes,' says Margaret. They sit, side by side.

'They're like butterflies,' says Dympna, without explanation.

'Yes. Yes, they are.' Margaret is still struggling. 'You've come about your James Hallow?' she says, and it's not really a question. Her voice is edgeless. She feels worn smooth by her sadness. A thousand years and still she grieves. How foolish. 'He arrived late this afternoon.'

Dympna's hair flames, as it always does. It moves on its own, bonfires around her face and shoulders, a bright, benign Medusa.

'We can't have candles at my hospital,' she goes on, ignoring what Margaret has said, not yet ready to talk about James Hallow even though she has so little time, never enough time. 'Well, there's no chapel. But even if there was, we couldn't have candles. The red tape that would be involved in allowing open flames near my patients . . .' Dympna trails away to a pause. Margaret watches her friend watching the candles – small sputtering hopes. She looks at them herself. They *are* lovely. An oasis in this place of hard light. But she is used to them, now. She hasn't considered their loveliness for a while.

Her hair still crackling, Dympna begins over, 'Not much prayer at my place. But lots of dreams, which are similar. Or better. It's cold in here, Margaret.'

Margaret turns to Dympna and smiles, with rare and real affection. It stings her heart. 'Cold? I no longer notice these things.' She puts a brief hand on Dympna's soft, goosebumped arm. It sends a surge of warmth and surprise through her as if she had forgotten what it was to touch.

'You feel cold, too,' says Dympna, and Margaret doesn't know why, but she suddenly feels awkward.

'James Hallow,' she says with firmness. 'You have come about James Hallow.'

Dympna laughs, and the chapel is grateful for it, its walls heave relief. 'Yes, I've come because of Mr Hallow.' She looks into Margaret's pale, glacial face, as different from her own as December from fruit blossom. 'Am I not getting to the point?'

The laugh helps Margaret to calmness. 'I don't mean to sound impatient,' she says. 'Forgive me. My heart feels stiff tonight.' She sighs, and decides to smile, and continues. 'I have been thinking foolish thoughts,' she says, 'I cannot stop myself. I am a lost cause. I should put myself under the care of St Jude.'

Dympna laughs again and the chapel, one would swear, illumines briefly with a russet autumn light, a millisecond season easing the burden of the tiny room, that has to hold so many winters.

# 2

Remembering is something that hasn't been easy for Margaret. Of course she knows, what her life was, of course she has it within her. But bringing it to stand before her is always gruelling. She simply cannot isolate – faces, days, words. There is a brume about it all, and every time Margaret puts a hand into it, desperate to feel some contour or edge or patch of body, she comes out with nothing.

But after Dympna leaves in a rush of auburn, after Margaret walks from the chapel alone, a memory of an old afternoon comes to her without bidding and it comes in all its detail. Perfect, as if it were today. She stops, ambushed, and the memory encloses her.

She is in the space that looks out on to the hospice garden, through large glass doors. It is at once a room and a thoroughfare, connecting as it does the reception area to a wing of bedrooms beyond, being the door to the garden, and also housing chairs and tables and a tea station furnished with matching, faded cups, brown and orange, and packets of sugar. In front of her she sees a woman, a day, a situation so thoroughly disremembered up until this second that they had ceased to exist. And now, here they are again, from the ashes reborn.

Margaret sees the paper she was reading, on her lap, as she sat by the window. She looks up from it and sees Malcolm talking to the wife of a favourite courtier. At the sight of this woman's proximity to her husband she feels a gut of repulsion. She feels insulted.

The woman, the wife of a man called Dunsel, looks like a rat, topped with a freakishly tiny head – as if a child's head has been placed on an adult's body. Blonde eyelashes make her face appear bald and unblinking, and a flaring, upturned nose gives generous views into the nostrils. The eyes are round and protrude daintily, with a mincing and hungry look. Her figure is tidy, which makes the bulging rattishness of her face and the smallness of her head the more pronouncedly gruesome. There she stands.

The king is smiling at this woman, this woman so unctuous and ugly. And she is looking coyly but determinedly back at him, like a trinklet. It is grotesque – she is mooning prettily as if she is a nymph, a lily of the field, all the while eyes popping, nostrils blaring. It is unseemly, vulgar, laughable. But the king keeps talking. He seems animated.

Annoyance flickers against Margaret's ribs. She motions to one of her women, smiling immaculately, and asks for her things to be gathered and taken to her rooms. She rises, bows her head to the king, and turns her skirts to quit the room.

But the king catches his wife by the waist. 'Before you go, little bird,' he says to her, 'come to greet Lady Dunsel, she has arrived today from Carnoch.' Margaret, pressed close by her husband's hold, can smell the smell of him, earth and antlers, earth and honey.

'Of course,' says the queen, tipping her chin down as the woman curtseys, 'Lady Dunsel. We have met before. It has been too long since you were at our court – we have missed you.' Malcolm raises his wife's hand to his lips and kisses it. Margaret does not respond, she goes on spreading her light over the laird's wife.

'Have you been all this time at Carnoch?' she asks, smiling, tall and soft.

'Yes, Madam. I have two children, too young for travel, or for court. I cannot be away from them often.' As she talks, Lady Dunsel does not meet Margaret's eye. Her disrespect is open – she looks around Margaret's edges, as if the queen is quite simply not there. Malcolm, apparently, does not notice this. He watches, content, as this woman makes a show of her lack of respect for his wife.

'What pretty chickens they must be,' says Margaret, still smiling, while thinking of what ill-starred faces the two Dunsel piglets must have.

'Thank you, Madam,' says Lady Dunsel, her mouth smirking downwards, keeping her eyes turned away. 'Were they old enough I would have brought them here to pay their respects. They have heard many stories of Máel Coluim's handsome English queen.'

Malcolm seems not to register his wife's hand stiffening in his own – he continues cheerfully to stroke her palm. He does not notice the present courtiers congealing with surprise and amusement, at the open mockery.

Margaret laughs, glassily, clenching and controlling so as not to unleash the squall that is mounting inside her. 'Your daughters would be disappointed to find that their queen is a Scot, Lady Dunsel, and not such an exotic thing after all. It was daughters that you said you had?' Margaret does not wait for an answer, for she well knows that any Dunsel sons would have been proudly borne to court at any age. She changes her tone to end the conversation. 'It is a happiness to have you with us, and I shall look forward to seeing you this evening, at supper. Now, forgive me, but I have kept my own son waiting on me – I promised Edward time before the evening.'

Son, Margaret had said, deliberately – my own son.

'Madam,' says Lady Dunsel, and curtseys a third time. The queen lowers her head and bows once more to her husband, who drops her hand, finally allowing her to leave the room.

*   *   *

Two gossamer-fine lines run across Margaret's forehead, little silkworms of worry. There are two deeper vertical rivets between her eyebrows. But apart from these her face is clear, her skin does not otherwise acknowledge her thirty-six years.

Her insides, though, are stuck through with burrs. A new one caught against her ribs today at the sight of the fawning Dunsel wife, the wife with no sons. Another caught with fury for Malcolm, Malcolm smiling toastily at the oily woman, not noticing his own wife's distress. Not noticing his own wife.

They gum her up, these burrs. They multiply, until she hears herself rustling as she walks. And late afternoons like this they find her lying in a puff of sadness on her side. Sadness mixed with anger, mixed with the afternoon light that fills the room blueishly – there are no sunbeams, or patches of warmth; the sun is grizzled behind thick cloud.

Margaret finds her love for her husband difficult. It is nothing like her other loves. The children – the children! – the children are quite different. They are each one darling to her. Each one a shower of pride and protection, each one attached to her still as if their birth cords had never been cut. She has them all on ribbons around her wrists. Her birds. Her darlings.

Alexander, so like his father in his face, so determined to be fierce like his older brothers, yet still small enough to nestle himself into Margaret's crevices – underarms, waist, bent knees, neck – he would burrow his way into her.

And Edith, her longed-for girl. Held in wonder by her six brothers; a creature quite other, this little brown-eyed doll. As Margaret told them, they must be gentle with her, and patient. They must treat her as they would a flower, and stroke her gently – for not only is she a baby, but a sister, to be watched over and touched with careful fingers. When Edith was a few days old, Edward, the eldest, held her with such shock on his face, but such dignity in his young man's arms, that Margaret found tears starting to her eyes. Edward – her first child – his father's secret pride. Edward, whose face is more glorious to Margaret than any sight on earth. The boy that she and Malcolm made.

All of them, each one so, they are her darlings. Her birds. Sparrows and larks, hawks and robins among them. All her darling birds, tied to her wrist with ribbons. To love them is a privilege, a dance, a happiness. To feel them flutter about her and know that they are hers. And there may be another, Margaret suspects, on the way.

Seven healthy children, and now perhaps an eighth. Six princes for the kingdom, and a girl like a flower to sit on Malcolm's knee.

Malcolm.

To love Malcolm is not the same. It is akin to a rage,

an epileptic mist. Malcolm, who appeared to her when she was twenty-three years old – appeared through the rain like a warrior-ghost, and snapped her into pieces. Whose hands are padded with hard skin, and smell of honey. They touch her with such certainty.

Malcolm, whose other women Margaret tries frantically to drive from her mind. She does not know they exist – has admittedly not heard whispers of them, yet – but they are an inevitability. What man stays faithful to his wife? What king does not take a mistress? Margaret tries to shake away the ruins of her pride as birds shake water from their wings. But the images of the others stick in her, burrs, burrs, burrs.

She knows it is a madness to think like this, it is self-torture. For Malcolm will come to her, and put his hand with infinite strength around the nape of her neck, and when he dips into her she will know in every cell of herself that he loves her only. She will feel, down into her marrow, that it is she who is tied like a bird to his wrist. Choked to him by a silver ribbon.

By a silver ribbon, as she stands by the teabags and teacups, by the celebrity magazines on veneered tables – a ribbon strained taut, so that she is unable to move for this moment; colliding, downpouring moment in her ridging, furrowing, never-ending life.

# 3

Margaret's own deathbed had been dark. The curtains heavily drawn, no light but pools thrown by candles. Sometimes, in the sad light of the hospice rooms, she thinks that her dark death had been preferable. None of this lit up wallpaper, lit up tissues, lit up bedpans, lit up Get Well cards. As they shrink down into their mattresses, the dying here see each evidence of their deterioration, tubes of urine, skin turning grey and leafy.

The dark had protected Margaret from seeing the facts of death all about her. It had protected her from seeing her own lost beauty – for she knew, mirrorless as she was in her bed, that her looks, resilient through her life, flawless always, were finally crumbling with her arteries and lungs. It is best to go to James Hallow's room now, she thinks, while it is dark and she will see only outlines. Outlines will give the kindest impression.

The door of the room is hooked open, and the orange light from the corridor dribbles in. There is a blue nightlight by the bed, the small bulb the colour of a flycatcher.

James is asleep. His eyes are closed, the lids pulsating as if caterpillars are fidgeting under them. As Margaret walks in his breathing ruffles and then catches, as if a wind has blown over him, as if he has been surprised by something.

The sheet is folded neatly over his chest, and his arms lie palms up, inert, over it. It is a pristine sleep. No warmth or tumbling or creasing of covers. Stillness. Like many of the sleeps being slept in the rooms throughout the hospice – palliatively drugged, mercifully doped. The dying slumber unmoving, all vigour sapped by the heave of life's last moments.

He is dreaming of doors opening, doors closing. But Margaret, of course, doesn't know this. Nobody knows this except James.

The light is too dim to see him in detail. But the nose slants clearly to one side, and the hair is grey, almost white, and cropped close to the head. There is a slack brawn beneath his skin, where shady muscles run.

Margaret moves to the window. They are on the top floor here – the third floor. The slats of the blinds look down to the small walled garden, where on dry days visitors will talk, sometimes patients will eat their lunch, or just sit quietly. The patients here always seem cold – wrapped up come chill or come clemency in scarves and slippers. Tonight, of course, the garden is empty. It has long since been locked up.

Beyond the garden wall are the tips of the street-lamps. Occasionally at this time of night a bottle will drop and smash, or a siren keen. But mostly it is quiet, in well-to-do north-west London, quiet enough to hear the blood in your ears and the breath in your nostrils. Or the breath of the patients as it battles and rattles, or gives up and goes. So many sleeping bodies, with different noises, gurgles and sloops. Margaret left her disgust behind years ago. Now she watches and listens and waits, with a blank sense of peacefulness.

Through the angled blind slats the room is reflected in the windowpane. James's foreshortened body floats in mirror image over the garden, tipped by toes pointing upward whitely under the sheet. The bedside table with the telephone hovers beside. The armchair is suspended in the air, waiting for a passing ghost to rest his chains.

Only Margaret doesn't register on the glass. Like a vampire, she does not see herself in mirrors or pools of water. Like a vampire, she thinks ghoulishly to herself, she feeds on the dying.

Looking from the window in James's room, imagining herself as some Dracula, Margaret smiles a little: these thoughts are a game, a burst of glamour and silliness in a rolling existence otherwise so endlessly gentle.

Out of nowhere, a voice cuts across Margaret's imagination.

'Who's there?' it says. 'Who's there?'

Through the dark, Margaret can see, the dying man is looking straight at her.

'I am a lost cause,' Margaret had said. 'I should put myself under the care of St Jude.'

We were in the chapel, remember? Three evenings ago. Dympna had laughed, and the walls had glowed.

'Well,' says Dympna, bringing a finger to her lips, as if about to silence herself, 'I hate to think whose care I should be under. I suspect I'm half cracked, and should be admitted to my own hospital.'

'*Half cracked?*' asks Margaret, her smile spreading. 'Half cracked,' she repeats, wanting to try the words again.

'Half cracked. It means halfway mad.'

'I guessed. It's good.' There is a flicker of something feathery in Margaret's heart, something like delight; it feels like a bird might suddenly fly out from her mouth.

'I've plenty more of them,' says Dympna, looking steadily, curls flaming. 'And they may all apply to me. Because either I'm beginning to get a little, ah, moonstruck, or James Hallow can see me.'

Margaret knits her brow, her smile diffusing, unsure that she understands what Dympna has said.

'He has been in my care for over three years,' Dympna

continues quickly, 'and has been no more difficult than any of the others. No different, stupid as that sounds, as of course everyone is different.' Dympna looks at Margaret's face for a signal of understanding. Margaret nods. Dympna goes on, 'He came to us with dementia – Alzheimer's – and Parkinson's. He has deteriorated slowly – regularly, if you understand what I mean.' Margaret nods again. 'Until last month, when everything became that much faster. None of this is unusual, I know.

'When it was certain that he was dying, and space was found for him here with you, I went to sit with him for a while before he left. To acknowledge him. And give him up. Give up my care.'

'Yes,' says Margaret, understanding exactly, able to picture her friend by James Hallow's bedside.

'I am sure of it, Margaret, that he saw me. No, no, wait, let me finish,' Dympna shoots a staying hand to Margaret's knee. 'I stood next to his bed, and he looked at me, not through me, or around me – he wasn't looking towards the place where I was, by chance, as happens all the time. He was looking *at* me, like I am looking at you now.'

Dympna takes in Margaret's expression. 'I told you,' she says, 'I'm half cracked. But, Margaret, you know what it is to be looked at. It is the difference between being looked through, and the way I am looking at you now. I was being looked at. He was looking at me.'

'Dympna,' says Margaret, taken aback by this story, and feeling empty of any natural response, 'I don't know what to say.'

'I wanted to tell you. I felt I had to. Margaret, it's not fancy: he followed me from the room with his eyes, and head. He strained to watch me as I walked, tried to turn to one side to face me as I was leaving.'

'Yes,' says Margaret, still searching for a reaction. None comes.

'Yes,' she says, again.

James has woken, and he knows the door is open. He knows there is someone here.

'Who's there?' he asks, and his voice sounds old and frightening and tight, for his throat has silted up from so many hours out of use.

Margaret curves from the window in shock. James's arm is waving weakly, swinging at the elbow as if it is on a hinge. He is waving for a light, swinging for a light switch. He makes a noise through closed lips, of frustration.

There is a lady by the window: she has a lady's shape. She is casting angry looks about her, although it is dark, and he cannot see her. There is no light, no light, and James's arms torment him in a storm of flopping and falling, they will not be bid, they will not listen.

The lady is there – a lady's shape. The room is dark. There is a terror in the air, a promise of bad things to come. Where is it all – everything familiar? There is only this lady, standing and watching in the strange dark. Hannah, Hannah, come back. Come back, my Hannah, and turn on the light.

What does she want? Why is she here in the dark?

'Who are you?' says James, in the same gurgling, sludgy voice.

The lady is coming away from the window, she is skinning away from it like a strip of orange peel. But as she comes closer she comes thicker, and her shape is definitely the shape of a lady.

She is coming closer. Coming thicker.

James is gulped by a panic of wanting to see the thickening lady, in case it is a somebody he knows, and wanting to wring his eyes tight shut. The back of his head feels like liquid lead, and he cannot lift it. It gloops like mercury. It pins him to the pillow. Fear begins to wriggle over his skin, and there is no light to be had. The endless opening and closing of doors that slam through his dreams, the inability to move and run away, the lady growing large as she comes for him; these things squeeze at all James's parts. A painful trickle of urine passes, at the same time as the tears start to drip. His whole body leaks.

*Jamie*

# 1

Jamie loves food. He wakes up in the night, hungry for it.

Then he steps lightly down the stairs, in the dark, avoiding the fucking idiot dog, and finds something delicious to eat.

These moments are good. They are perfect, satisfied balls; they feel, to Jamie, like dough rolled between the palms of his hands, or like a thick door clicking exactly shut behind him.

Tonight it's two a.m., and Los Angeles twinkles, all promise, as it sleeps outside the kitchen. Jamie takes a large first bite of avocado, mashed on to brown toast. He has crushed sea salt on to it, as he does often. Less often, but still often enough, although not this time, he adds a shake of tamari, from a black bottle with a red label that inexplicably reminds him of England.

Jamie is English, although he was once Irish, a few

generations ago. But he doesn't like England, and he doesn't much know Ireland. When he was in his early twenties, he went to discover the corner of County Mayo that his family had supposedly come from, and it was a dump. Ugly, damp, and a suicidal shade of grey.

Jamie doesn't even like London – the greatest city on earth, quite probably. He certainly doesn't miss it – it's a place where everybody is rude and envious and too cool, where the air pulses with rain and cold eleven months out of twelve, where everything is expensive, and where some evenings each paving stone seems to hold a black memory. The farther from London Jamie is, the less frightened he feels.

Jamie lives in Los Angeles, and he loves it here.

What's not to love about LA? Warmth, width, water. A soft-top and broad streets to drive it down. Pretty, healthy girls with brown stomachs and white, white teeth. Old-fashioned bars, ribboned with newfangled, newly fashioned people. Life open to the sky.

Who, here, wants to be anywhere else? Who, in LA, doesn't wake up happy?

The dog, whinging and irritating by his feet as he eats the avocado on toast, does not belong to Jamie, and it does not belong in his house. It belongs to a friend, Beth, in her house. But she is in Boston for a fortnight, and so the dog is here, getting on his nerves. Why he agreed so smilingly to have the dog stay is a mystery to him – it's a dog devoid of any glamour or handsomeness. It's a whining, bad-smelling, needy irritation.

At first Jamie pretended to like the dog, but soon realised that there was nothing to be gained from doing this, and stopped. In fact, the pretend dog-liking, while it lasted, actually *diminished* the quality of his life: it resulted in licks on the face that left behind the fleshy smell of canned dog food, and squat little shites, curled happily in the middle of his bedroom floor. The dog craps outside now, and Jamie deliberately shows it no affection.

That the two go in hand is sad. That affection, to the dog, should prod it to take advantage, to provoke, to disrespect by defecating in Jamie's personal space, is sad. It is a small terrier of some kind.

Ignoring the dog, Jamie returns to his bed, post-avocadal.

He likes falling asleep smelling of avocado. He couldn't articulate this himself, as he hasn't realised it in a definite sense, but the midnight feasts of avocado leave a nutty, squishy fug around his face that he likes.

His bed, in a triumph of chance, fits exactly into an alcove that makes up a third of the bedroom. As a result, getting into it involves a quantity of clambering and feels like entering a separate room; like being a wealthy Chinese of another century, with a bed built into the wall like a treasure chest.

Yes, it is a triumph of chance. Jamie didn't buy the

bed for this alcove, for this house – he bought the bed years ago, when he was living in two rooms rented from a friend. There was no alcove in those rented rooms for the bed to fit into, it was up against a wall, as most beds are. It is only now, years later, that the bed fits with such millimetrical perfection into this alcove.

Jamie was not, *is* not, the type of man to start attributing *meanings* to things. That the bed fit so exactly – click! – into the alcove, was a nice chance. That's all.

Life is life, things are things. There's no meaning, no hidden equation or deft structure below any of it. It's all random, coincidence, chance: nice chance, like the exact fit of the California King, or bad chance, like illness. But chance, anyway. Chance. Like a baby having blue eyes or brown.

And that was fine, as chance could bring possibility, and open roads, broad enough for soft-tops. Chance could bring: a pretty girl, or a stubbed toe, or a broken plate, or a spaghetti carbonara, or a frayed grey sweatshirt, or a good book, or a bad movie, produced from London, with Jamie, straight out of drama school, cast in a lead part. And a doorway out of fucking England, away from all the shit, to a new world in Hollywood.

Chance.

The phone rings. The dog yaps from downstairs. It's two-fuckin' thirty in the morning.

94

– Hello.

– Oh, hello. Is that Mr Hallow?

– Yes. Who's this?

– I know it's very late there, but I'm afraid I had to call.
  The voice is English.

– Who *is* this?

– Sorry. My name's Simon Price. I'm a nurse. I work at
  St Margaret's Hospice in St John's Wood. Your father
  was admitted here yesterday evening.

  Jamie sits up cold, and he's suddenly aware of how
  dark it is in the room. He reaches to the light switch.

– Hello? Are you still there?
  says the voice.

– Yes, I can hear you.
  says Jamie.

  There's a pause.

– Mr Hallow,
  says Simon Price,

– your father's not at all well.

And so Jamie finds himself at LAX, waiting to board a
plane, even though with every scowling cell of himself
he does not want to be here.

  Why is he doing this, then? Why is he here, waiting

to board a plane to London, if he doesn't want to be? Why isn't he at home in the California King that fits exactly into the alcove?

Jamie is here because he was too ashamed to tell Simon Price the English Man Nurse that he didn't want to come to see Dad – that he had no interest in coming – that he hadn't seen Dad for five years, and that was fine by him. That whether his father was alive or dead, he didn't care. That St Margaret's Hospice could boil Dad in oil, and go fuck themselves.

The voice of Simon the Man Nurse on the line, apologetic and anxious, shamed Jamie. And so he called an airline.

A small campfire of vanity in Jamie had hoped that the girl at the check-in desk would recognise him and give him an upgrade. But the girl at the check-in desk turned out to be a woman, matter-of-fact and efficient, with a plump bosom and short fingernails. The girl that Jamie had hoped for, with too much make-up and a trim bosom and long fingernails, the kind of girl likely to watch *Do Re Me*, the prime-time detective show that Jamie had a guest part in this series, was three desks along, helping someone else. Even if this older, not-glossy woman had seen Jamie in something – he'd had a large part in a romantic comedy last year, taking billing just underneath two very A-list actors, and it had come out on DVD last month – she wasn't showing it.

The plane was full, sir, she said. It wasn't full when I booked a seat on it this morning, Jamie said. I can assure you, said the woman and her bosom in the stripy blue and red shirt, *acrylic*, that the plane is full. Jamie thanked her, and took his boarding pass. He was given an aisle seat.

He only had hand luggage, a sleek, chocolate leather suit carrier. Inside it he had packed:

4 t-shirts
2 cashmere jumpers
1 sweatshirt
5 pairs of underpants
7 pairs of heavy socks
2 pairs of sports socks
1 pair of running shoes
1 pair of jogging bottoms
1 wash bag
1 pair of black leather shoes
2 shirts

and 1 black suit, in case there was a funeral.

Jamie only planned on staying for three or four days, a week at most, and he knew that a death and its red tape and a funeral were unlikely to happen in that time, but he brought the suit with him anyway. Out of an irritating feeling of being obliged to.

He was wearing faded jeans, and a long-sleeved t-shirt, a navy-blue cashmere coat, a thick, soft, grey scarf, and a pair of in-between shoes, not quite sneakers, not quite formal. He had dressed for London. And for aeroplane air-conditioning. He had in one pocket his cellphone and house keys. In the other his passport and boarding pass. And in his back pocket his wallet.

Through security, zap, scan, tick, Jamie bought a coffee. A latte, a real one made with full-fat hormone-rich cow's milk. And a banana. He'd never been on a diet except for one role playing a mad, emaciated painter. He had no time for diets, even if they were called eating plans or lifestyle choices. He loved food. He ate it. His last girlfriend but one (there was a story there) had laughed with such animate surprise when they'd gone to eat sushi for the first time, and she saw that his eyes had fluttered closed in ecstasy at the first bite. *Watching you eat that*, she said, *is like watching pure happiness*. Pure happiness. That's what food did to him.

Jamie cycled at the gym a few times a week. He swam when he felt like it. He had a stiff back, and did a twice-weekly pilates-yoga blend with his physio, which had thus far kept the thirty-something spread in check. There was no need to be any fitter than this.

He bought a newspaper. Turned to page two. And then in a grunt of vexation – have I left the gas on? Did I leave the windows open? – he remembered the dog. The fucking dog. Who he had left cringing in the TV room. Fucking dog. *Fucking dog*.

Jamie rang Mike, a friend who had his spare keys.

- Shit, Jamie,
  said Mike,
- I'm really sorry. Don't worry about the dog.
- If you could just feed it when you can, and it needs
  to be taken outside to piss. I'm only going to be gone
  two or three days.
- Don't worry about it. Be gone as long as you need.
  The dog can live with me. I'll look after him.
- You don't need to do that, Mike. Just drop in and
  feed it when you can.
- Don't be stupid. I've always had dogs. I'll take care of
  him.
- I'm really sorry about this.
- Christ! Don't apologise, man. *I'm* sorry. The dog'll be
  a pleasure. We'll have fun. What's his name?
- Oh. Uh, Daniel. No, not Daniel. Denver.
- Denver.
  says Mike.
- It's not my dog, Mike.
  says Jamie.
- No, I know. You said.
  If there hadn't been a dying father hanging over the
  phoneline, Mike would not have let this slide. He
  would have, at the least, made a little fun – *you're*
  *looking after this dog and you don't even know its name?*
  *Fucking hell, Jamie.* But an aeroplane away James
  Hallow was losing his hold on his blankets, on his
  life, and so Mike let it go, and said no more than,

99

- No, I know. You said.
- It belongs to a friend of mine who's in Boston. Beth. It's some kind of terrier. I'll call her and pass on your number, so she can call if she's back in LA before me. But it's unlikely. I won't be more than a couple of days.
- It's cool, Jamie. I got the dog covered. Look after yourself.

On the plane Jamie was sitting next to a middle-aged woman in cycling shorts and a SYRACUSE UNIVERSITY sweatshirt. She smiled and said hello as Jamie put his suit carrier and coat in the locker above. This was to be nipped in the bud. Jamie gave a cursory nod, buckled himself in, and took out the in-flight magazine from the seat pocket in front.

The woman, he knew, was looking at him with interest; it was always this kind of woman who looked at him with interest. She had no evident reading material with her, apart from the two words on her chest. The movies wouldn't start until well after take-off. Her hands were folded expectantly in her spandex lap, as if a trans-Atlantic time-killer would drop from the ceiling like an oxygen mask. It was likely she would try to talk to him.

Jamie hated economy class, especially on American airlines where the likelihood of obesity quadrupled. He hated the proximity to these people, the fact that he could not cross his leg without brushing the pasty calf next to his. He hated the fact that if this stranger wanted to talk to him, to elbow him, to study him in detail, she could – he was three inches away from her, closer than most lovers sleep.

He could have flown Business. He could afford it. But why the fuck should he? Why should he spend thousands of dollars in order to see a vindictive, brutal old bastard, who had never done anything but hate him? Who richly, surely, deserved Jamie's hatred in kind? No fraction of this trip need be pleasant.

London. Pawing at Jamie with ancient fingers. Towering with ghosts too old for a Los Angeles head. Too much greatness, too much filth, too many crevices and hidden histories and things to forget. Too much. And now in one of its stone-carved, terrifying corners, it cradled the body of James Hallow, poisonous and malign. Jamie could feel them, his father's hands, pushing into the back of his skull, fingertips indenting into his head, the pain of it spreading. *Pray*. That was always the command. *Pray. Before those worms eat through your head completely.*

Other people, when returning to their home town – not that London would ever be labelled a Home Town, you belonged to London, not the other way – visited their primary schools, childhood haunts and playgrounds, the house where they grew up. Hand in hand with spouse they'd stand on their old street marvelling at how small it all seemed now, pointing up at windows, bittersweet remembrance, *that was my room*.

Not Jamie. The house where he grew up was to be demolished, the rubble burnt, its ashes buried. The only memory Jamie had of the house that did not cause the involuntary tightening of his guts and hardening of his mouth was the memory of walking away from it for the last time. He had thrown a cigarette butt on to the balding front lawn as he left, away from this street forever, leaving Dad, Mum, the stairs and carpets and cooker and wallpaper and bathtub and misery to rot without him.

# 2

The house on Bolan Street was dark, and there were things in the walls. Things with faces that oozed out of the wallpaper, that brushed your passing ankles with seaweed-scented fingers. Jamie would scudder through them to his bed, a magnet of horror. Through the night he could hear them breathing in the passageway, waiting hungrily for his bladder to burst, so that he would be forced out into them, sweating, sickened, terrified.

One night, he decided he had to wet the bed. It was the only thing to do. With eyes shut, he forced the bullet of tension in his pelvis into release, and the gasping, yellow warmth seeped into his pyjamas, into the mattress, down his legs. And then the warmth turned to damp, and Jamie realised that he had done the Wrong Thing. The rasping voices in the passage were coming for him like flies for meat. They were promising to do terrible things in scraping, guttural syllables. Jamie rolled backwards and forwards across his mattress, to distract the Wall People, and to distract himself from the Bad Mistake he had made.

He seemed to be the only one who knew about them. Or, if Dad and Mum knew, they didn't talk about it. It was hard to know what to do, whether to try to tell them. It may be one of those things that would make Dad inexplicably annoyed. Or make Mum look worried and sad and disappointed. Jamie lingered around the kitchen on an after-school evening to try and decide what he should do.

Dad was at the table with a cup of tea that Mum had made. He was filling in forms that were spread across the small surface, and that somehow made the room seem nicer. They were all white, the forms, and clean. Mum was taking little bites out of a biscuit, like a rat. Jamie watched powdery crumbs fall on to the forms, and wanted to wipe them away. He wanted to take the biscuit out of Mum's hand and throw it into the sink.

Instead he stood quietly, thinking his biscuit-throwing thoughts, by the door into the back garden. The top half of it was made from glass squares, three rows of three. The bottom left square had a diagonal crack across it, and Jamie ran his thumbnail in and out of it. They didn't notice him. Dad was looking at the white papers, and Mum was intermittently looking at Dad and concentrating on the biscuit.

He just needed to stay long enough to know Dad's

mood. That's what everything was made of. He just needed to stay long enough, quietly, unnoticed, until he knew whether Dad was having Wobbles or not. When Dad had Wobbles then nothing was okay. Then his mood was strong, and ugly. Jamie ran his nail – bump – into the crack, and – bump – out. Mum still had all that brown biscuit left, even though she had been nibbling, nibbling, nibbling forever. Spraying all the clean forms with biscuit sawdust.

Mum does that. She scatters dust everywhere. Like a Hansel and Gretel track, except grey, and chalky. Not fluffy breadcrumbs or smooth pebbles, but the kind of gritty, dead-like trail that you want to clean away. It's as if she's made of Dust Stuff, and is slowly crumbling around the house. She leaves her dust in the bath, Jamie has noticed, and over her own shoulders. It's as if it's her way of speaking, or saying Hello, Here I Am. Trying to remind everyone that she exists. Because she doesn't speak much. And she's always worried when Jamie speaks. In case Dad is in the wrong mood. 'Hush, hush,' she says, 'hush, hush,' breathing dust into his ears. 'You'll disturb your dad.'

James Hallow looks up from the forms he is filling in, and his wife's eyes scuttle quickly away from him. He is used to this. She is holding a gingernut biscuit between her fingers, mousily eaten around the top edge. She moves her other hand to her hair, and begins to scratch the left side of her head, as if she cannot stop, scratching compulsively. James puts his pen down and catches her wrist with his hand. The scratching stops.

'Eat your biscuit,' he says to her.

She fixes her eyes on the table, and puts the biscuit to her lips.

Jamie doesn't know what his father's forms are, and he doesn't know when will be a good time to move from the kitchen. He thinks it will be okay to tell about the things in the walls, as long as one of Mum or Dad talks to him first. But not now. He mustn't interrupt. Now they are together at the table, and Dad is busy on other things.

The moment comes later, when Dad is watching the television. His hand is on Hannah's knee, and it has put her into a rapture. She stares mistily at her husband's covering hand, as if it is a relic, with a look ecstatic, fearful, and reverential. A few times, her own hand wavers above his, wondering if it dare lower itself on to the sacred knuckles, but it is too frightened – it does not want to disturb this moment of bounty, so it flutters and fights its own longing for touch (it is a hand, after all) and settles back on the bouclé alone.

Jamie will never fully understand, even after both his parents are dead and he sieves old photographs through his fingers into boxes and bins, how she was before. In front of him, she has always been like waxed paper, slippery and dry at the same time, flimsy and transparent. In a housecoat, nervous and old, and

106

ridiculous on the three occasions each year that she emerges from her bedroom in two thin lines of lipstick, looking around with a mixture of trepidation and excitement. Always the same powdery-greasy dark pink colour, for Easter mass, Christmas mass, and on Dad's birthday. Mostly, Dad doesn't notice, and Mum wavers into a blank expression. But once or twice he has lifted her up and said, 'Look at you, Hannah,' or given her a kiss, or twirled her around a bit, or sung a song about a pretty lady who was a Sweetheart. And Mum has laughed and lit up for a moment, and Jamie has found it quite horrible and unnatural, like if a pigeon suddenly stopped on the pavement and gurgled an aria.

Jamie doesn't know that his mother's giggles feel to her like champagne against the side of a boat, the bottle broken in its own froth. Green cuts of glass among the bubbles. For there is as much terror, violence, and relief in Hannah's reaction as happiness. Her three days of lipstick are a bravery applied in dread, and undertaken for nothing other than her own soul's sake. Her husband is as likely to react to her made-up lips with a twirl and a two-step, as to come roaring at her like the mouth of a river, crashing over her with awful names, and catching her with a foamy clip. When he picks her up and calls her pretty and dances, the relief breaks in glass and fizz, and she hears herself laughing – a sound almost as curious to her as it is to her son.

Her son, who grows up by stashing himself in

corners, unnoticed. Hush, Jamie, hush, don't bear the brunt of your dad's sickness. The son who will never know what his mother was like before – before she was waxy and frail and silent, before lipstick looked ridiculous on her.

Even when flipping through dead photographs he will not quite grasp how joyous her moment of loveliness was. His mother bloomed like wildflowers, with disobedient pink in her cheeks, and hair that tumbled like dark surf. And she had James Hallow entranced. He looked at her with triumph, with disbelieving pride that this summer bird had come to eat from his hand.

When James began to be cruel, she faded quickly. Now, not even ten years older, she twitches and crumples, all the roundness gone, all the flight bent out of her. One, two, three days of lipstick, foolish and doddering. Clipped. Extinguished.

Jamie stands next to the television, waiting; he knows not to stand in front of it. His dad, after a while, gets up, pressing down on his thighs with his hands as he does. He switches the television off, and Jamie says, 'Dad.'

Mum looks up, with an air of confusion, as if surprised by this new voice in the room, as if Jamie was a stranger walked in from the street. She looks at him baffled and distressed.

'Can I tell you something?'

James turns to his son, looking amused.

'Go on then,' he says.

'There's something in the wall outside my room.'

Dad makes a face with his lips.

'What?' he says.

'There are people in the wall, outside my room.'

Mum has made a little noise, a breathy squeak. Hush, she is saying, hush, don't disturb your dad. She is a m-o-u-s-e.

'What do you mean?' Dad asks.

'There are people,' he says, looking back at his dad, trying concertedly not to get scared and turn his eyes away, 'who are in the wall at night. They whisper bad things, and try to touch you.' Jamie feels his heart starting to rush, with fearful memory of those chopped-up faces, and with developing fear of his father and his father's palm.

But the faces are worse than Dad. Otherwise he wouldn't be saying anything at all, he would be keeping quiet, counting tiles, looking at carpet.

Mum has stood up, and is now just behind Dad.

'Don't be so silly,' she says, talking fast, but quietly, always quietly. 'Don't bother your dad with such silly things.'

Jamie doesn't look at her. He looks at Dad.

The explosion doesn't come. Dad stands, looking with neon eyes at Jamie. After a few seconds he scrunches his mouth again, and says, still looking into Jamie's face,

'Hm. Go to bed.'

Then he turns towards the kitchen. Mum scurries after him. Jamie is left in the room alone, and soon obeys, taking himself upstairs.

They will start tonight as they always do. Jamie has taken a bucket from downstairs and put it in his wardrobe, in case he needs to pee. He lies facing out from the wall, with his desk lamp on for safety, and hopes that he will fall asleep fast.

But someone is coming down the passage and it is Dad.

Not Mum. She is downstairs somewhere nibbling and crumbling.

Dad stands, he is the King of this house.

'There are no ghosts in the walls, Jamie,' he says.

*They're not ghosts*, Jamie wants to say, but a black fog has seeped in with his father, and he does not feel clear enough to say anything. The air is charged with a soggy, mushroom-smelling thing, and Jamie shifts up to sitting.

'The only ghosts are in your head,' says Dad, still standing in the door, framed like a Leonardo Man, without the circle, without the stellated limbs, so not a Leonardo Man, no not at all. 'There is nothing in this house.'

It sounds final, but Jamie feels squirmy. Should he try to explain again? Better, this time?

Dad nods towards the desk lamp. 'Why is that light on?'

The fog is thickening into mulch, it is spreading out of Dad like locusts, a blackening, sticky damp with a tone of voice that sounds like – smack!

'Jamie, why is that light on?' Dad's voice is all fists. 'Have you been sleeping with that light on?'

'No,' says Jamie, and the air buckets into his mouth like wet ash as he speaks; he wants to choke.

'Don't lie,' says Dad, and comes in from the door frame, to the side of Jamie's bed. He reaches forward, and Jamie has learnt already not to flinch, because flinching only makes Dad feel worse; but he's not reaching for Jamie, he's reaching for the lamp, and he has picked it up, and screwed the bulb out of the lamp, while it is still on, which you're never supposed to do.

'You're a liar, and you've got devils in your head. Worms in your head, Jamie.'

Jamie is wide-eyed. The dark is too dark to make out any shapes.

'If I were you, I'd pray. Pray that God makes you honest, stops you from being a liar. Ghosts in the walls! There are no ghosts in this house.' Dad is hissing, rumbling hissing like a Snake God, *Kukulkan from Mexico*, who they're learning at school, who comes down the temple steps when the sun is in a certain way.

Dad's hand finds its way through the dark on to Jamie's head, gives him a rough shove so that Jamie falls clumsily into lying down. *How can he see me in this dark? How does he know where to put his hand in this dark?*

There are no smacks tonight, certainly no beatings, and Jamie no longer hears what Dad is saying to him. It is the same old Fear Talk, the stuff to make Jamie afraid. But tonight, in this reeling, snake-spitting dark, Jamie doesn't hear. As Dad gurgles on, letting forked poisons into the air, Jamie is thinking of the faces in the corridor. Ready for him in the dark, to straw him over with slick fingers. They will eat him into that wall. He will boil in it. Dad won't help. There is no light, and they are free to come for him.

Jamie sleeps that night quite close to frenzy for a little boy, gripped like putty by fear.

But one day soon all this will make him brave.

Jamie will go to war with his Wall People, alone, out of necessity. And when he does, he hardens like a chestnut against every other fear as well. The war against the greater fear conquers the fear of his father.

One day, not so very far away, he will say *fuck off, Dad*, and will wrest away sneering from his father's grip. The first to do so.

He will carry his head rearing upwards, like a horse. *Fuck off*. And then no one can have him anymore. His imagination will be his own.

# 3

Jamie's father looks at him wearily, with half-closed, heavy eyes, and then turns away to watch the ceiling again. Jamie wishes he wasn't alone here. But wishes are bubbles. Pop. No use wishing.

No relief from the dirty memories, fanning like pondmoss on the surface between Jamie and the dying man.

What should he say? Should he say anything? The nurse said that James Hallow could hear, and respond, and squeeze her hand, and eat and drink with assistance.

Imagine. Dad holding hands.

'Dad. It's me, Jamie.'

There is no response from his father, who continues to watch the ceiling, unmoving but for the occasional hooded blink, mouth slightly ajar. Jamie comes closer, a couple of steps being enough to cross the small room to his father's right – he's a god in here, cruising continents and running rivers in a single shuffle. The bed has standard hospital sides, three rods thick, to stop Dad hurling himself to the floor in some ecstatic passion. Hah. Jamie's instinct is to lean forward and hold on to these bars, but it somehow seems an obscene thing to do, so he just stands, dangling.

'Dad?' he says again.

The man in the bed creaks his head to the side, hovers on his son for a few seconds, and then, once more, looks away. His eyes do not even try to focus.

'Dad', Jamie says.

'Dad'. Again.

'Dad'. Pause.

*'Dad'.*

His voice gets harder each time, ashamed of itself unrequited in the silence of the room.

Jamie feels a fool. He could tear his clothes off, squat, pummel his chest and yodel, for all the effect it would produce. The thing in the bed would just turn its head slowly, as if through tar, and then turn back to the plaster cracks above him. The eyes would remain mudded in film, like a fish's.

He stands for some minutes. He is still. And like that – motionless – he looks more like his deathbed father than he'd care to.

Jamie is imagining all sorts of things.

He is imagining turning calmly around, pulling

down his jeans, bending over, and mooning. While pointing grandly to his bottom and singing an operatic free-form based on the word 'ARSE'.

He is imagining collecting every meagre item from the room and from inside his own bag – t-shirts, telephone, remote control, underpants, book, shaving foam, plastic cup – and piling them all on top of his father like sand, the sand that he was too afraid to pile on the old beach holidays. His father would be covered in hospital and Los Angeles debris, obscured completely except for two big toes pointing out, and two dead eyes staring up.

God, he could do anything at all, and it wouldn't make a difference.

He is imagining laying his body down on the bed, alongside, laying his face on his father's stomach. And then his father's hand would noiselessly animate itself, and bring itself to rest on his hair. It would be the most tender surprise of his life.

Jamie wishes his father had died a long time ago.

He grabs the rail of the hospital bed with both hands, shakes it, minutely but definitely, and leaves the room.

Meryl's interest is pricked by the sight of what she sees as a gorgeous young man, he must be about her son Ben's age, leaning outside the closed door of Room 414. He's about the same height as Ben, although less broad, with very dark, curly hair. He is wearing faded grey-blue jeans, a long-sleeved black t-shirt, and is drinking coffee. Or tea.

But there's no teabag string hanging over the edge of the cup, so it must be coffee.

Unless he's thrown the teabag away.

'Can I get you a chair, dear?' asks Meryl, walking lop-sidedly towards him, worrying mid-sentence about whether her lipstick is properly applied – whether there are smudges, or if it's on her teeth.

'A chair? No thanks.' Jamie looks up, smiling a mechanical smile of rebuffal at the lady in his habitual, slightly annoyed way – his nose lifts upwards, a backwards nod, his eyes glaze over so as no one can come in.

'Are you here visiting a family member?'

'My father.' Jamie juts his chin towards the door, and then turns his head away from Meryl, to look out of the window, down into the rectangular hospice garden. He takes a sip of thin, burnt coffee from the polystyrene cup. The one thing that might be helpful here, in a place of vigil and sleeplessness, would be a decent cup of coffee. For fuck's sake. And who is this bat?

'It's lovely having this greenery,' says Meryl, looking through the window along with the handsome young man, poor Meryl, always trying so hard, 'isn't it?'

It's always women who do this, never men. Men have an innate understanding of etiquette between strangers.

They nod, they may give a terse smile, they acknowledge, and then they get on with themselves. They don't prod their way into lives not their own. Always looking to talk, talk, talk. Jamie looks at the woman, concentrating his face into the instruction for her to *go away*. 'I suppose so,' he says, 'although, it really does depend.'

'My *dad*,' he intones, 'can only stare at the ceiling, so it's not that much use to *him*.'

Oh dear. Meryl's face scrumples. 'This must be a very difficult time,' she says. The young man doesn't respond. 'If there's anything I can do, you just let me know. My name's Meryl.'

'Beryl?'

'No, Meryl. Like Meryl Streep.'

'Ah, of course.' Jamie huffs a laugh through his nose. 'Meryl Streep.'

Meryl notices his amusement. 'Although the similarity ends there, doesn't it?' She laughs her deliberate laugh – punctuated Ha Ha Has – with her head forward and her eyes bright and expectant, eager to be liked. 'Doesn't it?' she says again. Jamie strains a smile. 'Anyway, you just come and find me, if there's anything you need.'

'Thanks,' says Jamie, before puzzling casually: 'Ah, do you mind me asking, though, Meryl, who exactly you are? Are you a nurse?'

'Oh.' Meryl doesn't know why, but this question always dampens her a little, it makes her feel somehow unimportant. 'I'm a hospice volunteer. I'm here to help in any way I can.'

Jamie looks at her, nods curtly, and then feels a moment of guilt.

'Thanks,' he says again, in compensation, before bending to pick up a suit carrier that Meryl hadn't noticed, and walking towards the lift.

Jamie had gone straight from Heathrow to St Margaret's, and now is in a black cab on his way to the hotel. The cab grinds through the dark evening, small mercy looking down on the lower cars so Jamie can feel elevated, removed from things. He is tired and blunt.

The hotel is large, and old-fashioned in its luxury. When Jamie had stayed here last, promoting a movie five years ago, he had been given a room with some hotel term for ritzy – 'deluxe', 'executive'. But this trip he is not part of a film, and is footing his own bill, and this trip does not want to pour any excessive comfort around himself. Things will be tolerable at best. Why should he enjoy any part of this ludicrous bloody mis-adventure? He has booked a standard room.

He has chosen to stay in this hotel again, liveried and expensive as it is, only because he knows he will be protected by its location and style as he was last time – he can disappear into it, and almost pretend he isn't in London, where he was born, where he hates more than anywhere else. London is hard faces, asthmatic air, punishing memories. The hotel provides escape.

It is directly on Park Lane, where the cars stream cruelly, incessantly past, where there are few pedestrians, and few reminders of London life. It is a hub, an artery, not anywhere where people stop, recognise one another, or lay any part of their characters into the pavement stones. Perched on Park Lane, Jamie can remain a tourist in the city where he grew up, look out of his windows at a London roaring, impressive, and unlike itself.

And inside it feels like a fortress. The hushed, plush spaces, high-up rooms, swipe keys and elevators cocoon Jamie in safety. Once inside, he is hidden. Like a rabbit in a hat, gone.

It was when staying at this hotel, five years ago, that Jamie had last seen his father. The meeting was certainly not at Jamie's instigation – Dad had managed to get through to him in LA several times, imploring with a voice that sounded like a stranger's, as if he had swallowed his own vocal chords. It was at Dad's third, bizarre phone call that Jamie had admitted with temper that he would be in London later in the year, and had promised to be in touch. Why he kept his promise, he didn't know.

He had then spoken to Dad on the phone in his deluxe, executive room, and arranged to meet him in the bar of the next-door hotel, which was fifty yards further down Park Lane. He would not have Dad come here, where he was staying. This was his space, his magician's hat to burrow into. Dad would be the worst possible invasion.

Plus the other hotel was modern, glass and steel grand, and bound to intimidate the mashed-up two-bit boxer from the dead end suburbs. Good. Stupid old bastard.

James Hallow had arrived at the place decreed by his son, the underlit, sparse bar, an hour and a half early. He had been preparing himself for the entire morning beforehand, putting money aside for the taxi, and then double-, triple-, quadruple-, countlessly-checking and rechecking that the money was there. He had to see his Jamie, he had to see his son, and he absolutely mustn't get lost or waylaid.

James summoned and entered the taxi two hours before he needed to. He must not get caught out by a blackout, or a twitcher fit. He must not get misty and lost. He must not forget everything.

*He must not get lost and go black and start twitching, okay?*

He left home two hours early, and had put money aside to have a taxi, because he mustn't get lost in the mist on the buses.

He wore a suit, spruce as he could manage, and had told the bar staff on arrival that he was waiting for his son. He said it in a loud voice, and didn't see or didn't care to see the smirking glances that were swapped around him.

'I'm waiting for my son.'

It was the truth.

For an hour and a half he waited, looking into a glass of coca-cola. He'd intermittently forget it was there, and then, with goldfish surprise, would see it again, and lean in to take a sip through the straw.

'I'd like a straw, please,' he had said to the waiter. He had remembered to ask for a straw. That was habit now.

Although, actually, he did sometimes forget. He sometimes forgot everything.

But not this time.

When Jamie arrived he was wearing a pale grey t-shirt and jeans, and looked so very like he did when he left home all those years ago that it was confusing. James made a move to lift himself from sitting and go towards his son.

– Dad,

said Jamie.

– Don't get up.

His father's face was the same: crooked, with blinking eyes, the face of a bully. But it had aged terribly; aged and gummed up, as if Dad were wearing a Halloween mask of himself. Its flesh was fallen and hanging, as if melting from the bones. And he was unsteady, struggling to get up and then sit back down again. His hands were shaking.

Jamie had seen his father in all sorts of states, but never like this. Clearly, he wasn't well – there was something beyond the usual sickness that was wrong.

But Jamie didn't want to ask. He didn't want to see.

Without a smile he sat down opposite his father, his heart rampaging in his chest with such force that he was convinced any passer-by could hear it. Why he was so nervous, and so appalled, he didn't know – his father was a buffoon, a sad old git, and Jamie was immune to him. It was just the weirdness of the sagging face and the frail movements that Jamie hadn't been expecting. He felt lynched by them.

Dad had started to do something, it wasn't apparent to Jamie what:

He was lifting his hand and holding it above the centre of the low, round table between them. It wobbled horribly, waving and spooling as if part of a haka. Jamie looked at the shuddering hand with incomprehension, and felt his awkwardness rising. The hand was fluttering like some strange voodoo, as if Dad were about to incant tribal ancestors from the sand-blasted glass.

Then he realised – Dad was offering his hand. Dad was offering to shake hands.

Jamie was baffling inside himself, at the severe change in his father, who apparently, suddenly, couldn't even shake hands. As if watching from a far away point he saw his own steady hand reach out and with speed shake Dad's. He felt his palm skin push against the palm skin of Dad, briefly, smooth and dry. Dad drew his hand back and placed it, still quivering and dipping, under the table. He was looking down intently into his glass.

A much-denied part of Jamie, small and curled up and unprotected, was in shock. He had never imagined anything like this, and all he could do was ignore it; ignore everything; ignore and move on.

– Dad? 're you alright for a drink?

Jamie asked, folding his arms, his chin jutting backwards.

Dad, still looking into the brown liquid of his coca-cola, said,

– Your mum died last year, my son. She's dead. I had to tell you.

It took a minute for Jamie to process.

*Your mum died last year*, my son.

*My son?* What the fuck was this *my son* business? Had Dad been watching mafia movies?

Jamie felt his face nastying into a smirk. The combination of Dad's honey-sticky, slurring words, spoken as if each syllable were an assault course, and the *my son*, had Jamie wanting to spit with laughter – laughter and shock were boiling up in him like witches' brew. But he kept his expression in order, pulled his head back further, pushed the boiling down and dipped his face in stone.

– I know, Dad.

- There was a funeral. I went to it. But I didn't have your phone number. I only found it from your mum's book after your mum died. Lots of numbers. I called you. I called you, remember?

Jamie suddenly felt a rush of fury sap up his gullet. He snaps,

- I know there was a funeral, Dad. Who the fuck do you think paid for it? I spoke to you on the phone, the day after she died. *I* called *you*.

James Hallow looked up at his son blankly, with blockish incomprehension. He absorbed nothing of what Jamie had said. The mood around this small table was becoming dangerous, and bizarre.

- You're on the tele, now. My son, an American.

James said.

Jamie looked at his father in disbelief.

- You didn't come when your mum died. May God keep her soul. May God forgive her sins. May God forgive her. May God forgive her.

These last two May God forgives are muttered.

- May God forgive her for what, Dad? May God forgive her for *what*?
- You are my son, and her son. But you weren't at her funeral.
- I paid for the fucking funeral.
- Fucking? Don't say *fucking*, stupid boy. *Fucking* get you down. My son, with worms eating his head inside out.

These were old words; Jamie had heard them, in variation, throughout his life. But the difference this time was that James had said them without violence, without passion of any kind. He said them almost apologetically, plaintively, looking down at his hands that pathetically clutched the edge of the table. There was a crush of embarrassment in his expression, as if he hadn't wanted to say the words at all.

But it was too late. They were out.

Jamie leant forward in his chair, resting his elbows on his wide-apart knees, his hands knitted together in their centre. He flexed his fingers, extended and balled them, as if preparing punches. Who did he resemble?

– That's right, Dad. Worms in my fucking head.

He pushed up from his knees, ringing ear to ear with upset, and walked away from the table.

– Don't go!

said James, who had been waiting here for so long. Who had put aside taxi money. He had shaved his face at six a.m., bloodbath.

But Jamie's back had already pushed through the door – might as well have pushed into a magic wardrobe and out into Narnia.

– My son,

James said, miserably, as quietly as the mouse he had married and buried. His words once more struggled as if through mortar.

That was the last time Jamie had seen his father.

Jamie woke at twenty to eleven the next morning, and thought about calling the hospice to see whether his father had died in the night.

But instead he called room service and ordered breakfast – eggs benedict, a latte, croissants, grapefruit juice, and a yoghurt. After a shower with pygmy hotel products – even in a place this expensive they couldn't give you a fully grown bottle of shampoo – breakfast arrived, on a trolley with a big silver dome. The room service man extended the leaves of the trolley so it became a tableclothed table, removed the dome so that it became eggs benedict, and Jamie saw that places had been laid for two. He didn't comment on it.

He ate everything sitting on the edge of the bed, except one croissant and half the bowl of yoghurt, and then got dressed. It didn't look cold from the window, but inevitably it would be. Jamie thought of Beth's dog and of Mike. The dog's name, he now remembered with certainty, was not Daniel or Denver, but Buster.

At the hospice he strode straight past reception and into the lift, up to the third floor. The reality and strangeness of the situation collided inside his stomach with his breakfast, and a shadow of hot vomit grenched into the back of his mouth and then sunk back down again. Why was he here at all, walking alone into a London hospice to stand in silence by his estranged father's bed, as if making some sacred vigil? What, exactly, was he supposed to do?

Back in the room and his father is, if anything, less responsive than yesterday. His eyes are closed, his head falls back into the pillows and his mouth is ajar. His breathing is a gritty, rasping rattle, filtering into the room from his throat and sinuses. He looks like he has been recently shaved, which accounts for the smell of soap that sits faintly in the air – but not for the smell of meat, as if somewhere close by is a butcher's shop.

James is in a deep sleep, drugged and drowning and exhausted from his waking agitations in the night and morning. He hears nothing when Jamie talks. Nothing. There is a decay of glue in his ears, behind which his munching, treacly dreams crash and scurry for space in the imploding head.

Jamie is standing white knuckled by the bed. Breakfast vomit comes up his throat again, and he thinks he might do something dreadful, like wrench the television from its wall bracket and bring it crashing down on to his father's head.

One morning, a winter morning much like this one only thirty years ago, Jamie had opened his bedroom door and there was a hat outside it. A hat, sitting on the carpet, right in front of his door; made of rough knit and thick-striped in grey and dark red. The shop label still poked up from its crown like a twig.

He had never seen this hat before, and he did not

know how it came to be sitting here, so definitely. It had not been dropped or left by accident, you could tell that from the expression of it. It had been placed there, on purpose.

Jamie looked at it for a moment or two, and then bent to pick it up. It was a soft hat, and it felt friendly. He put it on his head.

And then he whipped it off, faster than he had put it on, and in a panic fixed his gaze on a patch of flocked wall. If Dad caught him here, with a stranger's hat on his head, it could be bad.

But what was he to do now? As he stood still as a statue with the stripy, soft thing in his hand? His fingers grew hot. What was he to do? With this hat? This mystery hat, arrived from nowhere?

Dad was not well today, just as he wasn't well yesterday or the day before. He was not getting dressed, and he was mostly loud and sweaty in their bed, the bed of him and Mum. So he couldn't go to Dad with it, because Dad wasn't downstairs making toast and syrupy black coffee, Dad was in bed, all day most probably, with dark shadows in his face and all twisted up in the bedsheets.

Even if Dad were better, Jamie would have to think twice and many times about going to him with this hat, as who knows Dad could accuse him of stealing it, of doing something dodgy, of being a rotten apple with a worm stuck in.

And Mum? What was the point. Even at seven years old as he was today, Jamie knew it was pointless going to Mum about anything, as she didn't exist. She was just a shape.

Jamie didn't know what to do so he stuffed the hat into his pocket with a soaring feeling of guilt, and this hat, that for a second looked like it might have been a nice surprise, became another worry, another potential accident to avoid.

Four days later during the night a packet of Fox's Crunch Creams found their way to the receiving patch of carpet outside Jamie's bedroom door. Again, there was a purposeful air about them; again, Jamie did not know what to do. After anxious deliberation, and a little agony, Jamie snuck the Crunch Creams, un-opened, into the kitchen cupboard as if they had always been there. He later saw that Mum had opened the biscuits without challenging them; it was a relief. Even then, though, he didn't have one.

He didn't have one because he didn't know what they were, and his instinct was to be afraid. In this house where Dad was barricaded into their bed by goo and evil, where he watched you and set traps for you with a terrorising magic – you could not eat the biscuits. Not even one. You could not keep the hat on your head. Not even for a minute. Because they could be the thing to send you to the floor with a reeling whack. They could turn the tables on you. They could spoil it all.

No good biscuits, no happy hat, were possible in Dad's house. And even while they *looked* friendly, even though they *seemed* like a wonderful enchantment, Jamie could not trust them. He was bewildered by them, in a painful way. He did not understand how they could possibly appear at his door, and his head hurt with thinking of them all day long, upsetting himself with the horrors they might hold.

Then, two days after the Fox's Crunch Creams, the culmination came. Jamie woke up and opened his door – it was *not* Christmas, it was *not* his birthday – and standing upright facing him was a red and blue and gold bike. It had gears – loads, and reflecting bits in the pedals, and thick padding on the handlebars, and like something out of a movie like a flash of brilliant light it knocked the stuffing out of Jamie's eyes. Next to the bike, lined up neatly on the carpet, was a white helmet, still in plastic wrapping, and kneepads and wrist guards, both black.

He just didn't know what to do, he just did not – know – what – to do, so he sat down cross-legged on the floor where he was. His desire for the bike – to go to it, to touch it, to fling his arms around it as if it were a friend or a brother – coupled with his fear of doing so, made him cry.

Jamie was not a loud boy – au contraire he was quiet, so quiet at home he sometimes startled his mother from her biscuits just by being alive – so when Hannah heard tears she had to come out to see. There he was, her son, and there was the bike and its laid-out safety bits beside it and she covered her mouth with her hands.

Jamie stood up when he saw her, still in his pyjamas, still crying, and said,

'I don't know about it, I swear. I swear, Mum, I've never seen it.'

He wished now he had kept the hat and the biscuits, as proof, as evidence of what had been happening, to show that it had nothing to do with him.

Hannah was shaking her head, not knowing what to do for the best. Except, of course, to not wake James, who had had another night of jittering and shouting at himself and dragging her soul over hard ground with the noises he made in the dark. She did not understand the bicycle and the crying son, and she had to screw her head on and think as fast as she could.

Dad had been in one of his proper sicknesses for a while now, one of the fortnights or months when Jamie barely saw him, except perhaps for a few horrible moments coming out of the bathroom, crossing in the passage; moments Jamie would rather forget. Dad was nutty and crowing in bed, slicky-sweaty and scary and the worst of everything; Dad couldn't've done anything like this. And wouldn't've, besides. Why would he do something like this? Why would he Boo Radley in the night?

Ill, savage, calloused men have their reasons, even as their blackest monsters visit. James Hallow must have had his reasons. Protection for his small son, who was vulnerable and preyed upon by bad things. Who saw bad things in the walls. Who was a sitting duck. A hat to keep him warm, good things to eat to make him strong and loud, and in the absence of wings a chariot to fly away on, fast, from all the danger.

Although she had taken her hands from her face, Hannah had still said nothing, and Jamie was getting desperate thinking of all the possible outcomes to this disastrous morning of surprise, of this bike gleaming at him like an angel.

'Mum?' he says.

Hannah takes a step towards him – just one. 'It looks like a nice bicycle,' she says, and Jamie's face expands in incomprehension. She touches the left handlebar with a weak hand, and Jamie with every churning bit is jealous of the action, and he still doesn't know what is coming, or what might ever happen ever again. He can't bring himself to say anything else, lest his heart squelch out of his mouth with a burp, like a frog.

'Whose is it?' asks Jamie, and every part of him contracts as if preparing for a blow.

Hannah is silent for a long while, and, once she has removed her limpy hand from it, she says, 'It's for you. You must be quiet, now, though.'

'Is it from you?' he asks. 'Is it from you?' and the little

132

boy's face is so lit up with amazement and – what's the opposite of horror? – joy; joy – that in another lifetime, in a parallel dimension, Hannah Hallow's tired, dusty heart might have cracked to see it.

She shakes her head, and Jamie's tummy at once plummets with disappointment, and wheels with hope.

'Did *he* get it for me?' Jamie asks, his heart, that frog, leaping.

'Shh, you must be quiet, now. You can't wake your dad. You've got to keep quiet, now.' There is panic in Hannah's voice, a tremble beyond the usual. 'You best not talk to him about this. You just take it downstairs, now. You mustn't wake him. Don't talk to him about the bicycle. You just take it downstairs. Quietly. Quietly. Take it downstairs quietly. You mustn't make any noise. Just play with it quietly and don't talk to him about it.'

Him, him, him, him, Him. James Hallow is asleep in ugliness in his bed, behind a door expertly, silently closed by his wife. He must not be woken, by his son's joy. Even though he has been the maker of it.

Jamie reached out and touched his bike, blue and gold and red. It felt just like he knew it would have felt.

'I would like you to tell me, in your professional opinion, if there is any point in me being here.'

Jamie is standing at the hospice reception, one arm extended out, its fingers drumming on the counter. As if he is holding the desk at bay.

'Mr Hallow, as I've said, your dad is very ill—'

'Please don't repeat yourself,' cuts in Jamie, 'I heard you the first time. I don't think you're understanding my question. I don't think you're understanding the fucking situation here. My father is as good as dead. He's lying in that bed like a fucking corpse, staring at the fucking ceiling.'

'Mr Hallow, when you arrived yesterday we explained the advanced state of your dad's illness. I'm sorry to press this point, but he is in the last days of his life. In order to make his passing easier, we're giving him morphine. It's a high dose, and, as I explained, he will not be conscious, or what you would call conscious, for a lot of the time. If it would help, we can sit in private and I can explain it to you in more detail.'

'I am not a moron. I don't need any more fucking detail. It's all pretty clear. I've apparently crossed the world to stare at my dead father staring at the fucking ceiling. For no fucking reason at all.'

Jamie's voice is not low, and the nurse underneath her calm manner is uneasy.

'Mr Hallow, I know this must be difficult. But your dad, in his clear moments, must be very glad that you're here. And I imagine it's because he's so ill that you are here, isn't it?'

'No. It fucking isn't.' Jamie's voice is towering higher, rougher. 'I'm here because someone from this hospice called me, in the middle of the fucking night in Los

Angeles, and told me to get on a plane. So here I am, only to bloody discover that Dad can't fucking see me, just lies in that cot as good as dead. Old man monster. Fucking monster, he's a fucking *monster*.'

At this moment Jamie finds himself, to his horror, to his mortification, suddenly in tears. Gulping tears, of a kind that he hasn't before shed on screen or in life. He is sobbing.

The nurse has come from behind her counter, and places a soft hand on his arm.

'It's alright,' Jamie says, wiping his cheeks with rough, surprised fingers and drawing back, 'I'm not crying.'

'Mr Hallow.'

'Jamie, Jamie, my name's Jamie.'

'Jamie, if you just come with me.' The nurse is without any force leading Jamie to one side, with a hand now on his back.

Jamie doesn't want to go anywhere, wants to go nowhere, is thrown by his watering eyes, lost in his constricting throat and his dipping, distending chest.

But somehow he is ushered into a small room, and is sat down and brought tea that he hasn't asked for and doesn't want.

And, through the corridors runs the whisper, rising, rising, *This is a job for Meryl.*

# Meryl

# 1

Meryl was indispensable. Which was a satisfying thing to be. Although she made light of her indispensability, of course:

*Who*, she'd say, *Me?*

Yes, Meryl, You!

*Who*, she'd say, *Little Me?*

Yes, you, Meryl, you. What would we do without you?

*Oh, you'd get along just fine. Who needs Little Old Me?*

We do, Meryl! We do! We'd be lost without you!

*Oh*, Meryl would say, with a wide smile, *I don't know about that.*

Meryl was a volunteer at St Margaret's Hospice. She came in on Wednesday, Thursday, and Friday afternoons, which allowed her to go to her Samba-cise classes in the mornings beforehand, try to shift some of those kilos!, and have a coffee and a gossip in the gym café with the girls afterwards. Once she'd got home, dried her hair, taken the dog out for a short walk and a poo, and had a light lunch, she would take the bus the twenty minutes south-east, and spend the afternoon from one p.m. until five p.m. visiting with the patients, playing games, reading newspapers, and chatting. Sometimes she also helped out with administration – you wouldn't believe the constant stapling, and filling out, and photocopying that had to be done in a place like St Margaret's to keep it going, to keep on providing the wonderful service that it did. Where do all the paperclips go when you need them? that was Meryl's question! Hoo!

Meryl had some lovely cards from family members of those who had passed.

*Dear Meryl, Thank you for lightening my father's load in the last, precious days of his life. We shall be eternally grateful, The Welch Family.*

Isn't that just beautiful? With everything they have to think about, to take the time to write a card. It's just beautiful, don't you think?

*Dear Meryl, It has been an emotional few weeks, and we couldn't have done it without you. We always knew Nana was peaceful and happy left in your kind, capable hands. Thank you so much, you are a special person. With love Karen, Pete, Damian, and Penny (Allison).*

Isn't that just beautiful? I think that's just beautiful. Don't you think that's just beautiful? Just beautiful.

Beautiful, beautiful, beautiful. Don't you think?

The cards would stay on the dining room side table until they became morbid, and then Meryl would put them away in a drawer, another layer to the clutter in the house, and Jo, her husband, would be unintentionally relieved. Not that he didn't think it was a great thing for Meryl to be doing – it *was* a great thing to be doing, all their friends said so – but sometimes, the thought of all those dead people. Well.

Today, Thursday, Meryl arrives at the hospice five minutes late, thanks to a sprain in her ankle that has been slowing her down for over a week now. She hobbles into the staff kitchenette, where her wonderful friend Simon, who is a nurse, and also gay, not that that makes any difference you understand, offers her tea.

'Oh, no, not for me, dear. Don't you worry about me. You just go ahead and make tea for yourself. I might have some a little later. If I've time. You just go ahead.'

'You sure, Meryl? All it takes is a bag in a cup.'

'Oh no, darling, you just go ahead for yourself.'

Meryl is tall, especially for her generation, and wide around her lower-middle. It is not fatness, much as Meryl frets about losing weight – it is just natural width; long, solid bones; a brawny constitution. Hips. She is a village girl in her genes, an inescapable hereditary reality no matter the urban accoutrements, shopping bags, theatre trips, and butter-free butter. She lowers herself awkwardly, shifting her weight on to one side, and then allowing gravity to push her to sitting.

She puffs. Lifts her leg, places her foot on a chair opposite, puffs again. Simon stands by the counter, drinking his tea, and flipping through a tabloid newspaper.

A minute passes.

Meryl pulls back her grey trouser leg, and pushes off her shoe with her other foot, to reveal an ankle swaddled in a gravelly-pink sprain sock, fraying around the edges. 'Oh dear,' Meryl says, almost (but not quite) under her breath. She begins to squeeze the ankle with her hands, to massage it. As always, there is an ache in her lower back as she leans forward.

Simon looks up from his paper. 'Ankle still bad?' he asks.

'Yes dear, I'm afraid so. I tell you, it's not good – *not good*.' Meryl rolls down the sprain sock. 'See?' she says. 'It's still so swollen.'

Simon peers over. He sees that the ankle is thick, although not necessarily any thicker than its colleague. The skin does look rather taut and meaty, though. And – *foul*! Simon's sense of the pristine *shudders* – Meryl's bumpy, cuticle-covered toenails are licked with a coat of lilac polish. That she has applied polish to such untended, crusted feet is dreadful to Simon – it would be better if she left them naked. But instead she has chosen to *ornament* them, and this repels him. Colostomy bags and catarrh Simon can meet with a cheerful, sometimes even a wry, straightforwardness. There is no awkwardness with patients, because he is so uncomplicatedly unbothered. But *this* – foul! Toes ghoulishly sprouting crumbling lilac nails, ragged and warped. Decorated dirtiness. *What is wrong with most women?* Simon stands to tip his half-drunk tea down the sink.

'You need to rest it for a few days, Meryl. It's probably staying swollen because you're using it too much.'

'Oh, I know, I know. If only I could. But there's just too much to do. I can't sit at home all day with my feet up. If only, eh? No rest for the wicked.'

'It would only take a couple of days to heal – not forever. Then the problem would be solved.'

'Oh, well, I don't know about that.'

'You need to look after yourself,' says Simon, giving Meryl a pat on the shoulder and a smile, before excusing himself back to his shift.

Meryl looks at her watch, and pushes herself to standing. She pulls her top down, examines her trouser legs (sprain sock just peeking through, check), and takes a lipstick from her handbag which she applies without a mirror, smacking her lips together as in the adverts. She is not a bad-looking woman, Meryl; there is something refined in her profile. But any natural elegance has over the years been whittled down and buried underneath aspirational mannerisms and big, learnt, fake smiles, a physical clumsiness and nervousness that has grown from a lack of self-love. She has aged fast.

Meryl's first stop today is with dear old Mary on the third floor. Mary, like many of the patients here, has cancer, hers is in her ovaries, and spreading. She is very old, but she is well enough yet, and will be for a week or two before the real deterioration starts.

'Hel-lo!' sing-songs Meryl, rounding the corner into Mary's room. 'How. Are. YOU!'

'Oh, Meryl, hello,' Mary smiles. 'Not so bad, I'm not so bad.'

'Glad to hear it!' says Meryl, angling the chair around to face the bed, as per routine (routines establish themselves quickly here). 'You're looking very well. And LOOK at those gorgeous flowers!'

'Oh, yes, aren't they lovely. My daughter Em brought those for me. Aren't they lovely.'

'Oh they're just beautiful!' says Meryl. 'Gorgeous!'

'She came in with them at a bad moment, I have to say,' says Mary, wincing a little at the memory, but nonetheless continuing in good cheer. 'I was having my, whatchamacallit, this thing,' she says, shaking her catheter tube, 'changed, because the other one had gone all, whatchoo call it, blocked up.'

'Dearie me,' says Meryl.

'Oh, I never mind it. But I must have looked a fright. I was a bit trembly afterwards, you see, and Em got worried. Even though I told her she shouldn't worry, she got worried. And she brought these lovely flowers for me.'

'Yes, they are just gorgeous,' says Meryl, reaching and taking a tulip petal between her fingers, rubbing gently.

'Amazing,' says Mary. 'You can get all sorts of flowers all year round now! Anything you like.'

'Oh I know, they're hothoused. Grown in a hot-house. All year round.'

'Yes,' says Mary, 'that's right.' She sinks back into the bed a little, enjoys the feeling.

'Well,' says Meryl, 'I tell you, I've been hobbling around all week!'

'Still your bad ankle?'

'There you go.' Meryl rearranges a blanket that had slipped. 'Yes, I'm afraid so. The ankle is not good. Really not good.' Her face has assumed a look of harassed, tragic resignation. 'I don't know when it's going to be right again.'

'Are you using crutches?' Mary's voice unintentionally wavers over 'crutches', giving the word, the question, the moment, a Tiny Tim quality.

Meryl doesn't really know how to answer. Is she using crutches? Well, no. Of course not. Evidently not. Does she need crutches, though? That's a different question. Different to whether she is using crutches already. Which she isn't. Even though she'd quite like some, just for a little while.

Everything seems suddenly a little gloomy.

'Oh, no, no. No crutches, dear. You know me! Up and at 'em, eh? And the doctor has given me anti-inflammatories, which keeps me up and about. My son knows a lot about these things too, he's always been a very active boy. He does a lot of exercise. And sport. He says I've got to keep my ankle moving, otherwise it'll seize up. So I turn it in circles, you know?' Meryl rotates her wrist in a circle in the air, to demonstrate to Mary, no question of hoisting her whole leg up to show. 'And flex it,' her wrist flexes, back and forth. 'Best to keep moving.'

Mary smiles, and listens to Meryl talk. Such a nice woman, Meryl. Mary likes listening to her voice, full of inflection and opinion. It's nice having it in the air, like a merry-go-round.

'And I can't sit at home all day with my feet up! If only, eh?' Meryl laughs, her undulating hoo hoos. 'Wouldn't that be nice! Lemon could do the washing up!

'You must think I'm crazy. Lemon is our dog,' Meryl huddles her vocal chords into babytalk. 'And a very naughty doggy he is, too.'

Mary didn't need the explanation – it doesn't matter to her whether the thing doing the washing up was citrus or animal, she just likes all the words, accepts them, grateful for such warm company that does not ask for anything back.

And the talking is good for Meryl, too. The more she talks, the more relieved she feels. She starts by injecting her voice with energy, to sound cheerful, to bring a little pizzazz, but soon enough the energy comes on its own, without forcing, and Meryl talks on about her ankle, with the relief swelling out of her. It is small things she talks about, but they feel bigger. They feel like stones, heavy and important. Meryl feels that her life might stop if her talking stopped. And if not her life, then at least the point of it.

Mary is hovering into sleep. Meryl looks at her and waits a few moments, to make sure. Then she smiles, and as gently as she can rises from the chair.

Of all the things she is, Meryl isn't vain. She doesn't mind if people don't listen, or tell her she is wrong, or fall asleep. As long as she's useful. As long as she can sit somewhere and exist and say something, it doesn't matter whether people listen or not.

In the quiet Meryl hears a wheezing from Mary's chest as it rises and falls, like a punctured accordion. Maybe she won't have so many weeks left, after all. Meryl's hand sparks out, on instinct, and lightly touches Mary's leg, all hard, narrow shin under the knitted blanket. She feels – of course she does – she feels sad.

It is later in the afternoon, the light is starting to fade, and Meryl hears a ruckus. With polar force she is drawn to it. It calls her. Her eyebrows gimble upwards, and her mouth pushes forward into a fanatically curious beak –

as if her lips are magnets, pulling her, leading her towards the source of interest, or gossip, or whatever you want to call it.

She catches the last of it – flaming ankle to be thanked for that – and sees Terri, one of the senior nurses, a lovely woman but a bit bossy if you ask Meryl, with her arm around that gorgeous young man from yesterday. He is crying quite hard. His shoulders are shaking.

Terri takes him into the Quiet Room, which is tucked behind and to the right of the lobby. She stays in with him for a short time, and then comes out again. She is making a call from the reception desk.

Meryl decides to go and interfere. But before she reaches the desk, Terri has hurried down the corridor into the staff kitchenette, from where she emerges two minutes later with a mug of tea. She softly opens the door to the Quiet Room with her free hand, and comes out again almost immediately having left the tea inside. She walks the ten-odd steps back to reception, and registers Meryl waiting.

'Hello Meryl,' she says.

'Oh,' says Meryl, 'hello, hello! How are you?'

'Not bad. You? Is there anything you need?'

'Oh, no, no. I just noticed that lovely young man was quite upset.'

'Right,' says Terri, 'yes. Well. Give me one minute, Meryl.' At this moment another nurse has walked behind the reception desk. 'Nisha,' Terri says to her, 'thanks for this. I don't know how long I'll be, but no more than half an hour.' She turns back to Meryl. 'He is upset. His dad's on his last legs. I'm actually about to go in and keep him company for a while. Was there anything else? Did you specifically need to talk to me, or can Nisha help?'

'Oh, no, I'm just fine. I don't need any help. I just noticed that the, er, he looked very upset.'

'Yes, Meryl.' Terri has lifted the watch from her chest pocket and noted the time. She waits a few seconds for Meryl to finish, or make a point, or leave, and is beginning to turn herself away when Meryl blurts:

'He's a friend of mine, the young man in the Quiet Room.'

'A friend of yours?' says Terri.

'Yes. I mean, I know him.'

'You know him.'

'I met him yesterday. We had a lovely long chat. He's a lovely young man. I'm very happy to sit with him for a while, if it'd help.'

Terri and Nisha exchange the briefest of glances.

'You don't have to do that, Meryl. Nisha is covering reception for me, so, it's fine.'

'Oh. But I'd like to!'

There is a pause. Terri sighs a small sigh through her nose. She thinks for a minute.

'Do you know the situation with his dad?'

149

'Yes,' lies Meryl.

'Well. I've gone through the entire medical situation with him. We did that when he got here. He's clear on that. Right now I think he needs a bit of quiet, and to be offered some grief counselling. You know about all that?'

'Oh, yes!'

'Right then,' Terri looks pointedly at Meryl, 'his name is Jamie Hallow,' she says, and then she turns to talk to Nisha.

Meryl couldn't even admit it to herself, but her heart is tripping a little pitter patter.

Right then! She should go in and talk to him.

Right then.

*Jamie Hallow.* James Hallow? Yes, better. Always nicer to call people by their proper names, Meryl felt.


Looking around this room with his tears passing, his sobs slowing, Jamie finds it to be absurdly reminiscent of a lap-dancing parlour. It is small and windowless, with low lighting and burgundy walls. Some Colour Consultant was probably hired at great expense, to come determinedly in with wheels and charts and command that this cupboard be painted placenta-red. Soothing, womb-like, comforting. Seamy, sexy, liverish. Jonah slipping in the stomach-lining of a brothel.

There is even the necessary box of tissues on the coffee table – the only equipment apart from a sofa, a chair, a plant, and pamphlets on *Grief: Squaring the Circle*. Jamie smirks to himself, expecting a perfume-smelling stripper with sweaty breasts and a pan-stick face to come sidling in.

Instead, a soft knock and a grumble at the door reveal Meryl.

'Hello,' she says, 'it's James, isn't it?'

'No. Jamie.'

'Oh, I'm sorry. Jamie. I'm Meryl, we met yesterday.'

'Yeah, I know. Meryl Streep. Look, I really don't think I need to be in here.'

'Oh, you don't have to be. The nurses thought you might just need some quiet time.'

Meryl says this with such kindness, such straightforwardness, that Jamie feels ashamed for a second. And immediately afterwards, tired. He feels tired.

Into the bizarreness of the moment, the inappropriateness of the room, the ridiculousness of everything, he says, 'It's like a lap-dancing club.'

'Excuse me?' Meryl stops with her hand on the back of the chair.

'This room,' says Jamie, 'it's like a room in a lap-dancing club. With tissues. No windows. Purple.'

'Oh, gosh, I wouldn't know, dear. But now you say it, I can imagine it.' Meryl looks around the room, and palpitates and sparkles a little. 'Oh, dear, yes, I can see it.' She pauses, looking at the tissues with an intent face before sitting down. 'But what would a nice young man like you know about those sorts of places, anyway?' Meryl smiles at him.

'Very little,' says Jamie, 'very little.' He shifts his position, and pulls at the back of his neck. 'Look, Meryl . . .'

Meryl feels she is about to lose this handsome boy, this young man, this man Ben's age at least, and something rare and reckless in her raises its head.

'So, I hope you're not expecting me to dance for you? What a thought!'

Surprised, deeply – *deeply* – by her own chutzpah, Meryl laughs a great nervous hoo hoo, that ricochets around the small room. 'Let me tell you,' she blurbs on, her cheeks rising pink, 'with my ankle!'

Jamie looks at this woman, whose wrinkles are tight with laughter, and cannot help but laugh also. A little lump softens.

'Meryl. I appreciate you being here, ah, but I think the best thing is if I just go for a walk.'

Meryl nods. 'You just do that, dear. The high street is one street in that direction. There's a gorgeous coffee place there. Better than the coffee here!'

There is a pause. Jamie doesn't move yet. And Meryl still sits there. As if she's waiting for something.

Jamie feels as if he should ask her to come with him – but that's ridiculous – this isn't a *date*.

'You're a volunteer, you said?'

'Yes. Oh, yes. I'm not a counsellor,' although so many

of Meryl's friends have told her she should be, that she should do the training, she'd be so good at it, 'but we do have counsellors available. The hospice does. It might be an idea for you to speak to one of the nurses about it. Grief is a complicated thing, you know. We all feel it in different ways.' Meryl smiles. Jamie is tugging at his hair. His father always used to pull his hand away when he caught him doing that. Roughly, and without even looking in his direction. Dad could see in the dark, he could see even when his head was turned in the opposite direction. He would, without looking away from the TV screen, catch Jamie's tugging hand and pull it to a stop.

'I don't know why I was crying,' Jamie says, to close the conversation, 'but I'm not upset. I don't need to see a counsellor. I'm just jetlagged, and really tired, and don't really see the point in being here.'

'That's alright, dear. No one is keeping you here. We all understand that this is a very difficult time for you.'

Jamie knits his forehead, moves his hand from the back of his head to his temple.

'No, it's not a difficult time. It's just annoying. I'm just pissed off. I shouldn't be here. I should be at home in LA.'

'Oh, you mean being *here*. I though you meant being *here* – in this, what did you call it?, lap-dancing club!'

Jamie only smiles with the smallest corner of his mouth. Christ, he's tired. He shouldn't have said the fucking lap-dancing thing; it's made Meryl Streep into his friend. It's all completely weird.

'I mean I shouldn't be here at all. In this, *country*. I . . . look. I don't like my father. And he doesn't like me. And all he is now is a shrivelled-up . . .' Again, Jamie finds tears blocking his throat. 'This is fucking ridiculous,' he says, getting up brusquely from the low sofa, shoving the tears away, 'I'm going for a walk.'

The door clicks behind him. Meryl looks at his untouched mug of tea, and thinks, *that poor boy*. She reaches over with a soft grunt of effort, and pulls the mug across the table by its handle. Her sweetener is in her handbag in the staffroom, but never mind. If only there was a biscuit.

Julie, her daughter, is always on at her not to use sweetener – it's carcinogenic, she says. These days, everything is carcinogenic. The microwave is carcinogenic. Mobile phones are carcinogenic. Crossing the road is carcinogenic! It's all nonsense. Meryl remembers her ankle and lifts it, with a heavier grunt, to rest on the coffee table. Then she stretches forward to lift the mug, which, between sips, she rests on her knee.

# 2

Every family has its mythology. A hero, an eccentric, a beauty, accompanied by at least one story of greatness. These idols are essential – their place in family folklore says Look! We are special. Our house, of all the houses on this street, is special, because granddad once danced with the Queen.

It is futile trying to debunk these legends, as daughter or granddaughter will cling to them as tightly as mollusc to rock – granddad's dance with the Queen makes us different, removes us from the sentence of ordinary, allows us to fluff out our feathers and feel ourselves preferred in some small way. And without this fleeting sunshine of superiority, our lives are so much more squashable.

The Witter Family Hero was Noddy Witter, the father of Jo Witter, Meryl's husband. His USP, a source of pride to each Witter wife, child and grandchild, is that

155

he was, wait for it: *very handsome*. So wildly, magnificently handsome that he was asked to audition for *High Society*. Bing got the role because Doddy (the children named him that – adorable!) hadn't a voice. 'I don't know why they couldn't have just dubbed the singing bits,' says Meryl, indignantly. 'They did that in *My Fair Lady*, didn't they? For Audrey Hepburn, didn't they? Well, why the rules are always different, I don't know. If they could do it for Audrey Hepburn they could jolly well do it for Doddy, don't you think? Jo?'

There are many pictures of Doddy in the Witter West Hampstead Homestead. Many. A number of them are pro-fessionally taken, in soft focus: Doddy at three-quarters, looking into the distance; Doddy looking downwards and wistful; Doddy with the collar of a trenchcoat turned up. Why these photos were taken, who commissioned them, is unclear.

Then there are the family snaps: Doddy posing gorgeously for the lens, his head at a rakish turn, his back straight, his smile composedly identical in each photograph; Doddy with his arm suavely around whatever other Witter snuffed about in his shadow. 'Wasn't he something!' sighs Meryl, wiping the frame with her sleeve. 'He was a *very handsome* man,' agrees Jo, with a pomposity that doesn't suit him, but is necessary for him to experience every now and again.

The Witter children have been reared with belief and pride in Doddy's great good looks, they have been instructed that the man in the black and white was no ordinary dapper – he was as close at it comes to being a star. Ben, when he brought small friends home from school as a child, showed them pictures of Doddy with straightforward, juvenile smugness – the one he showed off most was an actual painting, in pastels and hazy strokes (again, nobody knows who commissioned it). 'That's Doddy,' he'd say. 'He was my granddad. He's really handsome. It's a real painting, see? Done by a proper artist.'

The blame at some stage must go back to the adoration of Doddy's wife, Jo's mother Pansy Witter. Pansy was a plated silver woman, if not quite sterling, short, with a small, round tummy, sturdy arms from stirring and kneading, hazel eyes, and firm, pink cheeks that in her fifties started to droop. She was a kind woman, who prized love, and it showed in her face.

But she was no Madonna, and that Noddy Witter, who knew how to talk to all the girls, and turned her words to air the moment he approached, should choose *her*, was an endless gurgle of delight and disbelief. She worshipped him. Prince Charming, she called him, and he would smile, as if to say: *Yes, that's right*.

Don't tell Pansy that Noddy was a man known among the strip clubs of London (in those days spruced up by being called cabaret clubs, or theatres, but still – strip clubs), too old for new beginnings, and never really in the running for much.

It would break Pansy's heart. She wouldn't believe it – jealousy, she'd say. Her Noddy was a catch, the handsomest man alive. He could've been a matinee idol, but he gave it all up for her.

Noddy in the end became a housemaster at an obscure but established public school, and Jo was brought up, along with his two brothers, in its corridors, and then as a pupil. He thought himself, to this day, tremendously privileged, and remembers with Mum-encouraged pride the way some of the other mothers used to look at Father, with a blush and a giggle. Jo still wears his school tie.

But now it is Meryl who is keeper of the Doddy flame, who keeps the Doddy wick tended and pure. And she is unremitting. Visitors are without fail confronted with one of Doddy's ten-by-eight framed headshots, and Meryl says, 'He was the most extraordinarily handsome man, don't you think? Don't you think?'

Lucy Pippins who'd just moved in next door said Noddy looked like 'an old-fashioned movie star', which pleased Meryl greatly.

There had only ever been one person who dissented, a surly teenage friend of Julie's whose skirts were always far too short. 'It's hard to tell from this photograph,' she had said, when presented with an enormous, gleaming frame. When Meryl had, as she often did, pushed, saying, 'Well, but you can still tell that he was very good-looking, can't you?' the girl had answered, reluctantly, 'Sorry, Mrs Witter.'

Meryl was so winded by this that all she could say was, 'Oh.' But later, with the children at the dinner table, she rounded on Julie with, 'What did she mean? I doubt she has anyone in her family so good-looking. Very few people do. Doddy was gorgeous. He was just a beautiful, beautiful man. And I'm amazed her mother lets her out of the house in skirts like that – she might as well be in her knickers.'

Meryl couldn't see it straight, and she couldn't let her family see it straight, either. The silly, soft-focus photographs of an ordinary man were Meryl's claim to specialness. She was evangelical over Doddy's outstanding face, and most of the Witters' friends had fallen into line long ago. Just as the Witters in turn had bought into the family legends of their friends, the uncles who had squandered great legacies, the aunts who had smoked cigars and worn trilbies, the older brothers who had been amateur tennis champions and lifted silver cups over their heads.

The dead make the best heroes – they are static. They don't stumble. They are forever established. They can't move from their frames.

But it is impossible to guard the mythology of a father who is alive, cruel, and sniping, and possessed by slimy things. Hannah Hallow tried, she tried to whisper to her son that Dad Hasn't Always Been Like This, but it was no good.

Jamie had never believed his father to be anything heroic. That Dad had been a boxer had never impressed him, and he didn't know much about it. There were plaques and trophies, and above the one low bookshelf in the living room a championship belt, with a gold circle in its middle. *James Hallow* or *James Meredith Hallow* they said. But so what? They were just dusty things.

Jamie had never seen a boxing match on the television. Dad watched them sometimes, and Jamie from his room upstairs could hear the yelling of lots of people and the ding dings of a bell, but that was it. He'd never been to see one in real life. The images of a fight were vague and stationary in his mind. That Dad was once involved in them didn't make him anything special. A few times at school a kid had said, 'My dad says your dad used to be a boxer,' or, 'My dad says your dad used to be a professional boxer,' or once, 'My dad says your dad used to be a famous boxer.' Jamie just shrugged.

It wasn't like he was a footballer.

Boxers hit people.

Heroes weren't shouty men who lay in bed dinning through the door about *God* and *forgiveness* and *worms*.

Jamie, of course, had made other heroes for himself, men he quietly admired. There were abstract heroes like Red Adair, a fireman captain who he and Mark Sander did a presentation on in class assembly. Then, later, there was Peter Stockton Smith, an American movie director who made reclusive, beautiful movies, and lived a reclusive life in Malibu, with a beautiful actress wife.

When grown up and brand new in Los Angeles, Jamie met him at a party. There he was, sitting with expansive walrus charisma in an old trapper's hat, with a bulbous glass of cognac in his spatulate right hand. He sat in a booth, in an empty corner of the otherwise bustling room, talking with animation to a man facing him. The man facing him had a reedy back.

Jamie marvelled at his life, that here he was in it, at a party with the figure of his teenage ambitions. Daydreams burst like birds at gunshot, of Peter Stockton Smith shaking Jamie's hand, looking quizzically into his face, studying his eyes, and saying in a deep-like-chocolate voice, *You're going to be my next movie*. The thought made his heart speed up, brought a blush up his neck that made him grab at the back of his hair, and then made him smile, at himself, at his own schoolboy fantasising.

Jamie walked over to the booth.

– Mr Stockton Smith, I'm so sorry to walk over and interrupt like this. But I've wanted to meet you since I was sixteen, and I couldn't resist. I could introduce myself as an admirer, or a lover of your movies, but basically I'm just a fan. A huge, huge fan.

– You hear that, Davey, I've got fans!

Stockton Smith is talking to the man with the reedy
back, who, it turns out, also has a reedy face.

– What's your name, fan?
– Jamie Hallow.

Jamie offers his hand to both men, and they shake.
The reedy man says,

– You're in Seshler Pitt's new movie.

Jamie nods, smiles, pleased.

– Well, Jamie, is it?

says Stockton Smith, in the fur hat. Jamie nods.

– This is Davey Fisher. He's a producer. A kerb-crawler.
The scum of the earth. Why don't you sit down and
finish off your drink with us?

The reedy man, Davey Fisher, slides up the leather
bench to make room for Jamie.

– You must have a sore ass,

he says. His eyes and words are dimmed and it's clear
he's drunk.

– A sore ass?

Jamie asks.

– From working with Seshler Pitt,

Davey Fisher replies, looking happy with himself.
Seshler had been easy to work with, had given Jamie
a big chance by casting him. He was unimaginative at
times, Jamie thought, but a decent man. If anything,
a sweet man.

– My ass is intact,

says Jamie, pronouncing *ass* the American way, a-s-s,

like a donkey, not a-r-s-e, the way that came naturally to him. The two men laugh.

– That's a first,

says Davey, and takes a slug from his glass.

Jamie lets it go. This guy is clearly an idiot, and drunk. It's pointless saying anything. It's Peter Stockton Smith that Jamie wants to talk to, anyway. Peter Stockton Smith who is swirling his cognac fast around its glass, before tipping it back into his flip-top head.

– I need another drink,

he says.

– What would you like?

Jamie asks, moving slightly sideways, about to get up and go to the bar.

– Si' down, si' down. I want it from that waitress, the one with the big face and the big tits. Hey, darling, over here!

He is waving his empty glass above his head, above the earflaps of his hat. She comes over, carrying a tray of already-made pink cocktails in large Martini glasses.

– Hello, sir. Would you like a Candyfloss Martini?

– I don't want any of that pink shit. Get me a cognac.

– Sure thing, sir. Is there anything else? Would either of you gentlemen like anything?

Jamie shakes his head. Davey Fisher leans over and takes a cocktail from the tray, spilling as he goes.

Peter Stockton Smith says,

- Well, honey, I'd like it if you could walk to the bar backwards for me.

The girl is thrown.

- I'm sorry, sir?
- If you could walk to the bar backwards. It's your best view, honey. Your best view.

The girl flushes, looks down.

- I'll be back with your cognac,

she says, and walks to the bar facing forwards.

- Saggy ass,

says Stockton Smith, loudly.

A few minutes later a different waiter, a young man, brings the cognac to the table.

Jamie suffered at the loss of Peter Stockton Smith. He took it personally. Don't choose living heroes – it was the lesson he should have already learnt. They turn out to be fat, or cruel, or crass, or short, or boring, or just too human.

Meryl had done well with Doddy, hadn't she? Doddy, safe from self-sabotage in black and white. Her children had a hero who would stay in his frame forever.

She had done well.

# 3

The house was lonely now. Where before it had always felt too small, cramped full of children and their clothes and their packing boxes and their mess – *you use this house like a storage facility!* – it now felt too big. These days the door to the spare room was permanently closed, as if the room no longer existed, and there was a fine film of dust on the bedsheets. A lonely house that they still didn't even own.

Meryl had never been brilliant at maths, but knew how to use a calculator and was numerate enough to know – even though money was Jo's territory, officially – that with all the redundancies, the months through the years when Jo wasn't working, the financial disruption – that they were in the doldrums money-wise. The mortgage had eaten into their savings, and would continue to do so for another three years until it was finally paid off.

As it was Jo was past retirement age, and was still

working whenever the office had a job for him, just to meet the bills without cutting further into their small, smaller, smallest savings. Jo couldn't work into his seventies. Even if he was up to it, the office wouldn't want him; as it was they didn't find much use for him. And then what? They'd have to scrimp every week even to pay the milkman.

'Dad,' says Ben, their eldest, 'you and Mum have got to be realistic. This house is bleeding you dry.'

'It's alright, Ben,' says Jo, walking with stiff legs over to the teapot.

'No, Dad. Listen to me. It's not alright. You shouldn't be living like this. You're sixty-seven years old and living with one eye always on the cost of things. For no reason. This area has finally gone up – if you sold the house, you'd have the money to buy somewhere smaller, a bit further north, and you wouldn't be struggling like this. You and Mum could relax a little. Dad, are you listening to me?'

'Yes yes, I'm listening.'

'Well? Do you have a response at all?'

Jo shuffles with his tea to the pale blue sofa, he's older than he should be, both Ben's parents are, ten years older than their years, it makes him sad. 'Your mother doesn't want to sell the house. There's tea in the pot.'

'Oh for God's sake. Would she rather live like a student? Dad, it's nuts. I'll talk to her.'

'No. There's no need. I can talk to her.'

'I know you can, Dad, but you won't. Where is she? I can talk to her now. Mum!'

'Ben!' Jo has raised his voice a little, an occurrence unusual enough to make his son pay attention. 'I said no. I would like to talk to your mother myself.' Ben looks at his father – a good man, who despite best efforts has never managed much. There is a wing of dignity fluttering in his face.

Ben sighs. 'Okay, Dad. Just please do actually talk to her. Today.'

'Yes yes. I will. I've said I will, Ben.'

Meryl has heard everything from upstairs, and when Jo begins the promised conversation that evening, she greets it sourly. She has been storing discontent over it all day.

'It might be an idea . . .' Jo says to his wife; 'Perhaps we should think about . . .' Sentences made fluff with conjunctives and qualifiers. Dissolving words. A good man, who is making a best effort, but whose best efforts have an apologetic history of never managing much. A nice man, a perfectly nice man, who can just never say anything with strength. And who feels keenly the shame of being sixty-seven years old, and mortgaged, unable to leave his job, or take his wife on holiday; a failure.

Meryl feels the shame of it, too. All their friends with their nice lives and holidays – the Klonks have a house on the Essex – Suffolk border, *and* a boat! – and here's she and Jo, having to scrimp every day, with two unmarried children, and one small house in West Hampstead. Why has Jo never succeeded at anything? Redundancy after redundancy. And there was Meryl thinking she'd married above herself! Look at them now. All their friends have started going to the English National Opera, and they can't even afford to do that. They couldn't even afford to get tickets in the circle, forget the stalls!

'You've never given me any kind of life!' Meryl is upset. 'You've never given me anything! Not one thing!'

'Merrie, don't get upset . . .'

'This house is the only thing I've managed to have and hang on to. This is *my house*! If you sell this house from under me, Joseph, I tell you, I tell you . . .'

'Alright, Merrie, alright. It wasn't my idea. I was just repeating what Ben said.'

'I don't care what Ben says! It's not his house! Ben has his fancy house in Kensington and he can do what he wants with it. He can mind his own business! Oh, and let me tell you, this is the house that Ben grew up in! Has he forgotten that? Or does he think he's lived in that fancy place in Kensington his whole life?'

'Alright, dear. Alright.'

They are both thinking it, but neither says it – Ben, with all his money, why doesn't he offer to help?

'I am not leaving this house! Do you understand me, Joseph? I tell you, I am not leaving it.'

'Yes yes, dear. Yes. I shouldn't have brought it up.'

'No, you shouldn't,' says Meryl, and begins to blink back tears.

When the children were still children, Meryl would day-dream of the life she would have after they were grown up. They would graduate, with first-class degrees of course, in Engineering, or Law, and everyone would give their congratulations and send cards, but behind the scenes be wishing that *their* children were as out-standing as the Witters. Julie could be a famous singer! She had such a beautiful voice. Beautiful, it was. Or a doctor – a surgeon. Such a shame surgeons had to drop the Dr and be plain old Mr. It didn't make any sense.

Ben could be a lawyer. A barrister – a QC! Benjamin Witter, QC. Or else a famous England cricketer – he was such a sportsman, and looked so handsome in his whites. Wouldn't Jo like that! They really were the most wonderful children. And so good-looking! Everybody says so. Everybody.

Meryl's daydream began like this: that once the children were grown up, and famous, celebrated, she would go and get her hair changed. She didn't know how, exactly, her hair would be changed, but it would change dramatically. A celebrity hairdresser would take her into his salon, and she'd have the kind of hair that you see on red carpets. No need for velcro rollers anymore! Her hair would be *glamorous*, very, very *glamorous*. It would be like in Hollywood. She'd look like a star! I tell you, with all those stylists and personal trainers, no wonder they all look like that. At her better moments, Meryl looks in the mirror and thinks that if she had all those stylists and personal trainers and nutritionists and whatnot, she'd look just as good as any of them.

The hair would be the start of it. After that she'd have the kind of shoes that she'd never been able to wear – with those high, thin heels. She'd *stride* in them, without feeling at all unbalanced. Without needing to hold on to banisters.

And she'd have a Chanel suit. She'd buy it from Bond Street and stride from the shop into a black cab with her stiff, shiny shopping bags. With the interlocking Cs on.

She'd become the kind of woman she'd always been baffled by.

And she'd pay someone to walk the dog.

Except, thinking about it, no, she didn't want to do that. She loved her walks. And she'd miss all her lovely doggy-walking friends. Although she wouldn't miss the pooper-scooping! She would certainly pay someone to do that! Wouldn't that be nice!

But now that the children are grown up, Meryl finds that she doesn't dream that dream anymore. It was too late for all of that silliness. She just got on with things. *Don't worry about me.* That was Meryl's mantra now, *Don't you worry about me.*

When Ben and Julie were over for lunch a few Sundays ago – a rare occurrence, now, to find a Sunday that they could both do – something occurred to Meryl. Julie was hectoring Ben about his t-shirt, she was saying he was *mutton dressed as lamb,* or some such nonsense, and Meryl said, 'You stop picking on your brother! Ben, I think your t-shirt's very nice.'

'Oh God,' said Ben, 'that's the death knell for anything I wear,' and both he and Julie fell about laughing.

'Remember that fleece Mum got you last year?' said Julie. 'With the colour-changing heat panels in the armpits?'

'They were not in the armpits! Don't be so stupid, Julie!' says Meryl, indignant. 'They were on the side! The man in the shop said they were the latest thing. They were very hi-tech.'

'Yeah. Along with bakelite.'

Ben is really laughing, but stops to say, 'Don't listen to her, Mum. I like that fleece very much.'

'Thank you,' says Meryl, seeing that the children have mouthed something across the table at each other and are off again giggling. Honestly, it's as if they're ten years old.

What had occurred to Meryl over this lunch, was how much she missed having the children around to reprimand. How much she missed them laughing at

171

her conspiratorially, or being impatient, or rude. Those old scoldings and mockings were actually made with such joy: they made Meryl a mother, and Julie and Ben her children.

Now what is she? Not Mum anymore. Hardly ever. Not anything. Jo begging the office for work to pay off a mortgage that should have been finished a decade ago. A sprained ankle. An empty house that isn't even theirs.

That night Meryl is tired, as always at this time. It shows on her face. The mania of smile lines – lovely, lovely Meryl, always, always sunny – are slack, unused. Her face hangs, and her eyes are dark. She is putting a heat pad for her ankle in the microwave, it smells of lavender.

Her ankle really isn't good. And if she could afford a pedicure, God knows she'd have one. Although it wouldn't be top on her list. The sports news is on in the background.

'Are you coming to bed, Merrie?' says Jo from the foot of the stairs.

'Yes. I'm just doing my thing in the microwave.'

'Right,' says Jo, and climbs the small flight of steps, the boards underfoot creaking harmoniously with his leg bones. How did he get so old, so soon? 'You're only sixty-seven!' Ben always says, 'but you and Mum hobble about as if you're ninety! You shouldn't be like this,

Dad. None of my friends' parents are like this. You've got to take care of yourself.'

*Only sixty-seven.* To think: 67. When he was twenty-five – thirty-five, even, forty-five – sixty-seven was incomprehensible. And yet, here he was. Scraping his way upstairs. With the voice of his grown-up son in his head, telling him that he's too old, even, for sixty-seven. Golly, wasn't life strange.

Once upstairs Jo begins his bedtime ritual, as his wife waits for the microwave to stop whirring. He can picture her downstairs tidying bits, folding things, putting stuff to one side. She is in faded salmon-pink slippers that are bobbly with age and moulded to the shape of her feet. If you put your hand into the fluff, as Jo sometimes does – Merrie's slippers are familiar creatures to him – you can feel the five toe indents, the arches, and the flat heel.

Jo will take off his jumper and trousers and lay them over the side of the chair, and tonight he will put his shirt with them also, as it hasn't got crumpled and is good for one more day. He will put his socks and underpants in the laundry basket in the walk-in cupboard. He will put on his pyjama shorts, and then go to the bathroom bare-chested to brush his teeth and splash his face and take his pill. Then, after towelling, he'll put on his sleeping t-shirt.

By this time the microwave will have binged and Meryl will be upstairs, making tired noises as she undresses and does her things. She will close the curtains, wondering silently why Jo never does it, why it always has to be her.

Jo will turn on his bedside light, walk to the door to turn off the main light switch, and then get into bed. He'll unfold his reading glasses, give them a rub if they're grubby, and then lift his book from its open, down-faced spot on the bedside – all Jo's books have creased spines. He'll wrinkle his face a little to focus, and then read, absorbed, yet always aware of Meryl's movements, her naked back, her grunts as she bends, the smell of her lotion as it turns her face shiny.

Meryl will sit on the edge of the bed, and sigh. She will sit like that, just thinking, for a minute or two, her shoulders in her white nightdress curving gently. Then she will open a small tube of lip balm that lives on her bedside, and apply it to her lips. She will chew her lips around elastically. She will close the lid of the tube, put it upright back on the table, and turn off her bedside light. She will lie down on her back, and arrange the covers over her, this time with her heat pad firmly around her ankle.

'It smells good, that thingy of yours,' Jo will say, his face still wrinkled to focus, his eyes still on his page.

'For heaven's sake, Jo. Bloody stupid the whole thing,' Meryl will say, irrationally.

Jo will not push it, will not find out what it is that is bloody stupid. Meryl will fuss a little. Then she will say,

174

'Goodnight, Jo.'

'Night night, Merrie,' Jo will say in return, and then will put his right hand on her thigh, over the covers. He will take his hand away to turn a page, or scratch the side of his nose, and then put it back on his wife. That's where his hand always will be. That's where it always is.

Eventually Meryl will turn on her side, with her back to Jo, and within a few minutes she will fall asleep. Her breathing will start to descend into light, adenoidal rumbles, and within fifteen minutes will be reverberating, fulsome snores.

Jo will read for a few minutes longer, until some natural break in the story, and then will move the blankets from his legs, and tuck them snugly around Merrie's back. He will mark his page, take his closed book in one hand, and turn off his bedside light so the room is in darkness. He will push himself upwards from the mattress with his fists, giving a small *gggrah* as he does.

Slowly, stiffly, navigating the dark, Jo will walk to the bedroom door, and then shut it behind him.

Now what will he do?

He will go down the stairs, in his shuffling sideways way, and put his book down on the coffee table. He will turn on the lamp by the sofa. He will walk through the kitchen and take the top two blankets from the airing cupboard. He will close the door carefully, walk back through the kitchen into the living room, and arrange himself on the sofa, with the blankets.

A few times over the years he has been discovered here, and has pleaded insomnia or a restless tummy rather than tell the truth – which is that he cannot sleep through his wife's snoring. Meryl's snoring began in her mid-fifties, and Jo, try as he truly has, just can't sleep with the noise.

He couldn't tell the truth; he couldn't tell her. It would chip away at her poise. He couldn't do it.

So the secret routine established itself, and for a number of years Jo has slept every night downstairs. The sofa is harder than the mattress of their bed, and, actually, he sort of prefers it.

At about five a.m. Jo will wake naturally, without an alarm. He will fold his two blankets and put them back into the airing cupboard. He will make a trip to the downstairs loo, have a glass of water in the kitchen on the way back, first rinsing his mouth out and spitting before taking a gulp, and careful to dry the glass and put it back in its place. He will collect his book and his reading glasses, make his way upstairs – the early daylight is at most times of year enough to see by – and quietly, quietly, creep back into bed. It will be warm, and softly welcome him back with its indescribable and specific smell, talcum powdery, fudgy. Merrie always grumbles a little in her sleep as he gets back in – it's not a big bed. Just a double.

Sometimes, she will have shifted in the night and be lying with her face open, not tucked sideways into her pillow. When this happens, it is Jo's favourite time of all. Then for half an hour, maybe a full hour, he will be able to lie uninterrupted on his side and look at his wife's still face, and remember. And recognise.

During daytime, Meryl's face will inexhaustibly lasso itself from one expression to another. It will beef itself into big, learnt smiles. Into round-eyed puckers of gossip and pursed pouches of being hard-done-by. It will be a parade of assumed expressions – stretching her face out, daily contributing to the astronomy of lines that deep-etches her cheeks. Meryl will constantly perform – BIG smile, look of SHOCK – to prove, largely to herself, that she is worthwhile, and does the right thing, and takes up space.

This morning time of Jo's, from five fifteen until six fifteen, will be the only time that Meryl is switched off. Or not switched on, if that puts it better. And he will look at the sleeping face, and there will be the face that he has loved since he was twenty-seven years old. The face that he knows. The one that lay exhausted and amazed after giving birth to Ben and then Julie. The face that got drunk and giggled and danced and fell over at parties – that was the smile Jo loved, the real one. The face that he caught glimpses of only now and then in waking hours, to remind him of his wife. And the life they had lived together. Here it was, his to smile at, on these favourite mornings, when her face is turned upward in sleep.

Not wanting to risk waking her, Jo will put his hand – rusty most mornings, like the rest of him – a centimetre or two from Meryl's face, so that it is touching her breath. The snores will still be juddering. Jo will feel tenderness of the kind that sometimes threatens to turn his reason to eggshell.

And then, in these last moments before morning, almost silently, so as not to wake her, Jo will say,

'Hello, love.'

# PART TWO

# 1

It is Friday now, morning.

Margaret has come again to James's room. This time she is transparently illumined by the sharp early sunshine; the three panes of windowglass behind render her a triptych.

The room is happier in this light. The medicinal objects – the urine bag pinned to the side of the bed, the oxygen tank with its unused mask, the drip dangling fatly on its shiny metal stand – are less looming. Margaret sees that somebody has brought a vase of flowers and put them by the bed, probably from the reception desk or another patient's room, a patient who no longer has need of them. Seeing this makes her proud, of the thought that her hospice carers spend, the pictures they hang, the flowers they distribute, the chocolates they offer, the cushions they arrange on the chairs. The women and men who work here largely know that death is an ugly business, devoid of romance, and yet they keep the illusion pink for the others, for the dying and their families. They work with kindness. Kindness is all there is.

Day noises filter into the room – movement, voices, television sets. The noises move the atoms in the air, spark and charge them, so the settled eeriness of last night is forced to shift into something more like normality. The sound of James Hallow's laboured breath no longer dominates the room. He seems less of a bogeyman, and more of a tired, old man, sleeping, ordinary, sad.

Margaret has decided what she will do, she decided in the early hours of the morning. Her hands rest on the fullness of her skirts, smoothing the material, comforting herself. There should be patches of worn thread underneath her fingers by now, from her daily smoothing, but there aren't. The dress continues intact, a part of its wearer's magic.

'James,' she says.

His eyes are closed, but he turns his head towards her, towards where, in half-cognisance, he has heard her voice.

He struggles to open his eyes. He has forgotten where his eyelids are, and what he needs to concentrate in order to lift them. They remain closed, and he cries out in frustration.

'James,' Margaret says again, her voice soft. She places

a palm as cool as picnics and summer evenings on his forehead.

James feels overwhelmed by the kindness of whoever is doing this. Whoever is helping him in this way.

If only the desperation of his body would open up, and explode outwards. It is a lacerating feeling, being shut up in this faulty appliance with nothing but an imbecilic, damaged brain for company. In a body that is full to its painful edges of salt balls and cannon balls and failed punches. A body that is a nail bomb. James wants to roar his way out of it; but all he can do is squeak, squeak, squeak.

This hand on his forehead, pulling him back to the certainties – there is a *hand*, on his *forehead*, his *forehead*, his *forehead* – provides a washing-clean relief that no morphine drip ever could. A hand as gentle as snow falling, as clean; a hand on his forehead.

James opens his eyes, and there, touching him, all seasons, is the lady who came before.

But today she is brilliant. Her every elbow and collarbone and crevice is an even line, lit up with the windows behind her. James can see all of her. There are no hiding places.

She is still. She is looking at his face – his face, *his face* – with eyes that look. Thank God she is here.

She is helping him back to himself. And he is not afraid.

For there is nothing to be afraid of in this dusk-lovely

lady. Retribution does not strike with cool, even hands, hands on foreheads.

He looks at her, without fear.

'Who are you?' he tries to say, but his throat is too dry to work, his words are hieroglyphs. Another frustration, he is caught in his throat – James wants to drag his throat out of himself, drag *himself* out of his *throat*.

Margaret, moving with evenness and steadiness, reassuring, calming, keeping her body still, takes her hand from his forehead. She takes up the small glass of water that is on the bedside cabinet. The glass has a stripy, bendy straw in it. There are several other straws, clean, not yet bent, in a cardboard tray that lies beside. She moves the water glass close to James's mouth and places the straw between his lips. His head is at a high enough angle to drink. She pinches the straw a little, so that he does not take too much and choke. James's lips pull on the straw.

There have never been rules, as such, in this place of Margaret's; from her inception here there has been no guidance. But she has instinctively known what lives within her parameters, and what lives outside, what is for her, and what is not. So, she has never touched a man or woman but for the kiss on the forehead as they arrive, and the blessing as they leave. So, she has never lifted a water glass to dry lips, never pinched at a straw and felt the water travel through it, cool between her fingertips.

But with this man who can see her, who looks at her

with startled eyes, all restrictions and boundaries have risen and dissolved like smoke. To do these things, now, that she has never done before, is alright. It is profoundly, trenchantly alright.

Margaret draws the straw softly away from between James's lips, feels the lip skin stick momentarily. She places the glass back down on the bedside.

James speaks again, his words, though hoarse, are clearer.

'Are you a friend of mine?'

He immediately creases his brow at his own question, because he doesn't remember friends for a long time. He cannot place them. Bodies in clothes and men in caps swim in front of him.

'I am a friend of yours,' says Margaret. 'I am a new friend. I know your name is James. You are staying here with me, James, and I will look after you.'

'I wish,' said James, 'I knew who you were.' He has taken too much air in, and begins to cough, a rolling cough, full and painful. He has spent most of the last weeks on his back, and a layer of phlegm has gathered, it lies horizontally on his lungs. He jerks with the coughing, it propels his upper body forward, more movement than his son would imagine possible. Margaret places a hand on his, with firmness, covering those protruding knuckles that have swung so many hard times through the air, her own hand smooth and perfect on top.

A nurse, having heard the coughing, comes in.

'Oh dear, just a minute,' she says, and comes to place her arms behind James's back as a support. She reaches over the front of him and plucks a tissue from a box on the bedside table. The tissue is cupped in front of James's mouth, and a frothy ball of mucus comes into it. The nurse wipes James's lips and chin, and throws the tissue into the bin. She rubs his back while he still leans forward – he does not weigh much anymore. Margaret watches from the other side of the bed, keeping her hand steady on James's.

'I think you've been on your back for too long, eh Mr Hallow? We should get you upright. That way you'll have more of a view, too. It's a beautiful day today, and you've got one of the best views in the whole place, here.'

As the nurse adjusts the bed upward with the touch of a button – all the beds are mechanised now, finally, after a long-overdue grant – she thinks again that the room is bare, and sad. The flowers have made a difference, but compared to the other rooms, that are full of knickknacks and familiar things, this room is barren. Were it not for the rug and the pictures, it would feel more like a hospital room than a hospice.

'There we go.' The nurse adjusts the pillows, pulls the squashed ones out from under James and beats them into shape and rearranges. He recognises that she is the one he knows and likes, from before. 'How about I open up one of the windows a crack,' she says, Felicity, 'let a little bit of fresh air in?'

James nods. He is exhausted by the coughing, and the moving, and just the concentration of it all, but fresh air would be nice. Allow in some sunshine. Maybe there was blossom outside, if it was spring?

'Thank you,' James says, barely a whisper, and he flicks his fingers up against Margaret's, because he is thanking her too. She feels the flick, and instinctively her fingers curl around his; she holds them; knuckles and skin; bones and skin; blue veins and soft, thinning skin.

'I'd like it outside,' says James.

Flop, ever quick, ever merry, replies, 'Well it's cold out there, I can tell you, Mr Hallow. But why don't we see how you're feeling when I pop back later? And if you're up for it we can get bundled up and take a turn around the garden?'

James nods, a small nod. 'You'll come?' he says to Margaret.

Margaret nods, and smiles, and squeezes his fingers.

'Thank you,' says James to Margaret. If he said thank you a million million times he would not tire of saying it. Thank you.

'Pleasure,' Felicity says. She does not comment on his words angled into the air, she does not think much of them. The dying, the ill, the tired, do not talk along straight lines. She has opened one window a crack and the brisk winter air is ribboning in, bringing on its current life, life, life, life, that Margaret can smell. This moment Margaret could drink the air like lemonade, gulp it. Ribboning in on the cold air are all the things she loved, her children, her husband, her life as it was.

Margaret does another thing she has never done before: she looks at the nurse, who is pulling and neatening and tucking the covers around James Hallow, and she too says, 'Yes, thank you.'

Felicity, of course, hears nothing. But Margaret has said it, and that is what lingers. What an odd moment of joy this is, for both of them. For Margaret, holding this human hand, feeling more substantial, more herself, than she has in memory. For James, with a feeling of thanks – thank you, *thank you* – ringing happily through him, tired as he is – *tired* – but with his hand feeling like a sprouting tree under Margaret's.

Felicity likes this man, and the thank yous he says with such intent. But she also feels sad for him. He has come to the hospice too late – he will not walk again, and it is unlikely that he will be able to come out into the garden with her this afternoon, even in a wheelchair. Although she will do her best, she will see how he is, and talk to Terri about it. Mr James Hallow has not the time to benefit from this place. He will die too soon. She doubts that he has many more thank yous in him.

Flop sits on the edge of the bed, asks James if he

could manage a little more of his milkshake, which she retrieves and helps him with. Perhaps he has half a teaspoon. It is his limit. She chats to him for a minute or so, and he smiles, and his eyes are weighing closed. She will leave him to rest. Would he like the tele on? No; a shake of the head. She'll come back shortly to close the window.

Meanwhile, Margaret has kept a hold of the hand, and looks at James Hallow as he lies. She has been looking at the lines in the skin of his face. There are not many of them, but those that there are are deep cut, and work around unusual shapes – high, wide cheekbones, and a broad jaw. On the right side of his jawbone, visible underneath the light stubble, there is a scar exactly like an indented fingerprint – as if he were made of clay, and someone had pressed their fingertip into his cheek. Margaret notes this scar. She is drawn to it. She wants to groove her own fingertip into it, to see if it fits. Like the hands on Hollywood Boulevard. She finds the scar beautiful.

*Beautiful*. It is not a word Margaret generally finds use for. Often enough, from the family and friends of patients, she has heard it said that Death is Beautiful. They have found in the passing of the person they love that there is a communion, a loveliness: something. Margaret has also read that Death is Beautiful, as if it glows with some kind of glamour, some glistening mystery. But Margaret has never heard it from the nurses, who deal in its actual minutiae. Because Death isn't beautiful. Death is its own thing. It is far away from all live words, words of loam and oil and beauty.

James's scar is not beautiful, either. Yet – this is the odd thing – Margaret still finds that it is. It is a strange feeling, feeling something so absolutely, while knowing it to be untrue. Perhaps this is what the visitors mean, when they stand and watch their beloved grimace into passing, and call it beautiful.

Margaret will keep this beautiful-not-beautiful scar in her memory, she will keep it alive, for herself, in its exact detail.

The nurse has left, and James, before he slips into sleep, slips away into God knows where, wants to ask again, ask the lady again,

'Who are you?'

'I am Margaret.' Still she holds his hand.

'You came for me. You came for me in the night.' His voice is so very quiet.

'I came to see you, yes. And you saw me. You saw me by the window. I then came to stand by your bed. You can see me standing here now?'

'I knew you'd come,' says James, and is momentarily hit by the panic that there is not enough time, that she has come for him too late. 'You know I'm dying?'

Margaret nods, and James nods with her, he is calmed by her nod, and he is tired. When she came he had been sleeping.

'What do I need to do?' he asks.

'Nothing,' says Margaret, shaking her head gently.

James nods again. He breathes, closes his eyes, then opens them.

'Margaret,' he says.

A nod, like a bell ringing.

'I saw my son?'

'Yes. He was here yesterday, and the day before.'

'My Jamie?'

'Yes. He has flown to London to see you.'

'From America?

'Yes.'

'Does he know?'

'Yes.' Margaret nods again. A definite nod.

James is satisfied, his eyes weigh closed, no fluttering, they are like sacks.

'Thank you,' James croaks, and as he closes his eyes he sees Margaret moving to sit in the chair, looking at him, and he knows that things are okay and alright and okay. *Thank you* is a good feeling. Thank you, Margaret. Margaret. Margaret, Margaret, Margaret.

# 2

Jamie is remembering one of the last face-to-face conversations he had with his mother, about a year and a half before she died. He had arrived at the house to see her – Dad wasn't in, he'd made sure of that beforehand – and suggested they go to a restaurant for lunch. He didn't come any further than the doorstep.

'Oh, but I've bought some nice bread,' said Hannah Hallow.

'You can eat it later, Mum. I'd like to go out.'

There is a hesitation.

'Won't it be expensive?'

'It's alright. I can afford it. We'll just go somewhere local.'

So Jamie had waited by the front gate smoking a cigarette, while his mother went for her coat and outdoor shoes and hat. She had already dressed up a little for his visit – she was wearing a brooch, some kind of enamel cheetah – so there wouldn't be any of that palaver.

Jamie had bought the cigarettes at the tube station, a packet of ten. He hadn't bought cigarettes for years. But there you go. He stood by the front gate smoking one, having rolled up the cellophane and foil of the packet and littered them into the gutter. He stood by the front gate, deliberately not by the front door – even in the brief minutes he had spent at the entrance to his child-hood home, the smell of the place had overwhelmed him, tendrils reaching outwards, upwards into his nostrils. Cloying and familiar. The smell of wet patches and digestive biscuits and cheap air freshener. He had seen the hall, exactly as it always had been, narrow and dark, the stairs at the back leading up to Mum and Dad's room, to his room, to the spare room for the sibling that never came, the visitor that never came, and to the bathroom. He hadn't wanted to see any of it in the first place, and he certainly didn't want to see any more. He remembered unexpectedly that there was always an open tub of cheese spread in the fridge. He could picture it in there, a yellow and blue plastic tub, with crumpled foil protruding from under the lid.

The familiarity of it all was crushing, odious. When Jamie had left this house that last time, he had left with the towering, blood-rushing feeling that he would never set foot inside it again – and he wouldn't; he wouldn't.

Even the view over Mum's head as she stood in the front door had been too much.

Mum came tapping her hard little feet behind him, with a rigid leather handbag in the crook of one elbow, a buttoned-up purple wool coat, and a knitted black beret over her hair. She wore glasses now, owlish and cheap-looking, with gold rims. Jamie noticed them, but said nothing.

Just as she noticed the cigarette being flicked away, but said nothing. That was the way – everybody noticed, but nobody ever said.

Mum, if she could help it, never said anything at all. Except Nice Bread, Too Expensive, Keep Quiet Now, don't annoy your father.

In a parallel life, where mothers loved their small sons enough to protect them, touch them and talk to them, Jamie, now grown, might have taken his mother's arm and walked the street with her that way. He was aware that there was something not quite picturesque about the two of them walking three feet apart. But taking Mum's arm would have been as outrageous and wrong as grabbing her bottom. They would walk separately.

They went in to a pizzeria, part of a clean, edible chain. Jamie ordered a glass of wine from the waitress as she presented them with big, laminated menus.

'And a big bottle of still water. Mum, would you like a glass of wine? Or something else?'

Hannah's eyes widened for a moment, before thinking better of it.

'I'll just have some water, yes. Or maybe a coca-cola. Yes, I'll have a small coca-cola.'

'Anything else?' asks the waitress.

'That's it,' says Jamie.

'I'll be back in a few minutes to take your order.'

Hannah was already regretting saying no to the wine. She would've really liked to have a glass of wine, in this restaurant, with her son. But what's done is done. She liked coca-cola, too. No problem with coca-cola, none at all. Coca-cola was a treat. It's just that she would've liked a wine even more. If she'd had a wine it would've been like she and Jamie were sitting having a lunch out like friends. It would've made her proud – that was it, *proud* – to have a glass of wine with her son, out the two of them, like old, sophisticated friends.

Jamie lights another cigarette. Hannah says nothing about this one either.

'So is everything alright in America?' Hannah feels herself flushing as she asks; she feels terribly shy – to think that this young man from America was her little Jamie, who used to wake with pink cheeks and stretch his arms up from his cot to touch his mobile. Who she used to have at her breast.

'Yeah, everything's fine.' Jamie is, between inhaling on the cigarette, tugging at the nape of his neck. He wants to stop talking right there, but makes an effort, breathes out, and continues. 'Work's been good. That's why I'm over here. We're promoting a movie that I have a part in. Interviews. It's a supporting role, but a good project to be attached to.'

'I think you said that on the phone, about the film. I told your Dad.'

'Oh, right?' Jamie cuts her off. He doesn't want to hear what she told Dad. 'We should probably look at the menu and choose our food.'

Hannah nods, obedient. The drinks arrive as the two of them silently look at their separate menus. If Hannah were still brave, as she once had been, she would take this moment to say to the waitress, 'And I'll also have a wine.' But those days, that voice, are gone.

'Do you know what you want, Mum?'

Hannah nods, still holding the menu in front of her.

'Well. Go ahead.'

'No,' she says, 'you go first.'

Jamie looks at his mother, wants to tell her to *order her fucking food*, to *say what she fucking wants*. But he doesn't. He looks at the waitress.

'I'll have a Fiorentina, and a small Caesar salad. Thanks.' He hands back the menu.

Hannah's eyes are scanning the menu rather frantically for her son's choice. She doesn't quite know what he has asked for.

'Would you like them at the same time? Or the salad first?'

'The same time is fine.'

'And for you, madam?'

'I'll have this one. The Margherita.' Hannah pauses, and looks up at her son, and flushes, and looks down at her menu again, and then blurts out, 'Can I have some more cheese on it? Do you do that?'

'Sure. Extra cheese. We also do a Quattro Formaggi,' the waitress signals to it on Hannah's menu with the end of her pen, 'that's a four-cheese pizza. Mozzarella, goat's cheese, parmesan, and gorgonzola. If you like cheese, you might like to try it.'

'Okay,' says Hannah, looking down at her knife and fork and paper napkin.

Once the waitress has taken the menu away, Hannah's fingers edge towards the napkin and start worrying around its border. She wants to ask Jamie which was the pizza he ordered, but doesn't. She doesn't know if she's done the right thing. She'd like a sip of her Coca-cola now, but thinks that perhaps she should wait a little bit.

Jamie, meanwhile, wants to snort at the cheese exchange that has just passed. There's Mum, more like a mouse than ever, fiddling and rootling and asking for more cheese, please. Cheese. More. Cheese. Please.

In retrospect, he can see the cancer in her face, as if something was digging and pocking away at her cheeks. But at the time, she just looked old; older. Almost a full-blown little old lady. And she probably wasn't much over sixty. Maybe she was even fifty-nine. Jamie didn't know. A papery, waxy, old-lady mouse, sniffing the air for cheese. Cheese and biscuits. Cheese. Cheese. CHEESE. He keeps an unsmiling face, but there's a sneer about it that his mother doesn't miss.

Jamie asks all the questions he should ask, in a controlled monotone, and Mum answers them with nervousness: Yes, No, Yes, Thank You, I Think So, Your Dad Says . . .

Jamie in return finds that he wants to launch into aggressive stories of his own Californian life, full of directors and actors and houses and shopping and restaurants and meetings and coffee and bars and girls in long, tight dresses. He wants to tell her all of this in a rampage, to see the look on her face – of incomprehension, shock, embarrassment. She would recognise none of it. She would understand none of it. Her son was from another planet.

But he keeps quiet. He eats his pizza, asks for olive oil for the crusts. Mum spends ages not knowing where to begin: how to use her knife and fork to penetrate the big round of cheese and dough. She eventually cuts a minute fragment from the crust, and starts to chew. Jamie finds the process excruciating. He pulls at his hair, trying not to look at her gnawing, or at the spidery strings of cheese that rise elastically from the pizza with her fork.

Her face harvests in and out of worry and covert

enjoyment, and Jamie wants to pull the plate away from her and smash it against the wall. What would Mum do if he did? Watch her beloved cheese mountain bilge greasily down the wall, nervously wipe crumbs from her lips.

Jamie does nothing but riot internally.

They are given pudding menus.

'It was very rich, all that cheese,' says Hannah.

'You should have said. We could have sent it back and got something else.'

'Oh no! No! No. It was lovely. I didn't mean I didn't like it. It was lovely.'

'Good.' Jamie nods, smiles rigidly, looks out of the window. Lights another cigarette.

'Will you have anything for dessert?' Hannah asks. She had managed to get through two-thirds of her pizza, rich as it was, and it feels good to be sitting here with it inside her. With Jamie. From America.

'I don't know. Maybe a tiramisu.' Jamie pauses, it's his fourth cigarette. 'It's a kind of Italian cake. With cream and sponge fingers.' He wants to say that the tiramisu here is probably from a deep freeze, and will be stodgy. But he doesn't. Hannah wants to say that she knows what tiramisu is, but she says nothing either, just nods.

'Maybe I'll have that, then. Will you have one?'

'There's also ice cream.'

Hannah nods. Looks at the menu card that she holds

in both hands. It is small this pudding menu, but she holds it in both hands.

'Which will you have, Jamie?'

He is surprised to hear his name coming from his mother's mouth. She hardly ever says his name. When she talks to him it is usually without a name: words without address, stamp or postcode. Mum's words go missing on the way to his ears.

Jamie hears, in the using of his name, and he sees, in her expression, how much his mother wants a pudding, how excited she is by the prospect.

'I don't think I want anything, actually,' he says, putting the menu down.

Jamie says this for no other reason than to be cruel. He sees how much his mother would like a tiramisu, and he is deliberately making it difficult for her. He wants to go on and say that he hasn't got much time left anyway, but saying that would be too much, it would make his feeling of cruelty worse, and it would be a lie. He has the whole afternoon free. And evening.

Jamie is concertedly not looking at his mother's face, that will be flushing, and perplexed, and disappointed – always, *always* disappointed.

Sitting in silence, the guilt comes – this always happens, a small jab at his mother and then a cascade of ill-feeling. 'Have something, Mum.' Jamie is trying to redeem himself. 'I'll have a tiramisu,' he says. He hears in response a sound like a little gasp from his mother, but doesn't look up. He's not interested in any more of her expressions and soggy feelings.

'I'll have one, if *you* do,' she says, 'as long as it's not too expensive. I've had a lovely meal already.'

Oh for fuck's sake, Mum, *for fuck's sake*.

'It's not expensive. I told you, I can afford it.'

'Pounds five, it says for the tiramisu. Ice cream is pounds four.'

'Mum, I'm going to have a tiramisu. Just order whatever you want.'

Why, *why*, is she saying 'pounds five' and 'pounds four'? Surely it is universally: 'five pounds', in that order? 'Five. Pounds.' 'Four. Pounds.' *Why is she saying 'pounds five'?*

The fury that Jamie has felt stewing since they sat down is now bubbling at his temples. His mother is ludicrous. Ludicrous and repulsive. He could pick her up and rip her apart with his hands. The way she crumples her face up as she talks is *disgusting*, as if she was a rat in a lab getting electric shocks. The way she dresses is *disgusting*, pinning brooches to her bosom in an attempt to look even more middle class. The way she eats is *disgusting*, looking furtive and taking the food off her fork with her teeth. The way she speaks is *disgusting*, pounds five pounds five pounds fucking five.

Jamie stubs the cigarette out, folding the butt over itself with such a pinch that his fingertips momentarily turn white. His mouth feels foul. Creamy and coated. He pushes the ash around the ashtray with the squashed cigarette butt, tidying it violently into a little pile. If he did anything else now, it would involve knuckles and bones. He wants to wreak Andronicus-style revenge on his mother. He wants to shriek *FIVE POUNDS* into her face. He wants to take her by the back of her crumbling, dusty head, and force it crashing down into the table. He wants to rip her apart with his hands.

Remembering this, remembering back, Jamie can see the cancer in his mother's face, although he didn't notice it at the time. There it was, pocking and digging and hollowing out. And it would continue its pocking and digging and hollowing out until she died, and was buried with Jamie's money.

And so what?

So what.

Remembering all this.

Jamie is in a Starbucks on the high street near the hospice. He sits on a brown sofa, with a burnt latte in a white mug in front of him, a white mug emblazoned with the Starbucks princess in her green circle. Light is pouring in from outside. As winter weather goes in London, it couldn't be lovelier.

Two deaths. One that he absconded from, paying for the funeral over the phone; and now this second death at which he finds himself in skewed attendance. If he was going to be there for one, it should have been Mum's. He never remembered liking her, he never remembered much love from her, but he supposed that sometimes in her own scrabbling ways she had been kind. He had nothing against her.

Not like Dad. Dad – he hated.

And when Dad died, as he would, surely, any second, then it would just be Jamie left. They would both be gone from his life and there would be no more ugly duties and old wounds. Then he would be free to be just Jamie, just Jamie in the world.

# 3

It is Friday, Meryl's last afternoon of the week at the hospice.

She feels, after her three consecutive days of volunteering, that she has earned her weekend. She sleeps on Friday night with a genuine tiredness, and wakes on Saturday morning taking genuine satisfaction in an easy, toe-stretching morning off.

On Saturday she makes herself toast with butter substitute and raspberry jam (a luxurious deviation from the weekday fare of muesli with fruit and skimmed milk, like in the picture on the packet) and a lovely pot of coffee. Or, if it's a nice morning and she's been good and gone to the gym that week and is not feeling fat, croissants from the patisserie on the high street. I tell you, just standing by the window of that place was struggle enough – they had the absolute best mille foilles – or was it *mille failles*? – with custard in between the pastry and sticky old-fashioned icing on top. If she were thin she'd eat ten of them, easily.

Jo loves croissant mornings, too. They're always better. Merrie is happier, the sun is out (otherwise she wouldn't have gone to the croissant shop), the house smells of coffee, the radio's on, and life seems to have lost its weights and stresses. If there was cricket on in the afternoon: well. That would be the perfect day.

But it is not Saturday today, it's Friday, so no croissants. It is sunny, though – the kind of sunny which looks like it might stay the weekend, which bodes well for the likelihood of croissants tomorrow.

Forgetting croissants, and focusing on today, though. Today, it's Friday.

Meryl has bought her coffee from Andreas, who owns the small café where she gets her hospice lattes – they're the best in the area. And Meryl values a good coffee. She can't stomach that Nescafé stuff.

'How's your ankle, Mrs Meryl?' Andreas had asked. He always called her Mrs Meryl, it was fun.

'Oh, Lord. Best not talk about it, eh, Andreas?'

'Still bad? If you were my mother, I'd make sure you were resting up in bed, none of this to-ing and fro-ing. Your children should be taking better care of you. They should be stricter with you, I think.'

'My children! You should give them a call, Andreas, tell them to look after me better! That'd be nice!'

'You give me their numbers, and I'm right on it, don't you worry.'

Andreas is smiling, he likes his Mrs Meryl a lot. She's always got a laugh in her, always takes an interest. Andreas is mostly not bothered by many of his customers. But Mrs Meryl, he likes.

And Andreas, in their small exchanges, seems also to bring the best out in Meryl. There were less complaints, more authentic smiles. Less agenda, more talk. Perhaps because in his careless, instinctive way, Andreas – such a marginal figure in Meryl's life, with his small pot-belly and baby-blue eyes – made her feel valued; made her feel real. More like a lady on her own patch of land, with words to say, and less like daft, irritating Meryl, predictable and uninspiring.

Meryl is walking – limping, hobbling – towards the hospice, having had a cheerful few minutes' chat with Andreas. Her latte is sealed, it will be just the right temperature once she has arrived and taken her coat off and organised herself, and in the meantime it is hot enough to warm her hand through her thin gloves.

She is thinking about Jamie, the young man from the hospice. She's thought about him if not often then more than once or twice since talking to him yesterday. All right, out with it – Meryl thinks he's gorgeous. Really gorgeous. With that lovely curly hair. Like a shepherd boy! Poor thing. It all seems very difficult for him. Poor boy. It looks like he's the only family, as well.

Bearing the brunt of this on his own. It can't be easy.

Rounding the corner on to Circus Road, holding her coffee and thinking thoughts of Jamie, poor Jamie, with his lovely curly hair, Meryl does a flash double-take into the window of Starbucks.

She can't believe it. It's him.

It's definitely him.

Jamie from the hospice. Jamie from her thoughts. Who she was *just then thinking about!*

He's sitting on a sofa in the window, in profile, with a newspaper spread on the table in front of him that he doesn't seem to be reading.

It's absolutely definitely him.

Meryl's decorum carries her on a few paces, until she is out of sight. Then she stops, with her coffee in her hand. Andreas would be so upset if he saw what she was about to do. Oh dear. *So* wasteful. She'd be furious if either one of her children did this, or Jo. Or anyone. It's a terrible thing to do. Oh dear. Terrible.

Meryl walks ten yards to the next corner, where there is a rubbish bin, and drops her untouched, lovingly made coffee gently into it. She thought about tipping the coffee first into the gutter, and then throwing away the empty cup, but she feels a little fluttery and urgent, and just wants to get it done. All Andreas's lovely coffee. She mustn't think about it too much.

Then she turns around, and walks back to the

Starbucks. Meryl thinks Starbucks are terrible places – not because of the human rights whisperings, she hasn't heard any of those – but because the coffee is not at all good. It's always burnt and watery, and Meryl can't stomach bad coffee. Lots of her friends like it there – it's like they have no taste buds. Of course she wouldn't tell them that.

Meryl goes to the counter and queues with her fingers and feet tapping, looking like a jitterbug over her shoulder every twenty seconds. She buys herself a latte with skimmed milk – now that *is* one of the benefits of this place, all the different milks. They have *soya* milk, too, which Meryl has read is very good for you. Especially if you're post-menopausal. Something about hormones? She bought a carton of the stuff from the supermarket a while ago, but hasn't used it yet. She must give it a try. What with, though? That's the problem. Maybe she should just start out adding a bit of it to her tea, to see what it tastes like.

Okay. Meryl goes with her skinny latte over to Jamie's sofa. She's feeling a bit palpitational.

'Oh, hello,' she says, sounding hopefully as if she has just spotted Jamie on her way out.

This is awkward. He hasn't heard her.

Meryl feels enormous standing there like that. Like an enormous great silent moo-cow. It's too embarrassing.

'Hello there,' she tries again, keeping the waver from

her voice with aplomb, she doesn't know why she feels so anxious, 'remember me?'

Jamie hears this time, looks up, and jerks his head back slightly.

'Hi,' he says, 'Meryl.'

'Oh, yes, that's right. From the hospice.'

'I know,' says Jamie.

'I was just getting my coffee, I was going to take it out, but I saw you over here and thought maybe I'd come and say a little "hello".'

Jamie nods. 'Hi. Ah, are you sitting down? Sorry, I've got my newspaper all over the place.'

'Oh, no, don't you worry dear, you just leave everything where it is.' Meryl puts her coffee down on the low table. She eases herself into the armchair next to Jamie's sofa with a muted *oof*, and then leans back, removes her woollen gloves. She feels much more comfortable now that she is sitting.

'How are you?' says Jamie, looking down, and then looking up. He's moving quite a lot now, whereas before, circled by his thoughts, he was – but for the unconscious hand through the nape of the hair – stationary.

'Oh, you know,' says Meryl, laughing, 'soldiering on! How about you, dear?' Something, maybe it was yesterday's faux pas, makes Meryl shy of saying his name. 'How's your father?'

'I haven't seen him yet today, actually. I was going in after this coffee.'

Meryl shakes her head, she feels the difficulty of it all. 'You just be brave, dear.'

Jamie's eyebrows move upwards.

He is quite taken aback by this, Meryl's counsel to be brave. Startled.

No one has ever before told Jamie to be brave. No one has ever seen cause, or had opportunity to. In his adult life, he has kept unscalable walls of Fuck Off around himself, he has not put fragile emotion on to friendship tables, so no amigo or passer-by has ever seen a frightened man, and so has ever felt the need to advise bravery.

In his childhood, it was just him and Dad and Mum, and nobody knew. Nobody knew that this was a child who needed extra reserves of strength and courage to survive the daily onslaught of grinding down and blowing up. So no one, when he was a child, mentioned bravery.

It feels like a caress of the funny bone; in telling him to be brave, Meryl is acknowledging that there is something to be brave of. For the first time, someone is noticing that Jamie has reason to feel buffeted. Scared. Buffeted and scared. Scared. Someone else has seen the monster. And Jamie is startled by it.

'Brave. Yeah. Thanks.'

'You remember I'll be right there at the hospice if you need me.'

'Thanks, thanks, I will.'

Meryl takes a sip of her coffee through its lid. She leaves a pucker of lipstick on the white plastic as she does, but it is not the kind of thing that she notices or is bothered by.

'How's your coffee?' she asks Jamie.

'My coffee? Unexceptional. Burnt. But most coffee you get anywhere is burnt.'

'I know,' Meryl is animated, she feels a whoop of good-feeling that Jamie knows, like her, about bad coffee. 'Isn't it terrible? When it's so easy to make a good coffee. I think the coffee here is just terrible. All watery and, as you say, burnt. And it's so expensive! Well, for a bad coffee, it's a lot of money. I can't stomach bad coffee.'

'It's better than the coffee in your hospice, though.'

'Oh, Lord! I know. It's just terrible, that machine stuff. I can't stomach it.' Meryl laughs, looking at Jamie. 'There's a very good little place just down the road here, though, literally just a one-minute walk down the high street. The Box Café, it's called. B-o-x. Andreas, who owns it, is such a gorgeous man. He must be Greek, I think, with a name like that. Although he doesn't look it. Anyway, he does the most beautiful coffee. You must go in there and get some. The Box Café,' Meryl taps Jamie's knee with her fingers and a flick of the wrist, 'you just go there next time and tell Andreas you're a friend of mine.'

Oh no. Oh dear. She's done it now. What a boo-boo. She's really done it now.

Meryl flushes. How could she go on about Andreas's place like that? Jamie would think it was very strange for her to be here in Starbucks, if she knew of a better place just a few doors down. How much more stupid could she be? Going on like that! As good as caught throwing her coffee away and coming in here just to talk to him. And saying Andreas was a friend of hers! As if she were trying to show off! She can't stand it. She never should have come in here in the first place, acting like a schoolgirl with some embarrassing *crush*. Oh, Lord. This was terrible.

'The Box Café. There's a place called the Box Café in LA,' Jamie is looking at Meryl, who feels sure her face is puce, but Jamie is just talking, doesn't seem to have noticed anything, oh thank God, thank God, 'but I doubt they're related. Anyway, I'm not going to be around for much longer, so I can put up with crap coffee until I leave.'

'Oh, I see,' says Meryl, her surprise taking over from her relief. 'You think you'll be going back to America quite soon, then? That's where you live, isn't it? In,' she hesitates, 'LA?'

'Yeah. I was thinking of going back today. After I've seen Dad.'

'For work?' Meryl's face is characteristically gathering in and out of expressions, and Jamie is trying not to become awkward.

'No, not work. I just think I should go back. There's no real point to me being here.'

'Are there other family members here?' Meryl seems suddenly to have lost her inhibitions, and is letting out questions as they strike in her head. If one of her children were here, they'd tell her to shut up.

'What, of my family? Er, no. Just me and Dad. Just the two of us.' Jamie tries to give a light-hearted shrug. But Meryl remains perplexed.

'Oh,' she says, 'well. Then, surely it would be,' this is a difficult thing to say, 'a good idea if you stayed here for a little while? Of course, I mean, if you can, I mean, I know it's none of my business. I'm not trying to pry. It's just that, if there's no one else. It's just you and your father, you say?'

'Yep, just me and my father.' Jamie is leaning his elbows on his knees now, with his hands locked in the middle, looking down at the floor. He is trying to remain frivolous in this conversation, he is trying.

'Well then, if you had a few days, don't you think it would be better . . .'

'Look, Meryl,' Jamie is bouncing one knee up and down, which bounces the elbow that rests on it, which creates a whole body bounce of agitation, 'I don't know if I mentioned this to you yesterday, when I was upset,' Jamie doesn't know why he is saying any of this, why he isn't just ending the conversation with a firm word and then leaving, 'but my dad and I don't get on. I know he's dying, that's pretty fucking bloody obvious. Sorry, I didn't mean to say *fucking*.'

213

'Oh, I don't mind.' Meryl's eyes are broader than usual.

'Yeah, well, look. Sorry. I know he's dying. Okay? I know that. But he'll die just the same without me – better, probably. He'll die better without me here. Look. He's never liked me. Never.'

'Oh, dear, I'm sure that's not true.'

'I'm telling you it is. My whole life, since the day I was born, he's made very clear what a waste of space I am. "Evil", he used to call me,' Meryl wants so very much to interrupt, to say *I'm sure he didn't mean it, oh, I'm sure it's all okay*. But she doesn't, she knows she mustn't, hard as that is. Jamie goes on, 'and a whole host of other stuff. Apparently, I have worms in my head. He bloody perforated my eardrum when I was thirteen.'

Meryl swallows a gasp. *Oh dear, Oh Lord*, she wants to say – but she doesn't, and it's the best thing she could be doing, continuing to not say anything.

'Look,' Jamie lowers his voice, looks over his right shoulder into the shop, and then back at the floor again, 'I'm not saying he beat me up all the time – he didn't. Far from it. It was just slapping and shoving and shit. It only got too much a couple of times.'

'I'm so sorry,' says Meryl.

'Yeah; no. That's not what I'm trying to say. Fuck knows a lot of people have had it a lot worse than me. A lot of kids get smacked. I'm not trying to say that. The

214

point is, Dad is completely wrong in his head. Miswired. That's the fucking thing. I've known it since I was a kid. He's always been violent, and hallucinated, and gone off into mad fucking fits. Parkinson's, they put that down to. Well, fuck it, maybe. But the bloody *satisfaction*, when he was finally diagnosed a few years ago. I've always known it wasn't just Parkinson's. Parkinson's doesn't make you a vicious bastard. He should have been in that institution for most of his life. Alzheimer's, they reckon now: well, whatever. He's been like that forever. So maybe he's had Alzheimer's since he was thirty.

'Anyway, look. What I'm telling you is that he's never liked me, and, quite apart from that, he is not right in his head. He's been demented and mental and religious for as long as I can remember. So it makes no difference whether I'm here or not. If he opens his eyes long enough to see me he'll probably tell me I'm Satan's progeny and then have a fucking epileptic fit,' Jamie blows a laugh through his nose, with no actual laughter in it, 'so it's best I'm not around. I don't want to be around. I've got no time for that man, and he's got none for me.'

Jamie remains looking at the floor – although he's not really looking at anything – with his elbows on his knees, jiggling. He feels self-conscious, nervous, dissatisfied, as if he has just given an audition speech. Although they were certainly not prepared,

215

these words, and he means them – he means them all.

Meryl's nerves, by contrast, have burnt off. She just wants to give this boy a squeeze (boy, *boy*, she must stop thinking of him as a boy; he must be the same age as Ben). She doesn't know about the hitting, she doesn't know about all that stuff. But the poor boy by the sounds of it has had a horrible time. You would never imagine it, what people get up to. And all alone, too.

Meryl hadn't spent any time with James Hallow, the father. And now it turns out he's a loony. Alzheimer's is always difficult, gosh, isn't it just! But this sounds like something else. Although that's none of her business, she must tell herself that; that's got nothing to do with her.

He had arrived at the hospice in a different stage of deterioration, mostly not compos mentis. She had poked her head round his door a couple of times, but both times he had been sleeping. There was something about him – about that point in the slipping away – that was best left alone. God knows why she did this, all these dead people.

'Have you any brothers or sisters?'

'Me? No. I've never had any. It's just me.'

It's funny, that, thinks Meryl, to say *I've never had any*. 'Well . . .' She pauses, she still can't bring herself to say his name, *Jamie*. 'I'm just terribly sorry,' her hand shoots out and pats his knee, 'I really am. You're a lovely young man, and I know it can't be easy for you. I, I, oh dear. Of course, you know best – it's your father after all! What do I know?

'But, if you are the only one here. Well, perhaps you should think about staying. All fathers love their sons, that much I do know. I'm just so sorry. I really am. Oh, to be a little boy and have all that to cope with.'

'Look, it's fine. I don't really see the point in talking about this much more. I'm not trying to be rude. I appreciate you taking an interest. It's just all very fucking weird. And one thing I can tell you is that all fathers don't love their sons. They just don't.'

Jamie looks up and sees that he has spoken brusquely. Meryl is blinking, and her forehead has shot up into creases.

'I didn't mean that *you* were weird. You taking an interest. I meant the whole situation, *my* situation.'

'Oh, no, that's alright. Don't you worry about me, I don't mind.'

'It's very nice of you,' Jamie says, 'to take the time. Speaking of which, I should probably get over and see my Dad.'

'Oh, goodness, yes.' Meryl looks at her watch, holding its gold edge with her thumb and index finger. 'I should get off too, look at that,' she taps the face, 'half past two already!'

Meryl is the first to stand up, although she is shy of making too much of a meal of it. She doesn't want to

217

look ungainly. And Jamie feels suddenly embarrassed by all the things he's said, and angry with himself for having said them. It's nobody's business. And he has no business feeling sorry for himself.

'Are you walking over to the hospice?' he asks flatly. 'I think I might just gather my stuff up here, I have a couple of phone calls to make, and follow after you.'

As Jamie is getting up from the sofa, Meryl leans in towards him and gives him a hug. He is caught by her arms before he has straightened up completely – his legs are bent in a semi-crouch. It is an awkward hug, with Jamie half-squatting like this. He wriggles out of it fast.

Meryl had hugged him, and patted his back with one hand.

'You just be brave, dear, I know it's hard.' A platitude? An unthinking panacea? Jamie wriggled like a tadpole out of the hug, and straightened himself up.

'See you later,' he had said, and then watched as Meryl left the Starbucks and then walked past the window with a little wave. She seemed to have a bad leg, she limped a bit. It reminded Jamie of Dad. It reminded him of Mum, of his own mum, who he doesn't remember ever being hugged by. The feeling of the hug had made him wince.

# 4

Margaret has spent the morning in the chair by James's bed, watching him as he lies with his eyes closed and mouth open, placing a quiet palm on him if he stirs in discomfort. The only time she moves is when a carer comes in with lunch on a tray – then Margaret goes over to the window, making sure that James can still see her. He must know that she is not going anywhere.

Through the window Margaret looks down into the hospice garden, where a young woman of around thirty-five is being walked around the grass on the arm of a young man of the same age. The young woman's name is Nicola, and the young man is her fiancé. They are dressed warmly, with Nicola in an eccentric assortment of layers – tracksuit bottoms underneath a nightdress underneath a big, puffy jacket, with a shawl wrapped around her neck. Nicola is ill – she will only live for another three and a half weeks – but for now she and Clive, her fiancé, are laughing over something in the sunshine.

Margaret has a number of times seen Clive as he leaves the hospice, his face unreadable as he walks out fast, into the other world, the real world, the world he knows, where there is no Nicola anymore. Nicola always takes a t-shirt from him before he goes, protest as he might about the cold, so that she at least has his smell with her in the night. She swaps it back the next day, for the one he is currently wearing.

It is too cold, Margaret supposes, for her elderly patients to take a walk out, although she can just see a few of them sitting by the large glass doors into the garden, watching the sunshine, watching the green, watching the young couple as they walk. Like Margaret, they see only two people, arm-in-arm, laughing, walking, happy. Although it is there – in the faltering steps, in the grip on the arm – it would take a black imagination to see the sickness in this picture. For this moment it is simply, truly a young couple in a garden. Margaret sends a blessing down to envelop them, like a bird with big, warm wings. Long may this moment last for them.

She turns from the window, James's lunch is over, and he has managed none of it. He cannot eat. He cannot lift himself out of grogginess enough even to contemplate it. He has taken a sip from a new Ensure milkshake, vanilla flavour this time. It was cold, it brought sensation back to his throat. It will give him a little energy.

James asks, with closed eyes, 'Is Jamie here? My son?'

Margaret walks towards the bed to be closer to him. 'No, not yet,' she says. At the same time the carer, a large lady called Janine who has done all she can this lunchtime to encourage and nourish and help, answers,

'I don't think so, Mr Hallow. But I'll check with reception, how about that? You're expecting him, are you?'

James nods, still with closed eyes, his head instinctively angled towards Margaret.

'Well then,' says Janine taking the tray in her arms, 'I'm sure he'll be along shortly. If you have a good rest now, you'll be fighting fit when he arrives. I'll be back a bit later. Is there anything else you need for the moment?'

James shakes his head. 'Thank you,' he says, working to keep his eyes open, to thank this kind lady before she leaves. She gives him a smile and an, 'Alright then.'

Margaret is standing where James had thought she would be. He turns briefly to her, before closing his eyes and drifting into insentient sleep; as he falls away again he wants with dreamlike strength to raise his arms up and bring her towards him, into his arms like a cloud. His forearms twitch on the bedsheets, and Margaret comes to him, to place her hand once more on his.

Two boys of about nine and twelve are standing in the doorway of James's room. They have left their mother with their aunt in a room on the floor below, having said they would play in the garden.

They did this, for a while, before coming back inside to explore. They have taken the lift to each floor, found out where the cafeteria is, got a hot chocolate from the machine with change from Mummy, tried to find a chocolate dispenser like the ones you get in tube stations but failed, and then, for the past ten minutes, they have crept from door to door of the rooms on this floor, and tried to peer in.

The older brother would cajole the younger into looking in and reporting back. In the last room an old lady had said, 'Hello there,' which had caused them both to dash frantically away, giggling and nervy.

Now in the doorway of James's room, they are looking in uncertainly. The older one laughs nervously.

'Is he dead?' says the younger, who has been positioned slightly in front by his big brother to act as a shield, it is the usual set-up for them.

'No, stupid,' hisses the older. 'You don't get dead people in a hospice. This is for sick people.'

'Oh yeah,' says the young one, remembering Mummy's explanation. 'Is he just asleep then?'

'You have to go in and touch him to find out.'

'No *way*.' The younger brother takes a step back, to be prodded immediately and brusquely forward again by the older.

'You have to.'

'No I don't.'

'Yes you do. I dare you.'

'I don't care if you dare me. I don't want to.'

'If you do – just go up and touch him on the face – I'll give you ten pounds.'

'No way! No way am I touching him on the face. You're such an idiot! I have ten pounds, anyway.'

'Okay, I'll give you twenty, then.'

'You don't have twenty pounds.'

'Yes I do, I swear.'

'No you don't. How come?'

'From tooth fairy money and reward for my maths exam, remember?' The big brother is talking to the smaller as if he is a moron.

'Oh yeah,' admits the smaller.

'Go on then,' another prod, 'I'll give you twenty pounds. You have to go right up and stroke his face and then come back.'

'No way! I'm not stroking his face!' The smaller brother is feeling a mounting anxious heat in his stomach, as if despite himself he knows that he is coming closer to doing this thing. It's not about the twenty pounds, they both know that.

'I'll give you twenty pounds, I swear. All you have to do is to stroke his face for five seconds.'

'Five seconds! No way! *One* second.'

The older brother is softly giggling in delight. 'Three

seconds, that's my final offer. And you can't cheat. It has to be one-two-three.'

'Two seconds.'

'Three seconds. I told you, that's my final offer.'

The younger brother does not answer, is just standing, looking in, and the older instinctively sees his moment, 'Go on,' he pushes, 'go on, quickly! Now!'

The urgency of the older brother's whisper has done it, like a starting whistle, and the younger walks speedily towards the bed, his heart drumming so loud that he can't hear anything else. He stands by James, is frightened although he sees nothing in this old man to be frightened of, and watches his hand in prickly-hot slow-motion tremble towards James's face. He shifts from one foot to the other.

A small, sticky fingertip touches the still skin, in this moment monstrous and terrifying, and as it does a squeak from the door says, 'Charlie! Someone's coming!'

Charlie, with some of James's skin cells invisibly on his finger, like a bee with pollen on its abdomen, dashes horrified to the door, and the two boys tumble panicked away, with bursting hearts and burning faces and an endorphin rush of hysteria. It proves too much for them – they decide to go back downstairs to Mummy and Auntie Nicola. They stand by the lift giggling and flushed and exhilarated, the older brother denying, on grounds of time count and without accepting mitigating circumstances, the sworn twenty pounds.

* * *

Margaret watched this episode at first with her usual distant benignity, and then with an involved smile. In the last few days, all the people who pass in and out of the hospice have reminded her with molten quickness of her own people, and these two boys have conjured up her own children, Edith and Alexander, whom she so often found whispering together conspiratorially.

Margaret is glad that the small brother, who reminded her of Alexander, had come in to touch James's face. It was a blessing of its own kind, and, like daylight, would charge the motes in the air into a happier feeling.

The elder boy had behaved like her Edith, who had been such a little bully. She was always scheming matriarchally, bossing her older brothers with unique charm and naturalness, with Alexander forever finding himself the bewildered and courageous minion. Edith's cheeks had been year-round russet, like apples, and used to quiver firmly as she nosied and commanded.

Why were such vivid pictures coming to Margaret now? For so long she has felt a blind man's grief at the groping haziness of her memories, but now the fast-passing faces of nurses, visitors, patients, even the crown of a head in the garden, were bringing back all the faces of her own.

And James Hallow, who was a stranger to her, bringing back memories of everything. Carving a hollow into

225

her as if he belonged there, as if he had come to claim her. Or perhaps the other way – as if she were to claim him. What would Dympna think? Dympna whom she had doubted. Did Dympna claim this man, too? Or was it only she, Margaret, whose place was with him? Dypmna would come back, and they would talk. This time, Margaret would rise from wherever she was and take her friend in her arms, would take scoops of her blazing heather hair into her hands. Two women, not so alone.

Margaret saw that the urine bag was filling with a trickle. A minute later James had opened his eyes. He took a few more uncomfortable minutes to focus and register, and Margaret didn't rush him. She waited in the chair, watching him gently. What James needed was a sponge, wet with water to quench his tongue and throat. But this Margaret could not do; she could not flutter the corridors like a ghost, sponge bowl floating in midair. Instead, she reached for the water glass.

This time, more so than that morning, James's mouth furrowed to suck the water up. He clicked his tongue, which seemed swollen, up against the straw. His lips pushed outward and in, suckling at the straw like a baby, with his eyes looking up at Margaret. The noise his lips and tongue and cheeks made was chomping and squashy and gruesomely comical.

Margaret wanted to look away.

She had seen this before – adults looking lovingly up

at other adults, as if they were being breastfed – but she had seen it always from the sidelines. She had never been on the receiving end of that suckling, smiling look from a patient, as, to them, she had never been there. But this dying man could see her, and he gazed up as his lips puckered. Margaret found it grotesque.

But she didn't look away, she kept her eyes firm and warm. She focused on the scar – her scar – still beautiful on this unbeautiful face. A fingerprint.

She told herself that this rapt-looking, loud-puckered face was not James – it was Death, drawing closer. She remembered what it meant, this horrid feeding from the straw – it meant that James was worse and farther away. It meant he was disintegrating.

He was trying to push the straw out of his mouth with his tongue, a large tongue, coated in white. Margaret kept her eyes firm. She removed the straw, and replaced the water glass. She took her place in the armchair next to the bed. She looked at James as he swallowed a few times, coaxing his voice to work.

'I know you,' he said.

'Yes. I'm Margaret.'

'Yes, I know. *I know that.*'

Margaret registered the irritation in his voice. The change in James from enraptured infant to whining old man was swift.

'Do you need anything, James?' Margaret asks.

'My son? Where's my son?'

227

'He is not here yet.'

'Will he come soon?'

'I'm sure he will come soon.'

'How do you know? How do *you* know?' says James, his forehead creasing angrily. And then he looks at Margaret, and sees her white light, and draws himself back in. 'I know you,' he says again.

Margaret does not take this confusion personally. She cannot allow herself to, just as she could not allow herself to recoil from the suckling at the straw. She nods, sits forward in the chair so that James knows she is close, and feels strong. She feels strong and real as the chair she sits on, with legs of carved wood planted firmly on the ground.

'My son,' says James, 'needs to come. My son. Do you know him?'

'I saw him yesterday.'

'He's big now, isn't he?'

Margaret doesn't know what to say. The man she saw was tall enough, dark, and handsome in a tumble-down, angry sort of way. But he was no bigger than most people.

'Children grow up fast. One day they're children, and then they're grown.'

'Yes! Yes. That's what I mean. He visits me now, in that corner.' James gestures a weak, trembling arm towards the corner of the room behind the door. 'He comes like he did when he was a child. He's the only one that comes now.' James sighs, as if he has finished speaking, but then raises his arm again, agitated, and goes on, 'He was always so small. Hannah said no, he was an average size for his age. But I'm telling you he was small. He was pale. He never smiled.'

Margaret sees that James's face is gullied into a tense, unhappy expression. The corners of his mouth are turning down, and he is drifting between mixed-up, harmful realities. She cannot wade in. She must not make it worse.

'You remember him well as a child?' she asks, deliberately, soothingly, to draw his mind in one direction.

'Yes,' his tired arm flaps up again, still motioning to the corner, 'he was always there. I always saw him, from the corner of my eye. He was small. He was in danger of lots of things, bad things. Small children are – they're seen as weak by lots of bad things. I did the best I could.' James's eyes are flexing full of water, but they do not leak. 'He was my son, you know.'

'Yes,' says Margaret, smoothing the heavy, tightly woven material of her skirts, 'I have seen him. He is grown now.'

'Yes! He's big now. I can't find him, although I call him when I can. On the telephone. He's in America.'

'He has come to London to see you,' says Margaret. 'He has come to London from America.' The word *America* feels funny in her mouth, she is not sure she has ever said it before.

'America,' echoes James. He closes his eyes for a moment, before winching them open again with speed, afraid that if he leaves them closed too long he might not be able to open them again. 'I could wring his neck,' James says, 'like a chicken. That's how small he is. And always in danger. I used to tell him,' James's eyes are still wet, growing wetter, still not spilling, 'to look after his soul. His God's Holy Soul. To make himself stronger.'

Margaret sees the tears millimetres thick on James's eyes and marvels that they do not fall. She puts her hand on his arm, circles her fingers round it, and squeezes gently, as if she were wringing the tears out for him, from his wrists.

'But,' says James, 'I was wrong.'

He sighs, a long, rattling sigh, and yellow urine passes slowly through the catheter into the bag. James swallows thickly, with difficulty, and Margaret this time gives him some milkshake – he has pulled much energy from himself with his words, and with his shaking, pointing arm. He manages a small suck, before turning his head away.

'He was my son, you know.' James has closed his eyes now. 'He wasn't bad.'

Margaret nods, even though James cannot see her. She nods, and places a hand over his closed eyes, to help him rest.

There are old wrongs and old wounds in James's troubled incantations of his son, Margaret knows that.

She knows, too, that she cannot heal them. How many knots and trespasses do people take to the grave, unable, in this life, to even them out? Many.

Many. There is not often the time, once death comes hexing in, to iron all into amends. People pass unforgiven, unforgiving; it happens often, and Margaret cannot stop it.

Her own death left her howling for all the moments of selfish refusal in her life, which had built up into walls and years. She had been pricking and griefing herself since, for all the wrong-headedness she had allowed to build up; walls and years.

*Malcolm, Malcolm, forgive me.*

Forgive you? Little bird? For what?

*Forgive me, Malcolm,* she wants to say. *Forgive me.*

For what should he forgive her?

*Forgive me.*

If Malcolm could have heard his wife, from the heart of the clay empire in which he lay, he would have said, might he not? –

*Margaret. My love.*

He would rise up all eyelashes and silver, to say this to her. He would shake the dust from his beard and plough his fingernails through hard ground to say this to her. And she? She would smile for her own stupidity, and weep for the missing of him, her Malcolm, so far gone, so far away, irretrievable, lost. She would weep for missing him.

# 5

Meryl is looking shifty. She is poking her head round the door into James's room, like a meerkat, while her body remains indecisively in the corridor. It looks like she might dart away at any moment.

The truth is, as well as looking she's also feeling shifty. Jamie will be following her to the hospice from Starbucks any minute, and will be coming up to his father's room. He mustn't catch her here. She must only spend a minute. A minute, for curiosity's sake.

It's terrible to be doing this, visiting with someone only because you want to look them up and down, check 'em out, have a gander. If she's honest, she's not here for any other reason. It's not like there's anything she could helpfully do. She just wants a look at him.

To disperse the feeling of guilt, Meryl clears her throat as she comes in. She doesn't quite know where to stand. It's not like she wants to go up to the bed and really examine him – whip out a magnifying glass. She only wants to . . . Well. She doesn't know what she only wants to. She just wanted to come and have a look. Although now she's here, actually in the room, she feels stupid. And horribly conspicuous, as if she were twice her real size.

He looks awfully sunken in that bed. And awfully still with his head at an awkward angle. Gosh. I tell you.

Meryl's face becomes purposeful, and she walks to the bed. Look at these pillows! They're a mess! She removes the first one gingerly, and once sure that James will not wake, she removes another. The remaining pillows she bolsters with her fingertips, as if massaging them, and then as gently as she can she takes James's heavy, sleepy head – she can feel a jutting bone in the back of it – and pulls the most acutely offending pillow upwards from behind his shoulders, before releasing his head back on to it. A rattling has come from James's throat as she did this last part, but it is subsiding now. That's much, much better.

Meryl takes the two spare pillows and stands with them for a moment. She looks at James.

She can't imagine any of it.

'Well,' she says, aloud, 'I have to go now,' and then feels richly foolish for having spoken. She puts the pillows on the top shelf of the cupboard, where the other spare sheets already live. Inside the cupboard there hang on a few, lean hangers a couple of shirts and pairs of dark trousers. There are neatly placed blue slippers underneath them. Meryl clears her throat again.

'Oh dear,' she says to herself, aloud, but quietly this time. Oh dear, oh dear. Oh dear.

That poor Jamie, oh dear. Living in America, maybe on his own. She hopes he doesn't go back, just yet. His mum must have passed away, too.

She had really better go, now. So much to do! There's a new lady on the second floor she'd like to drop in to see.

It was terribly, terribly sad.

Meryl closes the cupboard, and looks back at the bed with something approaching wistfulness on her face, one corner of her mouth turned down. She leaves the room, propping the door a little more ajar than it was.

Meryl: if not busy, then always doing things, especially with pillows. She's an unlikely heroine.

Much more likely a heroine is the saint who has watched this all from the chair by the dying man's bed. The saint, Margaret, is beautiful – one of those rare constructions that could not be altered for the better. She has poise, and tenderness, and despite rages and confusions, despite a well-trod instinct to harm herself, Margaret always thinks of, cares for, and sacrifices to others. She has the power of certainty, Margaret, the power of belief, and she glitters when she walks, a peculiar, ethereal glitter. A better candidate for heroine all round.

Whereas Meryl is a fusspot. She has a large bottom and forgets how to be basically graceful. She feels unloved, which is lonely. She makes a meal of it, which is unattractive. But Margaret, watching her as she has over the past two years, thinks that Meryl, if more unlikely, is also a more authentic heroine than she.

When Meryl first started volunteering, Margaret recognised her type. The children had had a nurse like Meryl – a kind of woman who has existed throughout the centuries, before there were suburbs to put them in and book clubs to subscribe them to. Women like this set Margaret's teeth together. They smiled continually, needily, compulsively, as if a smile were a bow tie. They chimed, 'Don't you worry about me!' as loudly and demandingly as their lungs could manage. They formed opinions based on gossip and trend, and spouted them freely. They dragged and complained about their ankles while around them souls clung on to bodies by hairthreads. They quite set Margaret's teeth together.

Everyone else at the hospice, of course, had at first thought Meryl was lovely. Always smiling, always ready to lend an ear – she listened, Meryl, she made time. But Margaret had arched away from her in irritation, dismissive.

Then, over the months, as some workers at the hospice began gradually to feel oppressed by Meryl – never doubting her loveliness, but finding themselves making excuses and walking the other way, finding themselves joking about her between themselves – Margaret had found herself growing gradually more tolerant. She found herself growing fond, protective, and, eventually, growing proud.

Meryl may have come to work at St Margaret's for all sorts of self-interested reasons. But the fact was, whatever these reasons, she continued to come to the hospice on her three afternoons a week, and for these hours she worked hard.

Margaret soon came to recognise Meryl's gabble of self-pity as the spinnings of a wind-up toy; they were pathological, as ceaseless as a dervish. She ignored them, and instead watched Meryl's hands as they busied themselves, watched the smiles of some of the patients as Meryl came to see them, watched Meryl's genuine desire to make people more comfortable, to engage them in happy talk, to listen when they needed to speak.

And the reality was that people came here – were brought here – to die. Meryl would jolly along a patient for weeks, listen to their life, come to know them, and then return one day to find them gone. It wasn't easy. She had had family members cry on her shoulder, leaving white salt trails on the fabric of her clothes. She had said many goodbyes, *you take care now, dear, you just look after yourself. And don't you forget me! I'll be back next Wednesday and I expect a big welcome! Bye bye, then, dear, bye bye.* Bye bye bye bye bye.

Margaret had seen Meryl wet with tears, tears grooved into wrinkles. Standing alone by the sink in the staff kitchen. Simon, a very competent nurse, had come in mid-flow and muffling each of his qualms given Meryl a hug. She had said, between sniffles, 'Don't you worry about me, dear, I'm just fine. Careful of my ankle, now.' Margaret, watching, shook her head, smiled.

Meryl did not look young, to Margaret, and did not look that happy, either. She had long passed her years of immortality, when death and aches and pains were too far into the future to register with any great impact – Meryl must think of death, and life, and time, often, and with a creased brow. And yet Wednesday, Thursday, Friday, she readied herself, waited at the bus stop, took the bus, bought herself a coffee (and sometimes one of those large biscuits they have in the jars) and came here to help. No other volunteer had done this so continuously or reliably. Margaret appreciated it greatly. Margaret would, in fact, miss Meryl once she was gone, although, God willing, that would not be soon.

Margaret correctly suspects that Meryl's coming here just now, to James's room, might have something to do with the son, Jamie. Who, despite the hair, and the finer, more predictable bone structure, looks like his father. Who today has still not yet come.

James has been sloughing through morphine dreams and memory snippets, heavy despite their small size.

He keeps, with agitation, dreaming that the door is closed, and that Hannah and Jamie and that cunt Bill Forth will walk past and miss him. But every time the door is opened, he knows it is going to close again. Bill Forth had his Hannah cherry-picked. Bill Forth stopped him fighting. It was time to talk again.

But how could he? With the door shut up like that? They'd all walk straight past.

Pop-pop-pop: James's lips are sticky, and his breath comes through his mouth in pops. As he stirs from sleep his fingers pluck at the sheets as if sand were running through them. They pick the sand up, and it streams away. He must focus, focus. On everything he knows.

He remembers his visitor over the years, the small devil that used to come but stopped – when? – recently. The smell of his flesh, burnt. He remembers the house he lives in, with the wallpaper in the hall and the lampshade. He remembers his fucking leg not working, his hand, and everything, no more fights, no more money. Hannah. Jamie. Jamie and the monster. Jamie on an island of monsters, in a suit of some kind, with ears.

He knows he is not at home now, and he can *not* open his eyes and he wants to roar blood up with dismay. What does he know? – plucking at the sheets – what does he know? No more of this dreaming. He needs to remember what he *knows*. What he has tried to tell himself every day – remember the *facts*, remember what you *know*.

He knows that for twenty-five years, for nine years, for two years, for eight years, for thirty years, for three years, *for three years*. For three years he had lived at St Dympna's Hospital. He had been taken there – why? Because he couldn't look after himself.

He does not remember Glen Willow, a home for the elderly where he had first been taken. He stayed there for only three weeks, because it became clear that it wasn't only Parkinson's and religiousness that had him: it edged into something else. Doctors came, and James was moved to St Dympna's, where his room was more comfortable for him, and where the nurses were psychiatrically trained. He remembers it there. *Three years*. He knows it.

Margaret leaves James's disturbed hands alone – she doesn't halt their picking. But she hears the popping of his breath and frustration in his throat, and understands that he is struggling to rise up out of the syrup. So she stands, and slides her hand under James's skull, cups it there. She exerts the smallest pressure, so that James, she hopes, will feel he is being lifted. The pain he doesn't mind – he never has, a punch to the ribs, okay, okay – but when the body stops listening, when it winds away from you like evil string, when it goes and you cannot fight its going. Then he minds. Then he wants to split open his skin like that snake and rock-hew out of himself.

He wakes up saying,

'Thank you, thank you,' through sticky lips, 'thank you.' He could weep for all the thank yous. She is here, with him, she has not left. And the door is open a little: enough. Do not let it blow shut!

'Thank you,' he says, 'thank you.' His head is rolling from side to side; death, it seems, is an almighty battle. 'I am *trying*,' he says.

'I know,' says Margaret. 'And I will help you in any way that I can. I am here.'

'They are pulling at me,' says James, and Margaret's heart contracts to hear it, the brutality of what James is in.

'I have you,' she says. 'I am holding you, under your head, and I will lift you up. You can feel my hand under your head, it is holding you.'

James wants to cry, but even that he cannot command. The thanks, and the prayer, and the ratcheting exhaustion of this he wants to rid with tears. If only he had cried when he could. Cried when Hannah died. Cried for becoming a nothing from a sidewinder, he was a king, a king, a king of the ring, and then suddenly a no one, a no body.

James's whining, mumbling sounds calm themselves into quiet. His head stops rocking, his breathing deepens. He is out of the dreams, and in the room. She is here with him. There is sunlight, daylight. There are friendly things.

Margaret, after a few minutes, slips her hand out

from beneath James's head, and comes to sit by him. He is awake, staring up at the ceiling. She dreads the inevitable question, *Has Jamie come? Is my son here?* No, he has not yet come. No, he is not here yet. No.

But this time the expected question does not come. Instead James, still looking at the ceiling, asks,

'What about your children?'

'My children?'

This is a body blow; a hall of Margaret's heart has been ambushed. Her children? *Her* children? They are not for talking about. They live tucked under the folds of dust in her heart. She is caught, stopped, bewildered. She is amazed at the question.

'You have children.' James's voice is certain and low.

'Yes,' Margaret says, the word intoning upwards like a flock of startled birds.

*My children are somewhere else. My children died long ago, without me.*

*The first on a battlefield with his father.*

There is a feeling in Margaret's chest like a stone being rolled away from an opening.

'Are they here?' James asks, tired to have to ask so many questions, when all he means is one thing.

'No, no.' Margaret hears the distress in her own voice, and does what she can to check it. 'They are not here.'

'Please,' says James, he must keep looking at the plaster cracks, and not close his eyes, 'tell me where

241

they are.' He is gripping the sand-sheets now, without violence, but with determination.

'I am sorry,' says Margaret, 'I am . . .' She pauses, and is frightened for a moment of what she has done, in opening the gates to this man. She does not want to answer. She does not know where his questions have come from. What can she do? Dive from the window in a flurry? Remain here, swallow hard. There is an avalanche threatening to break in the corner of the room, behind the door – the same corner that James pointed towards, saying he saw his son. That she is here at all, talking to this man. And now he asks about her children. It is dizzying.

'My children,' Margaret's palms, without her knowing, have settled themselves on her lap, facing up, as if they are begging, 'looked after me when I was sick. Those who were there.'

James nods, nods for Margaret to please keep talking.

'They are not here now. Only I am here now. I try to think of them often, but I'm not able. I can't see their faces clearly enough. You see, James,' he is pleased to hear his name, 'they were my children a long time ago.'

The pain it takes to admit this – that in dying she let her children go, she severed the cords that bound them to her – is acute.

'I do not know them now, although I knew them when I had them, at the time. They,' she says to explain, 'are not here anymore.'

'Boys,' says James.

'Yes. And two girls.' Again she hears the upset in her voice, again she tries to stem it. 'I love them very much. I know what it is to love like that, your child. Your Jamie will come, he will come, James, soon.'

James's right hand is flapping over the edge of the bed, his fingers are pincering together, like clams or castanets. He is signalling to her. Margaret takes his fingers, and realises as she does, that this is a gesture: from James, to her, of understanding. Perhaps something more. He is, with his hand, trying to help her. She takes his fingers in hers and she holds them.

'Will they come back? Your children?' James asks.

'I don't know.' Margaret is turning James's hand over in her own, examining the fingers, the pads. 'I don't think so.'

'Your husband?' says James. 'Did he go with them?'

'No,' says Margaret. 'No,' she says, and to her surprise her voice has come out loudly, 'Malcolm did not go. I did not let him go. Malcolm is not gone.'

Her words have erupted with force, and they are words that she could never have predicted. Only as these words oxidise and plant their flags in the ground around Margaret's feet, does she look at them and realise they are true. She has never let go of Malcolm. She is not able.

Her children she allowed to fly away. But never Malcolm. Of him, she has never let go.

She has stopped turning James's hand, and now just holds it.

'Is he a nice man?' asks James, meaning so many things by 'nice' – was he good? did he say thank you? did he ever shout or hit her? did he do nice things, kind things? did he look after her? did he touch her gently? did he use other women? did he drink? did he say good things, kind things? did he know God?

'He was a King,' says Margaret.

A king, a king, a king of the ring.

# 6

The door to the new lady's room is shut, and Meryl peers through the round window like it is a porthole, and she a fish. She knock-knock-knocks, and comes through with a smile.

'Hallooo!' she projects. 'Can I come in?'

The lady is sitting up in the bed, supported by the angled headrest, and tightly placed pillows. There is something metallic about her, like a taut steel wire, and also something quietly fabulous, as if behind the pillows she is storing feathers and brandy and eyebrow pencil. She is old. Old like tracing paper.

'Yes,' she says, looking at Meryl with coolness, not moving her head or her body, but her eyes only, 'you may.'

'Hello,' says Meryl, in a Montessori voice, 'I'm just popping in to say hello.'

'Hello,' says the wirelike lady in the bed.

'My name's Meryl. I just thought I'd pop in and introduce myself, and have a chat.'

This inanity is very irritating to Mrs Maddox Brown, who is the lady in the bed. 'You're a nurse?' she asks, her expression unchanging.

'Oh.' Meryl is once again dampened by this question. 'No, I'm not a nurse, I'm a volunteer. I'm here to spend time with you, and just be of help in any way that I can.'

'I see,' says Mrs Maddox Brown, 'you're here on your own time,' and faint lines of entertainment spider in her thin, old lady cheeks, and around her rather curved, rather exquisite mouth. She wants to add, 'You have an amateur interest in the dying, do you?' but she doesn't, because saying it would throw this Meryl off kilter, and thus cause her to stay longer. What kind of a name is Meryl? American, probably.

'So, Marian, shall I just sit down here?' says Meryl, pulling a chair closer to the bedside, slightly lopsidedly, because of the blasted ankle. Mrs Maddox Brown has started at the use of her Christian name. Meryl notices. 'Is it okay if I call you Marian? Such a beautiful name,' a stroke of inspiration hits, 'like Robin Hood!' She beams.

Mrs Maddox Brown nods, curtly, and raises her lean, white eyebrows.

'So, dear,' begins Meryl,

*Dear?* Good God, Mrs Maddox Brown wants to throw a brick at this woman,

'You arrived this morning?'

Mrs Maddox Brown nods again, a single inclination of the chin.

'And how are you settling in?'

'Settling in?' Marian Maddox Brown's voice is reedy, breathless, but there is an authority in it, more rigour than Meryl is used to. 'I'm rather perplexed by that question. I'm perfectly comfortable, if that's what you mean.'

'Oh, good, I'm glad to hear it. New places can be difficult, at times.'

'Can they.'

Mrs Maddox Brown is looking unwaveringly at Meryl, which is, to be honest, a little daunting.

'Well, yes, I think so, don't you? Especially when you don't know anyone, and you haven't got your things around you. Don't you think?'

'I have, as you see, a few of my things around me – enough to keep me happy. And I have no desire to know anybody.' Rewind a few months – a few weeks, even – and Mrs Maddox Brown could have had a field day getting rid of this person, a fox at a rabbit's neck, a hound at a fox's. But this damned exhaustion, damned frailty that hit four weeks ago, signalling the end with a pointed finger.

'Oh, don't you worry, dear, it's easy enough. We're a lovely lot, around here. A bit mad, maybe! Hoo hoo!' This is the kind of laugh that other people laugh *at*, and aptly describe as *infectious*. 'But a really lovely lot. You'll get to know everyone by the end of the day, I'm sure.'

'Mrs . . . ?'

'Meryl.'

'Yes, you said. Meryl, then. To be completely clear with you, *Meryl*,' there is emphasis on the name, a rolling of the *r*, 'I really do not wish to meet anyone. I'm not here to have dressing-gown parties with whatever other geriatric geese you have penned up. When I say I have no wish to know anybody, I mean it.'

Meryl is thunderstruck.

Her eyes have bounced wide.

But she is also robust, and knows she cannot sit slack-jawed. 'Oh, I see,' she says. And then she adds, 'I quite understand.'

*I quite understand.* This is Meryl's usual unconscious mimicry of whomever she's with, whenever she's feeling underconfident. It makes her feel less insecure, to be like other people, to be heard as speaking in the right way. It just makes her feel more comfortable, and there's nothing wrong with that, is there?

Except that at this moment, she is further uprooted by the pitchfork truth that this lady, Marian Maddox Brown, sits in a significantly different social class than she does. An elevated one, an upper one, a one that makes Meryl squirm with longing and inferiority and discomfort and eagerness. Maddox Brown. Two surnames. Without a hyphen, which Meryl thinks sounds even grander. She read in a magazine quite recently that to have a hyphenated or *double-barrelled* name was actually now considered 'chavvy', which she took to mean 'common'. She had personally always thought so, but never said. The magazine was right.

But two separated surnames were different.

'I'm just here to help,' says Meryl again, aware that her ankle is becoming sore, 'in any way that I can.'

'You're very kind. I shall let you know if I need any help. For the time being I'm quite alright.'

There is a pause of about ten seconds, which Meryl can't cope with. It makes her prickle nervously.

'Can I get you a newspaper?' She realises that she has said this rather loudly, and modulates her voice. 'Or a book? We have quite a good little library here. Nothing magnificent,' she says, smiling, trying to sound conspiratorial, 'but one or two decent things.'

'No. Thank you. I really don't need anything at all.' Again there is a pause, and this time Mrs Maddox Brown breaks it. 'Is there something wrong with your foot?'

'Oh, dear, you've spotted it.'

'I'm not medically trained. But I notice without much sleuthing that you are massaging it.'

Meryl has, indeed, bent down to give the wretched ankle a rub, as it had been quite seizing up as she sat there – she could feel it getting stiffer, like it was turning to wood.

'Oh dear, well, yes. It just went, under me, like this,' Meryl twists her wrist around to demonstrate, 'a couple of weeks ago. It was agony, I tell you. I have these terrible ankles. And it just hasn't healed properly. It's still terribly swollen.'

'I feel for you,' Mrs Maddox Brown interrupts, her voice impeccably even. She really can't tolerate this any longer – this woman apparently pitching camp in her room, rabbiting on about absolutely nothing. She knows her temper – five more minutes and she will become apoplectic. 'Just as, Meryl, I imagine, you feel for me. I imagine you have noticed, through the cloud of discomfort in your foot, that I am dying. You may have understood as much simply by dint of my being here.'

'Oh, I,' Meryl straightens up, 'I, didn't, I, I didn't mean to upset you, I'm not trying to . . .'

'I am not upset.'

'Well, I . . .' Meryl is feeling low-level animal panic, as sticky and giddy as the panic she felt as a girl at school. Panic pushes her farther, faster into the inappropriate, so lost is she for the right places to fumble. 'I,' she says, 'my foot really isn't that bad, you know, I, it's just at this age things take so long to heal, that's what my son, you know. If. If you don't want a newspaper – although I'd be more than happy to read to you, of course I would, I've got my glasses right here – well there are lots of board games in the lounge area,' she is babbling now, burbling, 'there's chess, if you like, or draughts. Or cards, of course.'

Mrs Maddox Brown is growing angry, and her body feels desperate for some peace. This cannot go on.

'Meryl,' she says, smoke in her tone, smoke rising, 'listen to me, please. If I had seventy years ahead of me, I might conceivably give you, complete stranger as you are, some of my time to play draughts. With a full life ahead of me, I might be a bit more laissez-faire with my hours. But I am a few days away from death, and I have no time to waste, with you, playing infantile games.' She is carried by her own tide, raising herself into a fury. 'I *need* to be left to *think*. For God's sake, this place is like a damned library! You come because it advertises peace, but instead find yourself surrounded by chatter. Chatter! For God's sake! I need a bit of peace in which to think!' Mrs Maddox Brown's raised voice is feeble and shrill. 'I say, with no ounce of personal malice, that I would like you to leave. I want to be left alone. I would like you to leave, please. And I would like you not to visit me again.'

'Righty-ho.' Meryl wants to leave, too. She just wants to disappear. 'Right. Of course, dear, of course. I'm just here to make you happier, to help in any way that I can.' She is getting up in a hurry, afraid that she will fall over – she has always fallen over, at parties, at tennis, at every critical moment, she's always been just so bloody clumsy. Her ankle is sore. Her face. It's hot with humiliation.

'If you spent a dedicated lifetime trying,' says Mrs Maddox Brown to Meryl, with smooth certainty, 'you could not make me happier. It is not within your range.'

'Well, dear. Well.' Meryl is feeling tearful and crowded and hot, she can't quite grasp what has passed in the last few minutes. 'I'll leave you alone to think, like you said. You just let me know if there's anything you need, alright? If you need anything.' She is up, having leant on the chair for support.

*Good God*, thinks Mrs Maddox Brown, as Meryl the Volunteer quits her room with a faltering smile and a faltering walk and a faltering heart, *Good God, if only I had something to throw at her.*

And then, once the door has shut, she laughs at her own spitefulness; she laughs at herself as if she is another person. She didn't mean to get so cross. She really had wanted to throw something.

Mrs Maddox Brown goes on to think that even if she did have some suitably ludicrous object to hurl – a small dog, a music-hall pie, or one of those rubber chickens – she wouldn't have the strength to throw it. The dreadful reality was that she didn't have the strength to move her arms beyond the smallest movements.

Mrs Maddox Brown had lived her life occupied with its details. She, like the Princess of Pea fame, could not fall asleep if there was a crease in her nightgown where she lay on it – she would feel the fold of the material pressing into her skin, and couldn't stand it. So her ritual became one of evening out wrinkles until her sheets and her nightclothes were pristinely smooth. Then sleep was easy.

Her walls were painted with exact, crisp edges, or else they were repainted, and painted again. Never was there a thread dangling or a scuffed toe, for they would be an affront – to the minutiae, to the microscopic splendour of things, to every blade of grass that pushed itself immaculately upwards to make the world green. Mrs Maddox Brown was a lover, an admirer, of life. She recognised and honoured its perfection.

But now, alas, she had not the strength in her arms to push away a hair that had fallen into her face. Even a month ago the unruly hair, tickling at her skin like a cobweb, would have driven her mad. But now – not so. Were she to mobilise her energy and lift her arm and push the hair to one side, she would be exhausted for an hour to come. It simply wasn't worth it. She closed her eyelids and allowed herself to hate the fallen hair for a moment, before moving on to other thoughts.

There really was so much to think about. So much. And so few days left.

Meryl stands in the passageway and presses her lips together and forward. Her hands are shaking as they hang by her sides, injected from the wrists to the fingernails with nervous shame. Her hands have shaken like this only a few times in her life: before and after having to recite a poem on Governors' Day at school, which she botched horribly; waiting for the organ to start on her wedding day, terrified that she would fall over as she went down the aisle; being caught by a group of teenage boys weeing behind some bushes at the beach; and on her way to the hospital, having been phoned and told that Ben, then twelve years old, had had an accident playing football. Thank God it was just a broken leg – severely broken, requiring a four-inch pin – but still a leg that would heal, rather than internal organs, or, God forbid, spinal column or neck.

Her hands are shaking again now, and Meryl, in her distressed daze, could be mistaken for a patient. She is breathing noisily, in and out through her nose. She can't stand here forever, conspicuous, quivering, clumsy great big idiot – great big bloody idiot, I tell you, always have been.

Meryl walks the back way to the ladies' loo. Apart from the big washrooms on the ground floor, there is only one ladies and one gents on each of the other floors, as all the rooms have their own bathrooms. Amenities. WCs. Toilets. All these words for a loo, and Meryl never knows which one to use. *Lavatory* seemed to be out, although Denise said it. But Denise also said *serviette* for napkin and *lounge* for living room and said theatre as thee-*Ater* instead of theer-ter, which Meryl knew was wrong. Ben, her son, had called Denise *The*

*Potato-Ater* behind her back because of it. Meryl doesn't know where the potato bit came from, but told Ben to not be so snobby. Meryl hates snobbiness, she just hates it. But Ben went on, and Meryl gave up reprimanding him.

It's a loo, isn't it? A cistern for flushing and a bowl for shitting in. That's what it was, and who cared about the bloody word. Little girls' room. Powder Room. Meryl has used those two often. But it's a loo. A LOO.

Meryl is locked in and sitting on the closed loo seat. The light in here is greeny and cheap. The floor is dark and glittery, and Meryl's shoes look clompy and clumsy and enormous on it. She has never been, will never be, one of those women with beautiful little shoes.

All these stupid thoughts. Stupid thoughts that won't leave her alone. Silly, stupid thoughts.

Meryl looks down at her hands, whose shaking is subsiding, and then up at herself in the mirror. She never used to look like that. Sallow and hanging. And might as well bloody admit it – old. Old. OLD.

Meryl's mouth pulls downwards and thin tears start running out of her eyes. As she sees herself doing this, she is racked with a sense of her own ridiculousness, a snivelling old lady with great big clumsy shoes crying and screwing her face up in the mirror. Her own unsightliness makes the tears come even faster, and Meryl looks away from herself. Her nose is running.

That horrible, horrible old cow. Sitting like a statue in her bed, staring and making fun and being so bloody rude. As if Meryl were too stupid to know that she was being made fun of; *oh, so you're here on your own time, are you?* Meryl had a zillion better things to be doing with her time. She could be at home, with her feet up, or chatting with friends, or going to the shops, or doing a job that actually paid her, more's the point! But she chose to be here because she thought she could help, she thought she could matter that way, and then that bloody rude woman goes and tells her to go away.

It made her feel so small. So anchovy tiny. Small and stupid and clumsy. Everybody thinking she was an idiot.

Meryl wants to go home. She wants to go home and make herself a sandwich and eat it in front of the tele with Lemon, her dog. She doesn't want to spend a minute longer in the hospice.

But if she goes home Jo will be there, and she'll have to put on a brave face, and make him some tea, and go and watch the tele in their bedroom just to be alone. And then Jo would ask, 'Are you alright, Merrie?', he'd shout it from downstairs, and she'd get irritated.

Meryl won't go home. It's better to stay here. Pull herself together. She could have a cup of tea and a couple of biscuits in a little while. Forget about that horrid Mrs Maddox Brown and make her other visits. She'd never say it to anyone else, but she made a difference, she knew she did. Just look at all the cards she had! She might be a stupid old idiot, but she made a difference to some of the people here. She's not saying she changed their lives, or anything. Just that they appreciated her spending time with them.

If there was time after her visits, she'd see if anything needed doing for the Admin office. They were always so overworked in there, poor girls. And she might run into Jamie again; oh she did hope so. She did hope he didn't leave just yet, with his father about to die. Although, of course, it was nothing to do with her. None of her business, and she mustn't stick her nose in.

Meryl blots her damp cheeks and the edges of her eyes. She needs her handbag, which has her lipstick and powder and hairbrush in it. It's with her coat in the staff room.

'Oh dear,'

she says to herself.

# 7

Shrugging into his coat to leave Starbucks, Jamie is approached by a teenage girl, who holds a square brown paper bag in one hand, and a biro in the other. She is wearing a long stripy scarf, large silver hoop earrings, a lot of eyeliner, and must be no more than fifteen.

'Excuse me,' she says, polite, 'but are you that guy off of *Do Re Me*?'

'Er, yeah. Yeah, I am.'

'Is your name Jamie Hallow?'

'Er, yep.' This has taken Jamie by surprise, and he feels nervy, he pulls his head back like a horse. 'You're not going to tell me you hate the show, I hope.' He is trying to be blithe.

The girl giggles, more of a *heheh*, actually. 'No, the show's great. I watch it every week. Sometimes I miss it, but, you know, I watch it a lot.' She is staring at him, examining him.

'That's great,' says Jamie, pulling on a pair of sheep-skin gloves he bought yesterday, although God knows why, they'll sit in the back of a drawer in LA. He adds, 'I'm glad you like it,' when the girl remains where she is, saying nothing.

'So you're English, then? Except I thought you were American.'

'Yeah. Er, no. I am English, yeah.'

Jamie's communication skills have left him. He can't find anything to say – maybe he's caught it, like a germ, from the girl, whose name he definitely doesn't want to ask or know. Suddenly, standing here, having already wasted hours of the day, he feels time slipping and wants to get to the hospice. People at other tables are paying attention while pretending not to, trying to gauge whether they recognise him also.

'How come?' asks the girl.

'Um, sorry?'

'How come you're English?'

'How come I'm English?' says Jamie. 'You mean . . .'

'I mean, how come you're English in real life? In *Do Re Me* you're American, aren't you?'

'Yeah, yeah, my character's American,' it dawns on Jamie that this girl is not an intellectual leviathan, and, were he not feeling awkward, he'd be irritated, 'but I'm English. Born in London. I live in America, if that's what you mean. That's why I act in American shows.'

'Oh, right, cool. Do you live in LA, then?' The girl

says LA in an over-pronounced way, as if excited by the letters.

'Yeah, I do, actually.'

'Cool. What's it like there?'

'Well, ah, I like it. It's sunny.'

'Are there loads of famous people?'

'Look,' Jamie wants to leave the Starbucks and the girl with an urgency, 'er, yeah, I suppose there are. I really need to get on. Someone's waiting for me. But it was really nice of you to come over and say hi.'

'Is it your mum?'

'My mum?' says Jamie, narrowing his eyes and not understanding, not wanting to understand.

'Who's waiting for you? That lady who was here just now?'

'No. That's not my mum.'

'Oh, right,' says the girl, still eyeballing. 'Were you also in that film, *Love Hurts*?'

'Yeah.' Jamie smiles in disbelief, that this girl with the gigantic earrings is continuing in an undeterrable monotone, scanning him up and down. 'That was me.'

'I thought so.' She looks pleased with herself. 'So you must know famous people, then?'

'I know the people I've worked with, and some of them are famous. So, I suppose so.'

'Like who?'

Jamie takes his mobile phone out of his pocket and looks at the time.

'Look, it's really nice of you to come and say hi. I really appreciate it, but I've really got to shoot off now. I'm running late.' He doesn't know whether to extend a hand, or what, so opts for a short-distance wave. 'It was really nice meeting you.'

'Can I have your autograph?' says the girl, in an unabashed way that makes Jamie want to laugh – she says everything in the same tone, at the same pitch, with the same open-mouthed, fly-catching moronity.

'Sure, if you want it.' Jamie takes a glove off, stores it under his elbow, and takes the brown paper bag from the girl. She passes him the biro.

He leans the paper bag on the table, and signs his name. He hands the bag back, 'Here you go,' puts his glove back on.

'Thanks,' the girl says, looking at the signature, and then at Jamie.

'Nice meeting you,'

says Jamie, and leaves.

What on earth is that girl going to do with his autograph? Frame it? Put it up on her wall? Take it in to her special-needs school? Jamie is smirking. It's not like he's a household name – he wanders the streets perfectly unnoticed – he's only photographed or interviewed when there's a film to promote. People in LA might know who he was, because as actors went he was established. Respected, even. But, famous? Certainly not to the degree where his autograph would be worth anything. How fucking weird.

And that girl, dressed like so many other girls he had seen in London, with low-slung jeans and big belts and highlighted hair and dangling ears. Indistinguishable. With so little spark, so little apparent interest even as she made the effort to come over and talk. Maybe it was just stupidity, of a uniquely British kind. The kind that is happy to breathe through its mouth and stare. In California the same dumb questions would have been peppered with toothsome smiles and platitudes, niceties learnt in the cradle. Whereas this girl was content to stand and breathe like a potato in earrings.

And Meryl, his mum. What if, eh? If Meryl had been his mum – well, the thought was ridiculous. She'd be married to the silent body in the bed that was Dad. She wouldn't laugh, or chatter, or volunteer in a hospice. She wouldn't have hugged him just then. She'd sit inside all day with her eyes down, turning biscuits to sawdust.

His mum, Hannah. Was dead. And he hadn't seen her for years. He hated thinking about her. When he did all he could see was the cancer, that he hadn't known about, and it ate into every memory he had of her. She was never anything but the cancer. Maybe he should have said that to the girl, as an experiment, to see how she would have responded: *My mum? No, my mum died, infested, crawling, suffocated with cancer*.

*Oh right*, the girl would have said. *Who's the most famous person you know, then?*

Walking the short walk from Starbucks to St Margaret's Hospice, Jamie's stomach snarls. He is hungry, but he won't stop for anything – if he does, the afternoon will pass completely, and it will be dark before he is in his father's room. He does not want to be there in the dark. And the flight he has booked himself on to leaves Heathrow at twenty past ten. (He didn't tell Meryl that, that he had actually booked and confirmed his flight. But, then, why would he? She's *not* his mum.) He needs time after visiting Dad to go back to the hotel, shower, pack, and check out, plus get to the airport in good time.

He really is hungry. There's a lot of food he'd like to eat at this moment. He'd like Italian food, the old-fashioned, unadorned kind. Mozzarella in carozza, with concentrated tomato sauce. Linguine with oil and pepper and ounces of parmesan. Hot food, that he'd have to blow on before eating. That would fill his stomach with a numbing, straightforward warmth. He doesn't know restaurants here anymore, although there is that ancient place in Chelsea. There's no time, though. He'll just pick something up at the hotel.

As he gets to the entrance of the hospice, it occurs to him that he would also like one of those ice cream bars you get from the deep freeze in newsagents. The additive-rich multicoloured ones called things like *Fab!*

and *Radar*. If they still existed. They tasted of reconstituted milk and stale sugar, and Jamie had never liked them, not even as a child when they were proffered once in a blue moon as a treat – always by Dad, never by Mum. But, strangely, he would like one now. He'd like to go to a newsagent, sift around the deep freeze, and choose one; take it to the counter and hand over a series of ten-pence pieces to the man behind.

Does he want one badly enough to turn around and walk to the newsagent? No. No. It's three o'clock, and he's here now.

Thankfully, there appears to be a layperson manning the reception desk, not the nurse who he shouted at yesterday. Christ, he wishes there weren't all these people to engage with – it would be so much easier, in a situation like his, in a place like this, for everyone to remain faceless, instead of adding themselves to your consciousness, your associations, eventually your memories. Two days he'd been in London, twice to the hospice, and already he recognised people, as if he were part of some community. It was uncomfortable, and unnecessary. Meryl, who in the space of twenty-four hours was being mistaken for his mother. Fucking ridiculous.

Jamie's stomach rumbles again, as he presses the button to call the lift.

Pot plants, a waiting area, a lift. Visitors in thick jackets, old people in indoor clothes. Jamie did not want to remember any of it after tonight, and he did not want to look at anyone. Worse than a hospital, this place – no one in here with a hope, everybody here to die. He was looking at dead faces.

The lift takes him to the third floor, and he walks round the corner, to his father's room. Hello Dad. Same room, same bed, same body in it. But looking worse – that's a surprise. Looking like he's melting into the mattress, into his own bones. Like he's lost two stone overnight. Fucking hell.

Jamie walks to the window, looks out. Below there is the small hospice garden, past that the street, the buildings, the city, the sky. Jamie is seeing none of it.

He is surprised. Surprised at the overnight two-stone change. He doesn't want to turn around, but at the same time he doesn't want to have his back to the bed. Dad's skin looked shiny, and like it was pulled over the bones of his face. Jamie's heart speeds up: the more he looks out of the window at nothing, imagining his father's body behind him, the more monstrous the image becomes.

He goes to the side of the bed. He doesn't know why Dad is so thin, suddenly. It's not like he's dying of tapeworm. This thought makes Jamie smirk to himself, and then suddenly stop. He doesn't like the feeling of his face in the smirk. He makes it blank again.

Dad lies with his mouth open. His chin falls towards his neck, and his top lip looks heavy – it looks like the teeth underneath are horses' teeth, huge and bulky. Like they are false teeth, the wrong size. His head is making a perfect indent into the pillow, like a ghastly attempt at the Sleeping Beauty. With his hair cut short, Dad's forehead looks large, and polished. There are spots of skin discoloration on one temple – liver spots, they're called. He is breathing loudly – snoring, almost – through his mouth.

'Dad.' Jamie hates the sound of his voice in this room. 'Are you awake?'

No response.

'Dad?' He considers shoving the side of the bed with his thigh. 'Are you awake?'

Silence.

Silence.

'For fuck's sake.'

There is a sound from the back of his father's throat, but not even Walter Mitty could imagine this as communication of any kind. It is a glugging noise, a *bah bah bah*, as if bubbles were about to rise up from his mouth.

Jamie drapes his scarf and coat over the back of the armchair. He goes back to the other end of the room, and opens the large door into the bathroom.

Inside the door there is a string with a funny disc at the end of it, which Jamie pulls – the light flickers once, twice, thrice, before yellowing into life. For all its wheelchair dimensions and bars and handles, it is a small room, and Jamie is over-aware of himself in the mirror.

He closes the door behind him, and, he couldn't reason why, locks it.

There is another cord, a red one, with a sign by it that says THIS IS NOT A LIGHT SWITCH. Underneath that sign is another sign, EMERGENCY ALERT, Pull If In Need Of Assistance. Like the steward buttons on aeroplanes, that Jamie had accidentally once or twice before elbowed on.

What else is there? A shelving unit with a neat washbag on it. A plastic slatted triangle of air freshener. A can of shaving foam for sensitive skin, white with blue writing. Two glass cups by the sink, one with a razor in it, the other with two toothbrushes and a tube of toothpaste. One toothbrush is new, still in its plastic wrapping. The other is old, transparent red, with fraying, splaying bristles.

Dad's razor, clearly, and Dad's shaving foam. Dad's toothbrush, that he will have pressed hard, as he always did, on to his teeth.

Jamie hadn't seen any personal thing belonging to his parents for over a decade. And yet here was a toothbrush, and it was Dad's. And here was Dad, brushing his teeth hard and fast in the mirror, his gums peeled back like horses' gums, his wrist and arm flexing, working hard, no time to waste, a look of concentration on his face.

It feels clammy and intimate in this bathroom. Jamie pees and washes his hands quickly.

Back in the bedroom, he sits down in the armchair. He had forgotten, until just now, the stance and look of Dad as he brushed his teeth – Dad filling every millimetre of the space with his shadow and his chest and his movement, as he always did. Which is why, partly, this yellow-grey body on the bed was so disturbing, so – say it, Jamie – upsetting: because it wasn't pouncing its shadow all across the room. Dad had a shadow, and it was big. It took up space. You knew if Dad was in a house when you reached the front door, because you felt his shadow squeezing against the walls, ballooning them, reaching outwards through the letterbox.

This dead-like Dad on the bed was shrivelled in on himself. The room around him was empty. No shadow, no Dad, to be found.

Jamie had also forgotten, until now, that he used to watch his father brush his teeth – Dad, bare-chested or in a t-shirt, brushing with speed, breathing heavily through his broken-many-times nose, spitting, rinsing, drying his mouth. All of it done forcefully, no time spare.

Jamie would stand on one foot by the sink, clicking his finger in and out of the grout between the tiles.

– *Stand on both feet, Jamie*, Dad would say. Then,

– *Your turn now*, Dad would say, and hand Jamie his own toothbrush, with paste already on it.

Jamie loved the taste of that paste, it was chalky green and chalky sticky. If Dad weren't there, he would eat it, straight off the brush, straight out the tube. But Dad was there, and so Jamie would stand his turn in front of the mirror, not eating, but brushing his teeth and spitting, brushing hard like his father, while his father watched.

Jamie hears his Dad stirring, looks up from the chair. 'Dad?'

James Hallow's fingertips are plucking at the sheets.

'Dad?' Jamie gets up, looks at his father. His eyes are still closed, and he is breathing with a catch in his throat.

Jamie sits back down.

'I'm sitting in the chair by your bed,' he says, 'so you know I'm here.' He feels stupid having said this, and to make himself feel worse, to have a sneer at himself, he says, 'I've been remembering brushing my teeth with you, when I was small. You used to put the toothpaste on my brush for me.'

Jamie's right hand finds and holds the hair at the nape of his neck. He keeps it there, pulling downward. As if he is pulling his whole body down; he sinks further into the chair.

Twenty minutes have passed since James last stirred, and since Jamie last spoke. James has been lying in his death soup, struggling, and Jamie has been sitting in the armchair, his knees wide apart, his elbows on his knees, and his temples down in his hands. He has been staring at the carpet.

It pains Margaret to see Jamie sitting that way, as if he is sheltering himself, in a brace position. What harms and sorrows have passed between the two men, she does not know. But she can feel them, splitting the room.

If she moved forward from where she stands by the window and touched James, it would help – it might bring him upwards and back, help him surface from wherever he was sunk. But she won't; she thinks she mustn't. This is a father and a son, a duo as opposed to a trinity, with no room for a ghost, holy or otherwise. This is not her story.

Moments pass, and Margaret is finding it impossible to stay still. She shifts, and presses one toe on top of the other. She smoothes the front of her dress with her palms, a gesture she has not lost in her thousand years of being. Hearing her own rustles and scuffs irritates her – of course Jamie cannot hear, but she can hear herself, and she wishes to be still. She has always been able to be still as she watched, to retreat into her own thoughts.

But the boy in the chair – like Meryl, she cannot help but think of him as a boy – pains her, and so she moves with agitated movements, unable to settle, unable to stay put. And James – her unlikely confidant, her friend, maybe – is dropping through his layers, with fingers plucking and throat rattling. He is deteriorating rapidly.

Margaret has not kept count of the number of people who have passed through her hospice. There have been many. Some she has forgotten, and will forget, although of course she watched over them each one with diligence. Others she has taken to with fondness and interest – she remembers them, their expressions even years after they died.

Like the young woman, Nicola, who was earlier walking in the garden. Margaret will remember her, her animated face and ponytailed hair. She will remember the sight of Nicola sleeping, curled on her side with one hand under the pillow and one above, and her fiancé's t-shirt of that day as a pillowcase. She slept silently and prettily, like a storybook princess – Margaret imagined that it would be something her fiancé missed and thought of, when, years later, he slept next to someone else, someone who was not Nicola, and who did not sleep so prettily and silently. Margaret hoped Nicola would die like that – in sleep, in quiet, with the smell of the man she had chosen and loved underneath her face. Margaret did not want to see her tortured.

Death had come to the hospice in countless gradations. Of course the dying here were helped, in whatever way they could be, to pass gently. But still Death's scythe could not be controlled completely, and sometimes it swung heavy. Margaret had seen death at its gentlest, but also at the summit of its horrors. And every time she saw, after the heart had stopped and the soul had flown, the body become unrecognisable as it emptied out – a solid, brittle thing, all human aspect gone. She always hoped that the family would leave before that happened.

But then there had been moments that eclipsed all others, moments when love took flight like birds from a tree, filling the room of the dying with swift-moving wings and fluttery movement. In those panicked last moments, when there is so much more to be said than time to say it, Margaret has seen such love fill the space as leaves no room for pettiness, impatience, or any small thing. A lifetime of irritation – the way he chews his food, the countless times he's stayed out all night and come home in the morning smelling of beer – dissolves. A lifetime of white lying, taking for granted, gently ignoring – dissolves. In those last moments of being alive, Margaret has seen lifetimes of offence and hurt feeling dissolve as if they never existed. Pushing them out and replacing them, is love – beating its peregrine wings, yearning, enormous.

Those moments were something to hold on to.

But this – is different. This is different from all that. In this room on the third floor with James and Jamie, as Death draws nearer to James's body like a cold creature to a fire, everything is different. Margaret cannot stay still by the window, she cannot watch in quietude. For the man in the bed is more than a ward or a patient, a forehead to kiss, a body to bless, in-out-in-out they come through the sliding doors. This man is more than that. He is, with his fingerprint indent scar and his eyes that see her, a friend. Yes, a friend.

And the boy, the young man, the man of thirty-seven years who is stooped in the chair, is his son. Yes, James is her friend, and Jamie is his son, and this death is close to her in a way that no others have been.

During her own slow death she was watched over and guarded by a staff who reported to a court who reported to a country, with the faces of her children coming and going – she remembers it, sees it almost as if she were watching the scene from the corner of the room, a spider in a web in the corner of her own room, watching her own death. And those last grief-stricken days of her life marked the end of it all – all the things that were close to her.

Since arriving here, frothing in on the back of some sacred stream, nothing has been close to her – for this is not her life. Her life was buried in Dunfermline ground. This existence is something else – her purgatory, perhaps, through which she moves godless and alone. Perhaps she is her own avatar.

Until now – these men. Everything of hers, having been absent, and she marooned here, is suddenly in this room with these two. Like a storm of leaves, it has come roaring and blowing back. Her life is in

273

these men, even though one, the son, is blind to her.

She must stay steady. She must not run to the bed and cover James in her arms as she wants to, to wake him, leaven him, bring him back. Like the times she watched her children take steps that she knew would see them fall, she must stand back.

It pains her to do so. She wants to tip Jamie out of the chair, to make him look – to make him *look* at his father.

Jamie suddenly moves his head up, as if startled from sleep – there is a popping, fish-like noise coming from his father's mouth. His father, whose younger, virile self has been plucking at Jamie's imagination this half hour past – belittling, shoving, ranting and threatening from his greasy bed in Bolan Street. Humiliating Jamie daily, making him small, and see-through. Feeding him cruelties, denying him anything worth anything. Wobbling and dribbling like a drunk, staring with God-eyes, bulging and full of poison. Jamie was nothing more than a ragdoll of a child, for his father to throw against walls and leave to moulder.

Jamie stands. He looks over at his father, whose mouth still works and chomps, lips smacking together and then drawing out concertinas of spit as they open. A gurgle now is coming from his throat, which turns into a mild, huffing cough.

His eyes are opening, gauzy and disturbed. The cough is wearing down. He swallows, swallows again, he needs water. Jamie stands by the bed, Margaret stands by the window. Neither moves, and both find their hearts are going faster. The room feels warm.

'Jamie?' says James Hallow, the voice is horrible and ancient, stuck somewhere deep in the throat, deep as if the throat is made of granite.

'Jamie?' he says again, clearer this time, his lips are moving better.

James, through open eyes, sees his son's face;

misty, but it is Jamie's face.

'Jamie?' he says, and he hopes, beyond hope, that it is really him, that his son has come, that he has found the door, and it was open, and he came through, to be with him, to help him, to be here.

Jamie looks down at his father, at the filmy eyes blinking open and shut – and feels – nothing.

The voice that comes out of his father's mouth is broken and ghastly, and Jamie feels nothing. With the certainty of a hobnail, he decides – no more of this.

'Jamie?' says the father, his slow brain appealing desperately, haltingly for an answer, for a confirmation that this is his Jamie, that Jamie has come.

Jamie, Jamie, *Jamie*. He wants to shout it across the waters to his son.

And Jamie wants to rip his hair from the back of his neck. He looks at this candlewax man as if he is seeing nothing, and Margaret by the window finds that despite her better judgement she is walking towards the bed.

Jamie looks down at the fish-like eyes, groping in and out of focus. He looks down at the parted, papery lips, at this compressed face that he has hated all his life, and he says, slowly, firmly:

'No.'

The man in the bed looks bewildered, frightened, but Jamie says nothing more. He turns, and leaves the room.

# PART THREE

PART THREE

# 1

Every morning for decades Meryl has, after washing, put on her make-up. There is not a day she has missed. The tubes and pots have changed a few times, when a foundation has been discontinued, or a revolutionary anti-ageing ingredient has been added, or a salesgirl has been successful in her representation of a new mascara, that curls the *actual* lashes. But, apart from these moderate variances, the routine has been the same. Foundation, powder, mascara, and a light lipstick. Blusher and eye-shadow in the evenings, with a darker lipstick.

She uses her products to their last drop. She excavates the last globules of foundation and lipstick with a cotton bud. She uses her mascara until a crust has built up around the top, making it a struggle to open, and the brush unable to deposit anything but clumps on her eyelashes. She even reuses her cotton wool pads, drying them out by the side of the sink. When Julie –

who is her daughter, remember? – comes over and uses her parents' bathroom, she throws the old, used bits of things into the bin. Meryl always retrieves them when Julie has gone.

'Mum, why do you hoard those crusty bits of soap and cotton wool? It's gross.'

'Don't be so silly, Julie. What's wrong with reusing things?'

'Reusing a hairbrush is one thing, but a manky old piece of cotton wool is pushing it, Mum. I'll buy you a lifetime's supply of fresh cotton wool, if it'll stop you from doing that.'

'Stop it.'

'I'm being serious. And those ancient pieces of soap . . .'

'I am *not* going to throw away perfectly good bars of soap just to make you happy.'

'Mum, they're about ten years old. They've got cracks in them, that have gone *black*. I gave you all that lovely honeysuckle soap for Christmas – where's that?'

'I'm saving it.'

'Saving it for when? For when the oil runs out and we all have to keep goats on our roofs?'

'Keep goats on our roofs? What are you talking about?'

'Nothing, Mum.'

'Are you making fun of me?'

'No. I'm just saying you should use the soap I gave

you instead of hanging on to your ancient, grey slabs of carbolic.'

'For heaven's sake! They're not carbolic soap! The one upstairs is Imperial Leather.'

'I know, it still has the sticker crusted into it.'

'Julie, I am not a dirty person. Is that what you're saying? That your father and I are dirty people who use dirty soap?'

Julie laughs. 'No, Mum. I'm saying that you should use the soap I gave you instead of "saving" it.'

'I'm only saving it until the bar we have now runs out.'

'The bar you have now will never run out. It's been in your bathroom since I was thirteen.'

'Don't talk nonsense.'

Julie can hear her dad chuckling from behind his newspaper, and it makes her smile. 'Anyway, I've confiscated it. So you'll have to open a new one now. Don't look at me like that – you won't be able to fish it out of the bin because I'm taking it with me. It's wrapped up in bog roll in my pocket. I'm going to take it to a secret location – where you won't be able to trace it – and dispose of it.'

Meryl knows her daughter is winding her up, and folds her arms to show that she is not being sucked in. She takes a breath, and narrows her eyes. 'Thirty-five years old, and stealing soap.'

'Yep. Doing my duty.'

'Well, good for you.' Meryl turns to her husband in a blip of irritation. 'Joseph, stop reading the paper. You've been reading the paper all day. You must have read it ten times now.'

'Mum, it's Friday night. Dad's allowed to read the paper.'

'Friday night! You should see him on a Sunday! He'll have his nose in that thing all day! That's all he ever does, is read the paper! You'd think the whole world is in the bloody newspaper! There are people and things going on in the real world, you know, Joseph.'

'Mum, let Dad read the paper if he wants to.' Julie is looking over at her father, who has folded the paper slightly, and looks like he is about to get up. She looks at him as if she feels sorry for him. To have your daughter's pity like that – well. It doesn't exactly make you feel like a big man.

'Your mother's right. I've spent too much time reading newspapers today.'

'Oh, today! You hear that, Julie? Even your father agrees with me! Today, he says! If only. He spends hours every day with his nose in that thing. Hours. Every day. If I didn't say anything, he'd disappear into it.'

Julie looks down at her lap, so as not to focus on her father as he rises from his chair, where he had been happy.

\* \* \*

When Julie has left, her mother discovers that she actually has taken the soap from their bathroom. It's suitable provocation, not that much is needed, to begin the Boyfriend Lament.

'I do wish she had someone in her life. I mean, she's had so many lovely men – do you remember Jonathan? That lovely Jonathan? He was such a beautiful man. And he would have done anything for her. But she just won't settle. She gets rid of every single one of them.'

'She'll find someone, Merrie.'

'Huh, well. I don't know. You'd think if she was going to she would have found someone already by now. She's thirty-five years old, Jo. And all those lovely boyfriends she's had. I would have been so happy if she'd stayed with Jonathan. Or that lovely Scotch banker, do you remember him, Jo? That Adrian? Who worked at Goldman Sachs?'

Jo nods, his lips slightly pursed, thinking *Scotch banker, Scotch Egg.*

'And what about children? If she waits much longer the decision will be out of her hands.'

'She's got a bit of time, doesn't she? You were thirty-two when you had her, weren't you?'

Meryl does not like being reminded of this fact. Among all her peers, she had married the latest, at twenty-nine. She had given birth to Ben when she was thirty, and Julie almost three years later. At the time, she was the grand old lady on the ward – she had felt near-geriatric. Now, of course, it would be different. She would probably be one of the youngest mothers there.

'Having children in your early thirties is different, Joseph. I was *thirty-two* when I had my last child. Julie is *thirty-five*, and at this rate won't have her *first* until she's forty. You read about it every day, all the problems – Down's Syndrome, and all that. That is, if you can have children at all. All that dreadful IVF!'

'Well, she seems happy.'

'Happy! How can she be happy all alone like that! Doing nothing but work.'

'She's got lots of friends.'

'Friends! Well I wish she would marry one of them.'

Jo had tried his best. But this is what it always came down to. Meryl, more than grandchildren, more than boyfriends, more than happiness, wanted a wedding. A Witter wedding in a big country house with a big cake, to invite all their friends to.

For years now the off-white, curlicued invitations to the weddings of their friends' children had been landing on the doormat, each one feeling more like a slap in the face. Then the weddings themselves, with the brides looking so gorgeous, and whizzing off in Rolls Royces, and three course dinners, and all that champagne, and speeches, and, best and worst of all, that infusing, inundating air of success. Of success. Successful children, grown-up and married. Successful husbands, giving speeches that are funny and eloquent and impressive. Successful lives, with enough money to pay for the big wedding in the big house with the big cake. Caterers. Dresses. Cars. Flowers. Music. Invitations. Success.

More than anything Meryl wanted to be a Wedding Mother. And what would it look like in a few years? To be the mother of a forty-year-old bride? *Unseemly*. Awful. Ben, at least, was fine for a while. Being a man was different.

But, even so, it would be lovely if he found someone, too. Everyone was always asking: *Has Ben got anyone in his life? Has Julie found a man yet?* All Meryl could do was make light of it, and say, put-upon, 'Don't ask me, Denise (or Jenny, or Bee), I'm always the last to know!'

It was hopeless. Hopeless, I tell you.

And this is the irony: it had always been the Witter children who were the most impressive, the nicest looking – the best, quite frankly. They were always the lead parts in the school plays, prefects, in the sports teams, they went to the best universities. They were the cleverest and the best. And now look! Ben seemed to have pots of cash from his *financial PR*, that was something. Always going off to fancy restaurants. His house was very nice, and, would you believe it, in Kensington! Plus he had a sports car.

But, still. None of that directly benefitted Meryl, so it didn't matter. Ben was never around, apart from the odd Sunday lunch. He kept his life to himself, never saw any of the old family friends, even though she was forever telling him that they always asked after him, which was true. And even if Ben did find some nice girl, he'd probably take her to one of those resorts in the Caribbean to get married – forget a family wedding. Meryl was unlikely ever to have her showcase.

Looking over at Jo, Meryl realised, as she had done before, that even if a fairy waved a magic wand and everything went the way she wanted it, at the end of the day there wouldn't be the money for a decent wedding anyway.

'What would you know, Jo?' says Meryl to her husband. 'Bloody useless man!'

Bitterness, and the feeling of being small – squashable as a gnat – ulcer away in Meryl as she climbs up the stairs. The pastel portrait of Doddy is in the stairwell.

'How could a man like you have such a useless son?' says Meryl to the picture, muttering loud enough so that Jo might hear.

But he doesn't. Jo's feathers are slick with years of it, and the meanness slips right off. He just concentrates on fading further into the sofa, so as not to bother Merrie any more than he has already. Because, God knows, he's failed her enough.

# 2

Meryl sits alone watching TV in the bedroom. Dinner can just bloody wait. Jo can get it for a change, bloody useless man. Wouldn't that be something! *As if. Yeah right.* All those things that Julie and Ben used to say as teenagers. *Yeah right, Mum.*

And Julie drove all the way round here, and didn't even stay for dinner. And all that business with the soap! There were some nice steaks in the fridge, and bits of fruit that needed eating up. She didn't need to worry about it now.

And that stupid dog! Always curled up by Jo's leg even though it was Meryl, not Jo, who fed him most days, and walked him. Stupid bloody Lemon. It would be so bloody gratifying if Lemon had followed *her* up the stairs and was sitting against *her* leg now instead of Jo's – it would show some blooming loyalty, quite frankly. But he wasn't to know, I suppose. Poor Lemon, he's only a dog.

And he was a good dog, too. And darling Julie, she was such a sweetheart. And so pretty. (Everyone says she looks like Meryl. Everyone.) And very jolly clever, too. Imagine coming all the way over here, and not even staying for dinner! But it was a Friday night, and Julie probably had some trendy bar to go to with her friends.

Huh. Well.

At Julie's age Meryl had two children and a husband and a house to look after *and* a part-time job. Grown women now lived like teenagers, without a care in the world, going to parties, dressing up like sixteen-year-olds. Not that Julie dressed like that – she always looked lovely, respectable, although Meryl did wish she would sometimes wear something other than jeans. Jeans were fine, most of the time, and Julie looked very nice in them. But just occasionally it would be nice if she wore something different, like a skirt.

Last time she saw Julie's legs they had struck Meryl as being good, although that must have been years ago. Imagine! Not having seen your own daughter's legs for so many years that you didn't know what they looked like! Your own daughter.

They had had some very hot summers, and even *then* Meryl hadn't seen Julie's legs. She was still in jeans. Jeans, jeans, jeans. What would happen if jeans didn't exist? What would she wear then? Maybe Meryl could get Julie a lovely dress for her birthday.

Although, best not. She'd never wear it. She and Ben

would just giggle over it like they always did whenever Meryl gave them anything to wear.

Oh, bloody shit on it.

'Bloody shit on it,' says Meryl quietly to herself.

It was at times like this that she could just give up on everything. She couldn't believe she was sixty-seven. Sixty-seven . . .

A flush of denial and embarrassment creeps up her throat at the thought of it. A lifetime gone, with two lost, unmarried children – everybody else's children doing so much better, to be honest, putting aside Ben's job – no grandchildren, no house in the country, no opera tickets, certainly no boat – not even a bloody dinghy – and no Chanel suit. No Chanel suit. Not now, not ever. Who was she kidding anyway? I tell you, no designer suit would likely fit over a bottom her size. She's always had these great big hips and they've just grown and grown. Meryl doesn't even know why she bothers going to the gym and using up all that energy, fat bloody lot of good it does. There was the coffee with the girls afterwards, though. That was always nice.

What did she have, though, really? What did she have to show? Her happiest moments were when she was away from home, away from Jo and Lemon, at the hospice. The hospice was the only place where she felt remotely worthwhile.

And her happiest moments in recent memory were those couple of chats she'd had with Jamie –

Handsome Jamie as Simon her lovely gay friend called him. Those chats, in the Quiet Room yesterday, and in the café today. They had made her feel worthwhile. No, more than that – they had made her feel *herself*. If only she hadn't been so unsteady on her feet with her awful bloody ankle – I tell you, this ankle just won't get any better. It's been this bad for weeks.

Those chats with Jamie made her feel herself. Made her face feel tighter and her eyes more open. Alright, he'd been difficult, and brooding, poor boy, but he'd chatted with her and looked at her like she was herself, as opposed to stupid old Meryl, silly old Meryl, silly old bag with two unmarried children she barely saw and a husband who sat at home all day and a house she was sick to the teeth of, although it was all they had.

The news was finally over, the good weather looked set to stay (although, of course, it was still going to be cold) and the ads were on. An ad for a car that was rather funny, an ad for beer, an ad for colour printing or some such thing. Meryl turns the sound off.

Downstairs she can hear that Jo is watching the same channel, so the music and words to the image on her screen filter upstairs with metallic delay.

'Are you fixing dinner?' she shouts through the door, but there is no response; Jo hasn't heard.

'Didn't THINK SO!' she shouts down louder.

This time, 'What, dear?' comes softly up.

But Meryl chooses not to answer. Bloody useless man.

Hang on a second. *Hang on a second.*

Meryl looks intently at the small screen.

That's Jamie. That's *Jamie*!

Jamie Hallow! *Jamie*!

*Her Jamie!* On the television!

Meryl can't quite believe it.

She can't believe it.

Her eyes dilate rounder, and her lips press forwards into surprised concentration.

She is certain, absolutely certain that that man just on the TV was *him*.

In her exhilaration Meryl forgets that she has turned the sound off the little television, and all she hears is the delay from downstairs. For God's sake! Of all the times for the sound not to work!

'For God's sake, Jo!' Meryl hollers down, sounding slightly hysterical. 'Fix the sound!'

'What, dear?' says Jo again. 'The sound? I can't hear you . . .'

Oh for heaven's sake, of all the stupid things to do Jo had now turned the sound *down*, and Meryl could barely hear at all.

Yes! She was sure of it! There he was again – *Jamie* – in a sort of technological-looking room with another man and a woman, drinking coffee (or was it tea! Haha!) and looking amused. There was a close-up of his face.

*It was Jamie.*

'Jo!' Meryl gets up, walks to the top of the stairs, and bellows down. 'Turn the bloody sound up!'

Jo is confused. 'The sound up, Merrie?'

'Yes! For God's sake! How many times do I have to say it? I can't hear a thing up here!'

'What do you mean? Is the sound on the upstairs tele not working?'

Oh. That's right. Meryl had turned the sound off her tele. What a silly flap to get herself into.

'It's alright,' she says, somewhat chastened and so with less of a boom, 'I'm coming downstairs to watch.'

Meryl couldn't believe it, it really was him, her friend, Jamie Hallow, on the TV. She couldn't believe it! Her eyes are still round and her mouth still forward when she arrives at the bottom of the stairs. This ruddy ankle, she really must put it up.

'No! Don't switch it off!' Jo had reached for the remote. 'We have to watch this!'

'I thought you were saying the sound was too loud.'

'No, no.' Meryl sits down next to Jo on the sofa. 'Could you pull the coffee table a little closer, Jo, I need to put my leg up on it. And where's the remote? We need to put the sound up.'

Jo pulls the table towards them easily – his upper body thankfully doesn't creak like the lower, yet. 'Is your ankle not any better yet, love? You really need to stay off it.'

292

'It doesn't matter,' says Meryl. 'My ankle's all right.' Jo's eyebrows shoot up, but thankfully Meryl's eyes are firmly on the screen. 'Look! Look! It's Jamie! Gosh, doesn't he look gorgeous? He looks exactly like he looks in real life! I had no idea!'

Jo looks at the television screen, to catch the tail end of the short scene – a dark-haired man has another man up against a wall by his throat, in an underground car park. The scene ends as the man crumples down to the floor, and the dark-haired man stands over him, and flips open a mobile phone.

'Who,' says Jo, quizzically. 'Him? Who's Jamie?'

'Yes, him! Him!' Meryl is excited. 'That was Jamie!'

'Who's Jamie? That man on the tele?'

'Yes! For heaven's sake, Jo.'

'But who *is* Jamie, dear? I mean – who is he?'

'Oh.' Meryl remembers now. She hasn't mentioned Jamie yet. Although, of course, there's no reason why she should have. 'Jamie Hallow. He's a friend of mine at the hospice. His father's a patient there. That's him, that one who just had the other man up against the wall. I had no idea he was an actor! I'm so stupid! I should have asked.'

'Oh, right, right,' says Jo, clearing his throat and taking it in. 'Yes, I see. Very good. Well, I've seen this programme before, it's rather good. American.'

'He's not American, Jo, he's English. I should know. I've spent the last two days with him.'

293

'I'm not saying he's American, Merrie, I'm saying the programme is.'

'Well,' says Meryl, feeling irritated and possessive in her excitability, 'so what?'

'So nothing. I was just saying.'

'Well, thanks, Jo. I'm telling you he's English.'

'Alright, Merrie, he's English. I never said he wasn't.'

They watch in silence for a while, following the story, but also waiting for Jamie to come back on.

'So what's it about?' asks Meryl.

'Er-hm. Well I'm not completely sure; it's one of these hi-tech things. But I think the general idea is that there are a group of detectives trying to track down a mass-murderer,' Meryl frowns and knits her eyebrows at this, 'who's been on the prowl killing various high-profile politicians, or statesmen, I'm not entirely sure who they are exactly, but public figures, and your friend from the hospice, Jamie,'

'Oh, look! There he is!'

Jo keeps quiet while Jamie drives, with a cigarette between his lips, into a parking lot –

It's raining, and the man and the woman from the scene before are waiting for him under umbrellas. 'Got a present for you both,' Jamie says, in an *American* accent.

'This better be good, Bruce Wayne,' says the woman. 'Your midnight wake-up calls are seriously depriving me of beauty sleep.'

'It's not like you need it,' says Jamie, in an *American* accent – that's all Jo had said, that this was an *American* programme – and Jamie and the woman exchange a jokey sort of glance.

'Get on with it, will you, J.P., I want to get back to bed,' says the other man. Then Jamie – *J.P.* – grins and raises his eyebrows and flicks the cigarette into the dark. He seems not to be minding the rain at all, even though it looks heavy.

Then he opens the boot of the car and the other two look over his shoulders into it.

'Worth getting out of bed for?' says Jamie-J.P., without looking up. The other two are clearly taken aback.

'Jesus H. Christ,' says the other man. The scene ends. –

'What was in the boot?' says Meryl.

'I expect it was the man who he had up against the wall earlier,' says Jo.

'What, dead?'

'No, I don't think dead. But probably just bound and gagged and that sort of thing. Or unconscious.'

'Is he the murderer?'

'I don't think so,' says Jo.

'Then why's Jamie got him in the boot of his car?'

'Well, he must be a bad guy. He's probably involved with the murderer in some way.'

'So Jamie is one of the detectives?'

'No, I think he's an ex-detective who's been brought

295

in to help with this particular investigation. He's having an affair with the blonde woman.'

'Is he?' says Meryl, surprised. 'I don't think so. They didn't touch at all just then. If he was having an affair with her, surely they'd be more intimate with each other.'

'I think they're keeping it a secret. Not mixing business and pleasure and all that. I think they might have been married before.'

'What, to each other?'

'Yes, I think so.'

'Quiet, Jo, quiet, I want to watch now.'

Another young woman, probably Julie's age, is now on the screen. She has a telephone wedged between her shoulder and her ear, and a toddler in her arms. She's a brunette, and pretty, and trying to get her children ready for school. It's a whole new element to the story.

Although most of it is trash, there are a few of these American shows that really are quite good. Very well made and rather gripping. That was the word – *slick*. Meryl wouldn't watch a programme like this at all if it wasn't for Jamie, but now that she is watching it she's actually enjoying it. She just hopes it doesn't get gory, she can't stomach blood and guts and that kind of thing. It's still early, though, just after eight, so there can't be anything too bad.

Jamie! To think. That poor Jamie, with his father so sick and all alone in the bed like that. It was a happy place, the hospice – that's what Meryl loved about it – but seeing Jamie's father so sick in his bed like that and all alone brought home for a difficult moment what it was really all about.

And here he is on the television! Jamie. Gosh, she really should have asked. Such an airhead at times, she was.

It's funny how quickly you stop thinking of him as Jamie, and start just watching the programme. And it's really quite good, as these American programmes go. And he's excellent – *excellent*.

Jamie.

Jo and Meryl watch the programme for forty more minutes until its end. They chat over the ad breaks, and Jo makes tea. He brings the two full mugs in one hand, and a packet of biscuits, chocolate-covered, in the other, having to concentrate so as not to spill; 'Why didn't you just bring a tray, Joseph?'

Together they eat all the biscuits. Neither says anything about this – Jo knows better than to comment on his wife's biscuit-eating.

When the credits roll, Meryl says,

'See! Guest starring Jamie Hallow as J. P. Wayne! Did you see that, Jo?'

'I did,' he says, 'I did. Very good.' He nods decisively. 'I thought the whole programme was very good. Very exciting, anyway.'

'Yes! It was very well made, don't you think?'

Jo nods, takes his last slurp of tea. 'Yes, very well made. Jolly difficult to make, I imagine, these programmes.'

'And very difficult to act in, too – I'm telling you, Joseph, Jamie is *nothing* like that in real life. I mean, he's acting very well all the way through, because, I can tell you, he's absolutely *nothing* like that.'

'Mmm,' says Jo. 'Very impressive.'

'*Very*,' says Meryl, with an achingly serious face. 'Although I'm not sure about the blonde woman.'

'Carle.'

'Kylie, was it? Well, I'm not sure about her. Not sure how good of an actress she is.'

'No, well, she was a little weak,' says Jo, loyally.

'Yes, I thought so, didn't you? Maybe she got the job because she slept with the director. You hear about that, don't you?'

'The casting couch,' says Jo.

'That's right. Ug, it's disgusting, all that business.'

'But on the whole it was very enjoyable, Merrie, I thought,' good work, Jo, *deflection*, 'very enjoyable indeed. And your friend from the hospice.'

'Jamie.'

'Yes, I know, Jamie. He was very good.'

'He was *excellent*, wasn't he?'

Jo nods, with an affirmative frown.

Meryl pats Jo's hand happily. She is feeling proud of Jamie, proud of knowing him, and pleased that Jo is sharing in her enthusiasm. It wakes her up to her husband for the first time in days – she looks at him with uncrusted eyes, seeing her Jo, her gentle Joseph. She leans her head on his shoulder, and Jo, with no awkwardness only uncomplicated readiness, puts his arm around her shoulder and squeezes it to him.

'He was such a nice boy,' says Meryl, looking into the middle distance.

'Your Jamie?'

'Yes. Although I had no idea he was an actor. You know me, Jo. I'm such an airhead. I don't know why I didn't ask.'

They sit silently for a minute or two, and the weight of Meryl's head grows as she slowly relaxes it. She is happy. She wants to tell Jo all about Jamie, as if he is a child of theirs.

Jo is happy, too. He feels straightforwardly proud of this man, this Jamie, whom he has never met, who has put in such a good performance as a maverick investigator. None of it bothers him at all – good Lord! To think! Jealous? What a ridiculous thought. Meryl is as good and transparent as a window.

'He's all on his own, you know, Jo, Jamie is. Looking after his father all by himself. I mean, of course there's all the hospice staff, but there's no other family, or friends.'

'Is his mother dead?'

'She must be. And no brothers or sisters.' She pauses

a moment, thinking about something. 'He was really good, don't you think?'

'Excellent,' says Jo. Meryl smiles. A directionless smile smiled only for herself.

'I don't know why I didn't ask him,' she says. 'I'm such an idiot.'

Again a beat passes. Lemon, the yellow Labrador, is resting his head on Meryl's knee, and she is absent-mindedly stroking the side of his furry head.

'I don't know,' says Meryl. 'I had a lovely long chat with him today, in the Starbucks on the high street, before going back into the hospice,' Jo doesn't question this, 'and he told me all sorts of things.

'I think his father – you know, who's so ill – used to, I don't know the word, *abuse* him.'

Jo finds himself tensing. 'Hurr,' he says, 'that's a nasty business.'

'Oh no, wait a minute, I don't mean *sexual* abuse. No, no. I don't mean that. I mean, I think, from what Jamie said, that he used to hit him sometimes. Although not all the time. But sometimes I think he hit him quite badly.' Jo is tutting and shaking his head. 'Not, you know, a little smack on the bottom, but I think he used to actually *hit* him.' Meryl lifts her head from her husband's shoulder and looks at him.

Jo clears his throat. 'The father used to beat him, you're saying?'

'I don't know. I think sometimes, yes.'

300

'And what about the mother?'

'I don't know. He's not mentioned her.'

'If the mother was in the picture, surely she'd have put a stop to it?'

'Oh, Joseph,' Meryl is forbearing, 'that's so naïve! The mother is usually as frightened as the poor children!'

'Yes,' says Jo, 'well, I suppose so.'

'I think he was,' Meryl looks for the word, 'neglected, you know? Poor boy. He doesn't seem at all happy, you know, in real life.'

*Neglected*: Meryl has, in her own way, seen to the heart of it. A small boy in knee-high socks, who wanders his own house like a ghost. Loiters and examines and occasionally speaks up, to no effect. Mostly, it was: *shh, Jamie, don't bother your father. Ssh, Jamie, stop being silly. Shh, Jamie, shh.* A mother's fear that turned her child into invisible, that shut her love into a box, so as not to draw any attention. If only Jamie could disappear completely, and so escape his father's hard words and hard knuckles. A mother who counselled her child to disappear completely.

'And what's the father like?' Jo asks.

'Gosh, well, I have no idea. I've looked in on him once or twice, I went in there this morning and tidied up a few bits and bobs. But I haven't spoken to him, or spent any time with him – he's out for the count. I mean, he's unconscious most of the time. He really is very ill, Joseph. I mean, seriously ill. He only arrived a few days ago, and the nurses said that he was out for the count. So there's nothing I could do, really. You know, my time is much better spent elsewhere, with people who can appreciate it.

'Oh, that sounds awful! You know what I mean, anyway.'

Jo nods, proud of his Merrie and the work she does. He doesn't think he could do it – he wouldn't know what to say to half those people. No, he couldn't do it. More than anything, it would be so awkward. But Merrie – Merrie just gets through all that stuff.

'Oh you poor dog!' Meryl gasps suddenly. 'I should've fed you hours ago! Sitting here looking up at me, starving!' She pushes herself up from the sofa with both fists, puffing as she does. 'Honestly, Joseph! You could've reminded me!'

'This dog's getting fat, anyway,' says Jo, levering himself up, and following Meryl and Lemon into the kitchen.

'He is not getting fat! You are not fat, are you, Lemon? You're just beautiful. Don't you listen to a word he says.' Meryl is opening the fridge and taking out the roll of dog sausage.

'You *are* getting fat.' Jo rubs Lemon's underside with his foot. 'You great big fat dog. You're a porker! Your mummy spoils you, doesn't she?'

'What nonsense! Come here, darling, come here.' The dog sausage has been chopped and placed in the

terracotta bowl. Lemon's tail wags maniacally. Jo
laughs.

'Having dinner an hour late is not going to kill him.
I got too caught up in that show.'

'Me too! I tell you, Jo, what a surprise.'

'It was very good. He was excellent, your Jamie.' Jo
has placed the used mugs in the dishwasher, and
binned the biscuit packet.

'Yes, wasn't he? Don't you think?'

Mr and Mrs Joseph Witter, in their kitchen.

'Do you fancy any dinner, Merrie?'

'Oh, yes – meaning will I make it?'

'No, actually. No. They, ah, put a leaflet for a new
Thai place through the door this morning, and I
thought we could try it. Just take-away, I mean. Unless
it's not what you want.' Jo proffers the leaflet.

'Oh!' says Meryl. 'Oh.'

Thai food. Pad Thai noodles and all those crispy won
tons.

They could eat it properly in the dining room, set the
table and get the lovely green cloth napkins out, that
Julie brought them back from Italy last Easter. Or was it
Ben? No, Ben never thought of things like that. He
always gave electrical stuff.

'There's some steaks in the fridge that need eating up,'
she says, sounding regretful as she says it. For some
reason, if Meryl made the steaks, they'd end up eating
them on the kitchen stools. But if they got Thai food,

Meryl would set the dining table, which would be so nice.

'Well, that's all right,' says Jo. 'Steaks would be lovely.'

Meryl is still holding on to the menu leaflet. 'Sweetcorn fritters!' she says. 'They sound just gorgeous. And jungle curry! That's the one you like, isn't it, Jo? The awfully spicy one?' Her voice is still mournful, reluctant and unconvinced.

'Won't the steaks last until tomorrow?' asks Jo.

Meryl really, really wants to order the Thai food. She wants the Thai food badly. She wants the whole ritual of it: to mark what they want on the menu, and dial the number. She wants to order Thai food so much that she actually feels she might get tearful if they end up not having it, and making the steaks instead. Even though, of course, the steaks would be very good; Meryl only ever gets steak from the butcher, who she's known for ever, and never the supermarket.

But she can't come out and say it. She's got no cash in her purse, and she doesn't know if they'd take credit cards.

'Then let's get take-away,' says Jo. 'Merrie?'

She's looking at the menu. She doesn't answer.

'It's a curry, Merrie,' says Jo, delicately, 'not a box at the opera.'

Meryl feels herself welling up. She keeps looking down at the list of dishes. A box at the opera.

Jo has taken his wallet out of his back pocket – it

drives Meryl mad, that, the way he walks around the house with his wallet bulging in his trousers, instead of taking it out when he comes in and putting it in the bowl – and has taken out a few notes.

'We've got more than enough in cash,' he says. 'Come on, Merrie, let's have a look at the menu. Tell me what you'd like, and I'll call them.'

Through the perimeter of threatening tears, Meryl sees Number 41. *Choo Chee, a mild red curry with coconut milk, Thai basil, kaffir lime leaves and your choice of chicken, prawn or vegetable.*

The tears blot back in.

She smiles.

'*I'll* call them,' she says, and goes to get a pencil from the pot under the phone.

# 3

Jamie has gone, and Margaret knows he will not come back. The angular determination with which he walked away, the steady hammer-stroke of his 'No', made it clear: he has gone.

Margaret, at the foot of James's bed, feels as lost as a dust mote, completely inequipped for any of this. She had wanted to pull Jamie back by his arm as he strode past her, and shout at him to stay; but she couldn't. She wants now to walk out herself, and find that at the end of the corridor is her own door, her own room, her own lost bed, where she would, slipping her shoes from her feet, lie on her side and stare inward. For forty years she has not wanted so much to lie on her side, alone.

But she cannot do this either. The wood and cloth of her bed, her room, her door, are long since ash, and in the hospice there is no place that is just her own. She might walk its spaces as patroness, but she remains homeless within it: none of it is truly hers. She does not lie down here. Only stand, only sit.

At least it is a feeling Margaret knows, a feeling that is familiar from all those times she stood as Scotland's Queen, unable to crumple, obliged to remain straight. It is a feeling from that long-ago life, which has, since Dympna's visit, come again, suddenly so close.

This is a strange story, beginning on Monday with Dympna in the cold, candlelit chapel. And it is now bound up with Margaret's own. It has woven itself into her past, and woken all the threads about it. This man, this James, in the bed, with the fighter's face. He is part of her life, real and near. He is as real and near to her as the stone flags and the burning wood smell and the prayer bell of home. He is a part of her life, and he has woken up much that was dormant.

Margaret walks to the head of the bed and takes James's hand in both of hers. She brings it, warm and papery, to her lips, and kisses it.

He is looking at the door, where he still sees trails of his son walking from the room. He can see trails of Jamie leaving, like the plumes of sky-smoke left behind by an aeroplane.

But feeling the touch of Margaret's lips on his hand, he moves his eyes slowly to her. They are bulging. He squints, and then blinks once, twice, three times.

'I'm sorry,' he says.

Margaret shakes her head.

'I'm sorry,' he says again, 'I'm sorry.' It is catching at the back of his throat, gravelly and difficult. 'I'm sorry.

'I'm sorry.' He is pumping Margaret's hand with his, and once more, 'I'm sorry.'

It is desperate, this index of sorries. Margaret keeps James's hand in hers, looks at him. He is looking back at her intently, and with panic. But what can she do? These apologies are not for her to swallow down and regurgitate up with forgiveness. She has nothing to forgive. She shakes her head. She cannot accept his sorry, sorry, sorries, because they are not meant for her.

A nurse is coming in. Margaret lays James's hand gently down on his tummy. The nurse has brought a trolley in with her. On the trolley are syringes in sterile wrapping. Clipboards, more than one. Cotton wool and tissues. White plastic medical bottles.

'Are you awake, Mr Hallow?' she says, quietly. It is the New Zealand nurse, Felicity, Flop, who James recognises. He nods. He smiles.

'I'm sorry,' he says to her.

'Sorry? What for? Have you been getting up to mischief?' She laughs. 'You've nothing to be sorry for, Mr Hallow.'

James shakes his head.

'Do you mind if I sit here on the bed with you?'

James shakes his head again. He knows Margaret is beside him on the other side, but he does not look at her. He looks at the nurse.

Flop picks up James's hand and holds it in hers. 'Now. How are you feeling, Mr Hallow? Do you think you could have a little bit of milkshake for me?'

James shakes his head, with a different timbre this time – it is a definite no. No milkshake.

'How about a bit of jelly? If I go and get a nice orange jelly from the kitchen?'

No. No jelly.

'You're just not hungry,' says Flop, 'are you. I understand.'

James loves holding hands. He spent a lifetime not knowing it, how much his hand loved being held by another.

'How about a sip of water, are you thirsty at all?'

James swallows, and it hurts, everything is fast becoming heavier. 'I'm dry,' he says.

'You just hold on a minute,' says Flop, who leaves and returns in just over a minute with a bowl containing water and several small, pink sponges on sticks. Looking at him, she reckons James actually wouldn't be able to take or keep down any water.

'Shall I pop this in a minute?'

She holds a wet sponge on James's tongue, and he sucks on it for a moment, before nodding enough.

'And I'm just going to put a bit of Vaseline on you there, so your lips aren't so dry. There we go. That feel better?'

310

James wants to say sorry again, but in time he remembers his other word –

'Thank you.'

Flop smiles, pats his hand.

'No problem at all. Now, I'm just going to have a quick check of a couple of these bits and pieces, it won't take a second.'

After putting on disposable gloves and cleaning her hands with a blue gel in a dispenser on her trolley, she with straightforwardness lifts up James's sheets, checks the catheter tube, the padding of James's nappy that he doesn't know he's wearing, then the catheter bag, which is only a quarter full, and the cannula in James's arm.

'You're shipshape, Mr Hallow! All done. Would you like a little more water?' She takes off her latex gloves and puts them in the bin by James's bed. She sits down again, the mattress indents downwards with her.

James is losing sight of things, and cannot answer.

Flop takes another sponge stick and holds it to his lips. He allows it to rest coolly there, but does not part his lips.

She has placed her hand on top of his once more, this good, sturdy girl. 'Are you in any pain, at all, Mr Hallow?'

He doesn't answer.

'Because we can top you up with some pain relief medicine, if you'd like?'

James still doesn't answer. He doesn't know what to

say. The pain, the pain, the pain, so what? He has lost track of the pain. It is everywhere now. On his forehead, in the small veins under his eyes. In the arches of his feet and wallowing like a puddle at the base of his back. The pain is everywhere now. So what? So what.

He looks over to his right, slow, viscous movement, and there is Margaret. His fingers wave up and down on the mattress, asking her to hold them. Margaret takes them gently in her own.

Two women, separated by hemispheres and centuries, holding the hands of the same old man. He is lucky, he is lucky and in this moment he is blessed by the God that is Real, and he knows it.

He turns his head back to Flop. 'Mr Hallow?' she says, 'can you tell me if you're in any pain at all?'

He shakes his head. His head is dry. Is dry and old. And old and old and old.

'My son,' he says.

Flop looks at him.

'My son,' he says again.

'He was here, James,' says Margaret, 'just now.'

'He's gone,' says James, and a whistle escapes his lips, 'like,' the lips whistle again, 'an aeroplane.'

James looks at this nurse, lovely and kind, a girl he might have kissed one day before when he was not so old and dead.

'I'm not in pain,' he says.

Flop is worried about Mr Hallow in her undemanding,

professional way. She has heard his words about his son, although not understood them; she has heard this kind of disjointed talk so many times before. She knows the rattling breath, the clutching at sheets, and she knows that James Hallow soon will not be able to speak at all. His mouth is seizing up and disintegrating, and no amount of sponge will help.

He is a nice old man, and Flop smiles with a small sorrow.

'Mr Hallow,' she says, patting his hand with great softness, 'are you sure you're not in any pain?' There is no need for him to be in pain, and Flop wants to be sure he isn't. From now on she will check in on him on the hour.

'No pain,' he says.

Formidable thuds of exhaustion are wheeling in on James now, like a steam engine's comicstrip chug chug chuff. He'll just stand on the tracks and go under. That would be the best thing.

But he has something he wants to say first, and in this thin moment his desire to say it is stronger than the looming, thundering tiredness. James must say it, or if not he will corrode away into a leather man, a devil's man, a man made of leather. He will burst forth with what he needs to say, before allowing the train to hit.

'I,' he says, and Flop listens, her eyebrows up, 'used to be a boxer.'

He is not enunciating properly, as if the edges of his

mouth have dissolved; his words are blurred. But Flop has four years of translating behind her, and Margaret forty, and they both understand.

Margaret presses the hand that is in hers. Flop says, sounding impressed and indulgent, 'Did you, Mr Hallow?'

James nods, cannot return the press of Margaret's hand although he wants to and does so in his imagination,

'I was,' he says, 'The Sidewinder.'

And with this the tiredness rushes in and devastates like the chug chug chuff of one of James's old punches, and he closes his eyes with speed, his hands and the bottom of his left leg start to shake with the familiar convulsions that have come to characterise his days. He falls, a felled fighter, into hard sleep.

# 4

It is as if James has sunk through the floor, and is no longer in the room. He is in a different density of sleep, from which Margaret knows she cannot rouse him. She sits by him, on the edge of the armchair.

The light is passing – it is that painful ten-minute period of closing in that covers London in post-apocalyptic gloom. The clear winter sunshine is being chased rapidly away by the pulsating, mildewed dark, the streetlights take up their hunched, neon vigil, and the whole world walks with heads down. Margaret sits in the fading day, does not want the lights on yet, and feels exactly, bewilderingly as she did ten hundred years ago, when she would watch the light turn dark from her bed, her heart heavy with chainmail, at war with itself.

This feeling has returned after one thousand years of absence, and Margaret has a flash of startled recognition: a lump of amazed familiarity fizzes in her throat. She had forgotten that she used to feel like this. It is like having a mirror held up to her face, and seeing herself after so many empty decades of being without a reflection. This is how she used to feel when she was living, those melancholy, dunderheaded afternoons when she was Scotland's Queen, her husband's wife.

That lost, beloved life of hers has been coming closer these past days, coming closer and creeping on to the sidelines. But now, as the dark descends on St John's Wood, it surrounds her completely. She feels exactly, bewilderingly as she did then.

As Margaret steps from the boat, her hair whips into the air, and her skin stings. They have landed on the edges of a storm, on the brink of Scotland, a country she does not wish to enter. The rain is too thick to see more than twenty yards ahead. The landscape uprears in shadow.

Margaret is angry to be here. Destiny was driving them to Hungary, a country she has claim to, that she remembers from her childhood with the passionate, dreamlike certainty of a drumbeat. There are mountains in Hungary that reach past the cloud, her mother has told her, and prayers of such glory that even the priest dare only whisper them.

This forced detour, one foot slipping miserably in front of the other, brings bad feelings swelling into Margaret's head. The violence and loss of the England she has just left, the wrecking of what she always thought was her home, have only been bearable because of the boat they were on, that was guaranteed to take them to Hungary – where she was born, where she has a place. Where she will sit up high, on one of those mountains.

And now the weather has pushed them here. As the wood of the deck creaked and became sodden, the water claiming it, Margaret surprised herself, in her usual detached way, by feeling no fear. Only anger.

'I will walk alone,' she had said, unsmiling, as her turn came to quit the boat. Two men hovered. 'What can happen?' she said to them. 'I have survived the storm. All I have to do now is walk.'

Further up the bank, the Scots men see her through the rain. She is one of the princesses – she walks immediately after the prince. A man walks five feet behind her, but she is by herself. Her head is down, one hand holds up her skirts, the other is still.

Her feet are wet, and sliding in her shoes. Her dress is as heavy as if it were made of gold. At the last step to the flat, she stumbles.

Her man comes from behind to help, but she says, without turning, having to shout through the wind,

'I can get up myself.'

He retreats a step.

She puts a palm in the mud, to push herself upright. But from another direction an arm bolts around her back, and lifts her. A sleeve is offered, of dark, coarse material.

'Wipe your hand here.'

Margaret sees, her brow tense and annoyed against the rain, that the arm that has pulled her to standing, and now offers itself as a rag, the voice that speaks to her with a strange, particular weight, belong to the Scottish King.

She looks at him. He is smiling. His beard drips with water.

She inclines her head, dips her knees.

'You remember me?' the King asks.

'Of course,' Margaret replies.

But, in truth, she does not remember him like this. Not – like this.

His hand underneath her forearm is as strong as battalions, as determined. It makes silly this small tempest.

Together, they walk.

Margaret, who until now has had James's right hand wrapped in her two, puts it back down on the mattress, and brings her hands up to cover her eyes, nose, and mouth. This is a strange moment.

In this moment she does not know what she is. She does not know what dreamworlds she has been skimming in and out of. She could open her eyes and be anywhere – at home, with her children skittering about her; in St Margaret's Hospice, with James wading towards death in the bed; in Disneyland, with Mickey Mouse giving her the two thumbs up.

God help her, if only when she opened her eyes it was not James there, but Malcolm. If only she could uncover her eyes and see Malcolm, his head naked and split open from his last war, his scar rucked into his top lip. My God, she would crawl into the strange modern bed beside him; she would cover his dead body with her hands, she would grasp his broken head to her and refuse ever to move. They would rot together in the bed; Malcolm; God help her, if she could open her eyes and see Malcolm in the bed.

She never saw him dead; she died herself before his body was brought home.

Three long days of dying, and God did not listen. God did as He pleased, God had separated them, and then He claimed Margaret for something else. Malcolm, whose head split open like a bloody nut on a battle-field, and who died without his wife. She was not there to weep into his wound, his head, open and splayed like a Dutch tulip.

She cannot even speak of her son.

The saint sits, her face covered by her hands. One moment longer before she opens her eyes again. When she does it will be a different man before her, with a different scar, beautiful in its detail – in the number of hairs around it, in its precise length and colour and

319

depth. It will not be Mickey Mouse. It will not be Malcolm. It will be James, who looks straight at her, and with his looking has brought her old life back.

Since 1093 no living person has seen her. Noses have been picked, bras readjusted, trousers pulled up in her presence. She is a thing more invisible than a grain of sand. Made up of nothing.

One day, years ago, ten years ago perhaps, Margaret had brushed past a nurse, and the nurse had immediately taken a small step back and shivered. 'Oo,' the nurse had said, 'I don't know what that was about . . . A goose must've walked over my grave.' Margaret had whipped her head and her skirts away in surprise and anger – surprise at the nurse's shiver, and anger at the ugly expression. Its creepiness coated her like fuzz – *a goose must've walked over my grave.*

That was the closest she had come to being noticed, and it had been as a goose on a grave. With webbed, orange, make-believe feet.

But then: Dympna's visit. James Hallow looking fearfully at her in the night. Looking straight at her, touching her, hearing her.

Margaret opens her eyes and removes her hands from her face. There he is: he lies there still. Not Malcolm. James. She does not know what she will do once this man has died.

Margaret takes James's hand up into hers again.

'It is dark now,' she says.

'James?' she says, 'it is dark now.'

She sits, poised on the edge of the armchair as if about to take flight.

# 5

There's a movie theatre on Sunset Boulevard that Jamie
loves. The screens are huge, with that encompassing
magic of faces and bodies twenty times as big as you
are. The sound is surround, and fills the entire theatre.
The seats are sharply tiered, no heads or hairdos to
induce temper loss or belief suspension. With a diet
coke – because they taste better than regular, don't coat
your mouth in that pulpy, metallic way – and a seat in
the middle, just off to the side, Jamie is lost in good
feeling. Even coming out into the daylight isn't as
devastating as it might be, as the cinema entrance is
more of an atrium, with a Rockefeller-high glass ceiling,
and an unreal sense of space all around.

Earlier that day, Jamie has suggested to a girl that
they go see a late afternoon slot at this cinema. The girl
has a name, but Jamie keeps it to himself. Irrational?
Perhaps. But her name is not part of this story, and

Jamie doesn't want to let it out. Because it's irrelevant – that's why.

He buys the tickets, and the girl declines buttered popcorn and Twinkies and Milk Duds and all those other disgusting American plastics that are offered at the turnstiles. He buys his diet coke, shoots her a look when she says something about diet coke being worse for you than real coke, and is in a blast annoyed at himself for bringing her here, *here*, to one of his favourite places. They could have gone to any cinema the width of the city, but he brought her here, and now it will hold the memory of her. He won't be able to come with pure feeling on a bright afternoon, one of his few simple pleasures – not anymore. Because her hologram will tremble at the snack stand, flip round the postcard stack by the ticket desk, be in the dark of the theatre, one leg bunched up on to the chair. Jamie walks a pace ahead of her and wants to bark at her to Go Home. He climbs the steps up the banks of seats, sits down without consultation. She, only a moment later – she has kept up – sits down next to him.

Once upon a time, this girl had watched Jamie eat sushi in a small restaurant in Studio City, and had smiled at him and he had smiled – he had been all smiles, then – at her. That was the beginning.

This night at the movies is the end, and for two hours and ten minutes as they sit side by side with the light flickering on their faces, they do not touch. She wants him to touch her, and he knows she wants him to touch her, and it makes him angry.

The film they are seeing is All American, but not bad for that. It is about a boxer in a flat cap in the Great Depression, who from wine and crystal and parties and money now has to eat twigs and paving stones to survive, practically, before making an unexpected comeback and feeling the sun on his skin once more. It is about a noble man, who fights, and who goes rags-riches-rags-riches. It's a tear-jerker, at parts. It's schmaltzy.

'I liked it,' says the girl.

Jamie snorts. 'I thought it was shit.'

'Oh. Hm. Why?'

'It was predictable, banal, crap. For fuck's sake, don't tell me you *liked* it.'

'It had a heart.'

'Every gimp on the street has a heart.'

'Gimps aren't movies. I'm talking about the movie. It had a heart, and I found it touching.'

'That's deeply depressing.'

'That I was touched? Is depressing?'

'Yes.'

'Okay.' The girl shakes her head, and her earrings catch the light and in that moment Jamie is a bit dazzled by her.

'My dad was a boxer.' Jamie has absolutely no fucking idea why he has just said this.

'Was he?'

The girl is surprised, she looks at Jamie in the face, something these two have not done yet during their exchange. She forgives him a little, looking at him.

'I didn't know that,' she says. Her eyebrows knit together.

'Why would you.'

There is a pause, another look, of a different kind.

'Why would I. I don't know, Jamie. I don't know. Why would I, indeed. I didn't even know you had a father. Why would I?'

'I'm not a scientific miracle, obviously I have a father.'

Again, a pause.

'Who was a boxer.'

'Yep. Why are we standing here?'

'As opposed to what?'

'Walking to the car.'

They walk, close but apart. They are clearly together, although, still, they don't touch.

Jamie had parked at a meter two blocks away from the cinema, not in the multi-storey, which he doesn't like. It is a warm evening, and her heels are soft on the sidewalk, they don't make a sound. Her arms are folded, as if there is a wind.

'I'll tell you what,' says Jamie, moving between tenses and feeling reckless, 'you'd be hard pushed to find a boxer with a story like that.'

'Are you taking about your father?'

'I'm not talking about anyone.'

'Am I allowed to ask about your father?'

'You can ask about whatever the fuck you like,' says Jamie. The girl, with the name locked somewhere inside Jamie's chambers, keeps quiet. Jamie's look is hideous and sneering, his eyes are weirdly lit.

'Um,' he says, as they reach the car, scratching the back of his head, 'there's something I forgot to tell you.' She looks at him. 'I came straight from my physio appointment to the cinema, and my physio gave me this ball to take home with me. It's on the passenger seat of the car. So you're going to have to sit with it on your lap.'

'What?'

'This ball.'

Jamie opens the passenger door to his two-seater soft-top, and occupying the seat entirely is a big, blue Swiss Ball, for bending over and rolling muscles along – for Jamie's back, which twinges occasionally. For his wellbeing. For his flexibility. For the fact that he is in his late thirties.

'I'm supposed to sit with that on my lap?'

'Yeah, look, I'm really sorry.' Jamie wants to laugh and his lips twitch. 'I know it's not ideal.'

'How do you suggest I do this? Your car is barely big enough for a human being, let alone with that fucking thing.' She is annoyed, upset, stuttering in humiliation at the prospect of being mashed under the ball, looking, feeling, an absolute prick.

'Look,' Jamie's tone is hardening, as if something is her fault, 'what do you want me to do about it? I didn't know my physio was going to give it to me this session. But I had to take it, so here it is. You just have to have it on your lap until we get home.'

'Home. Your house. That's where we're going is it?'

Jamie just looks at her, with a dark, raised eyebrow. His face is tart.

She puts the ball, enormous, on the sidewalk, and gets in the car with one hand on it. She pulls the ball in, on to her lap. Jamie shuts the door on her.

Unless she were to push her nose up against the blue plastic, she has to keep her face turned sideways, with a cheek pressed up against it. In order to stop it from falling on to the gearstick, she has to keep her arms around it as if she is giving it a hug. She imagines how ridiculous she must look from the outside of the car. She feels mortified. She can't believe she is allowing herself to do this.

As Jamie gets into the driver's seat and glances over at her – dwarfed by the inflated blob, squished up against it, her graceful legs made clumsy by their forced akimbo straddle – he suppresses a smirk. And who wouldn't? It's pretty funny.

'You knew you were coming to meet me, but you still brought this thing?'

'Look. What do you want me to do?' Jamie has

pulled away from the kerb, is melting into the glittering Friday night traffic. The ball will leave marks on her skin.

They meet a traffic light. They turn right. Air blows in through Jamie's open window. He doesn't take the top down, although he is tempted.

They can't touch now, can they? There is no room to put a hand on her. She wriggles underneath the ball, and her skin squeaks against it.

They wait at another light, turn left, and drive upward into the hills. The road winds. Los Angeles catches the light. It dazzles.

'What's the matter?' the girl says.

Jamie looks over at her, with derision. She looks unbelievably foolish.

'What do you mean?'

'What's the matter. I mean: what's the matter. What's wrong.'

'With me? Nothing.'

'Something has happened, and you're not here.'

'Where am I then?'

'Not here.'

'What do you mean?'

'Something's the matter with you.'

Jamie looks over at his girl, hugging the giant ball, face pressed against it. He juts his chin at her,

'Nothing. Is. The matter.'

There are five beats of silence, and then the girl says,

'I don't have the energy to break through all your walls.'

Jamie smiles; it's not nice.

'What makes you think you could?' he says.

'Stop the car, will you.' Her voice is soft, like her shoes on the street.

'Where? Why?'

'Anywhere. Just pull over.'

'Are you going to get out?'

'Yup.'

'Don't be so stupid. How are you going to get home?'

'I'll get a cab.'

'You won't be able to get a cab. It's LA on a Friday night.'

'Just pull over, Jamie.' The girl sighs.

'What are you going to do? Walk for five miles?' Jamie keeps glancing over at her as he drives, and is not seeing the Big Blue Swiss Ball anymore; suddenly he is seeing her eyes, even though they are turned down.

She doesn't say anything else, and a few minutes later Jamie brings the car to a halt. She opens the door – she has with silent difficulty spent the last moments feeling for the handle so that she doesn't have to have him do it for her – and pushes the ball out gently. His hand is on the gearstick; she puts her hand, mysteriously cold, on to his. He pulls it away immediately, on the pretence of rubbing his head. She nods. She has decided something. She gets out of the car, and places the ball back on to her seat.

'Okay,' she says, looking briefly down into the car through eyelashes, at Jamie, before closing the door.

Bang.

She starts to walk back down the hill.

Jamie drives on up, his heart is fast in his chest, his hand, that she touched so lightly, is shaking with a feeling – can you name that feeling, Jamie? Can you name it? – and he watches her in his rear-view mirror for as long as he can, legs and shoes and hair and clothes and hands, until she is gone.

She is gone.

Jamie and the Ball drove home alone, and ate crackers, shared a frosted bottle of vodka, until sleep came.

As the cab grinds towards Heathrow and Jamie sits cross-legged in it, he thinks for the first time since leaving LA about the dog. Beth's dog, whose name is Buster. And for the first time since – since when? a long time ago – Jamie feels a wash of guilt. He feels guilty. It's an unpleasant feeling.

The dog was stupid. Okay, it was stupid. It scraped its little claws along the kitchen floor, sliding like a first-time ice skater, and scratching through the varnish. Its breath smelt. It did near-liquid poos, that Jamie had to scoop up and dispose of. It sniffed at Jamie's crotch.

It wasn't his kind of creature. But nevertheless he had agreed to look after it, and had instead treated it badly.

He had yanked at its lead when it had stopped to smell or examine something. Sharp – yank. When it had tried to come into his bedroom or study, Jamie had hissed at him, with a 'chah! yhah! hsttt!', and Buster had retreated, whining quietly. When he had tried to lick his hand, Jamie had taken it away roughly, and given the dog a shove with his foot – not a kick, definitely not a kick – but a shove, a displeased shove, nonetheless. He had told the dog to fuck off countless times. Had left him closed in the TV room for hours, hearing his begging noises from the other side. And, final unkindness, he had abandoned him. He had left him trapped, alone, homesick, and probably frightened, while he had carelessly got in a cab to the airport.

Jamie had treated Beth's dog, Buster, with cruelty. He had known it at the time. Cruelty, there was no other word. It made him feel sick at himself.

Fuck, when did he become like this? He wanted to apologise. He wanted another chance with Buster. He'd stroke him behind the ears and let him hop up on to his lap. He wanted another chance.

When had he become like this, so heartless? A walking toughnut shell of meanness? He wasn't supposed to be mean. He was stand-offish, he knew that. Dismissive of a lot of people, especially in LA, which was not exactly a city of Einsteins. But – mean? Cruel? Heartless? He didn't want to be any of those things.

He wasn't mean as a kid – he just wasn't. He was quiet, and pale, and got on with things. He wasn't mean when he left home in his early twenties for America, to make his first film. He was angry, certainly – why the fuck wouldn't he be? – and triumphant, and full of a feeling of powerful possibility. But not mean. Dad hadn't touched him for years, then. Not since he grew and started to talk back. The religious fuckery was still a daily grind, and the bouts of raving like a possessed cartoon in bed, throwing ugly nonsense at whoever passed the bedroom door. And the physical fits, Jamie continued to hate witnessing those. Through the years they had got steadily worse. But he was no longer frightened – when his dad, whose eyes were growing weekly smaller and redder it seemed, stood and looked at him, told him of the worms in his head, the evil in him, the need to pray, Jamie was tall and looked him in the eye. He sneered back, reared back, and told his father to Piss Off.

And he wasn't mean to Mum. He just ignored her, like she ignored him. When he was leaving, he wasn't rude, or unkind, he kept things even.

She was having a cup of tea with the biscuit tin at the kitchen table, and Jamie stood in the doorway behind her.

'Mum.'

She turned around on her chair, her gingernut in one paw.

'I've been given a part in a movie. It starts filming in America in April. In Los Angeles.'

The biscuit and the hand have lowered to her lap, the eyes are big.

'My agent has an office over there, who want to continue representing me. They think that off the back of this movie, I could do well in LA.'

He never knew how much Mum understood, about agents and movies and filming, but he went on,

'So I'm heading out there in two weeks. I'm leaving London – moving out. I'll take all my stuff with me.'

Mum is silent for a moment, and then says,

'You're leaving for America?'

This exasperates Jamie, but he just says, 'Yeah.'

'You're going to be in a movie?'

'Yes, Mum.'

She is looking at her lap, down, the biscuit still in her damp hand.

'Oh, well that's good, isn't it? That's what you want?'

Jamie doesn't say anything.

'Have you told your dad?'

'Yes, just now.'

'What did he say?'

'Nothing.'

'He didn't say anything?'

'Nothing. Nothing. Not one word.'

'Well, that's good. That's good, isn't it? It's what you want?'

Jamie does not say anything. But he sees that his mother has subtly wiped away a tear – she disguised her movement as a scratch, a scratching mouse movement; she has become adept at hiding tears. But Jamie notices, as he always does. He notices but says nothing. Mum is quite an actress, it's in the genes. He says nothing.

'Maybe you'll be a famous actor,' she says.

'Maybe,' says Jamie.

'Well, we'll miss you round here,' she says, and takes a fast, violent, tiny bite of her biscuit, before lowering her hand back down heavily.

Jamie looks at his mother, swivelled in her seat, looking down. The nibbled biscuit. The lino floor, red and white.

'Yep,' says Jamie, who is also a fine actor, he rubs his hands together, walks to the sticky fruit bowl on the counter and takes an apple that he doesn't want. He rinses it. Peels the label off. Takes a bite. End of conversation.

He hadn't been cruel; he had kept things even.

He wasn't mean, then. He had told her, evenly. He had told her over the next days what his plans were. He had packed. He had given her a kiss when he left. He had not been unkind. It had been a struggle, and a welter of emotion, but he had not been unkind. His anger had stayed poised inside him until he had closed the front door, lit a cigarette (he had smoked in a studentish way then), and as he walked down the short front garden path, tossed it back behind him as if it were a petrol bomb.

He had not been cruel to Mum, then, when it would have been easiest, when he was burning at his highest gas.

But that pizza, years later. Alone with Mum. Saying he didn't want pudding, just to disappoint her. Smoking cigarettes, to seem like more of a stranger. He had been mean, then. Then, he had been cruel.

He hadn't taken any pleasure in it, just as he hadn't taken any pleasure in neglecting Buster the dog.

He wanted to take back what he had said to Mum, 'I don't think I want anything, actually.'

He wanted to take back leaving Buster in the TV room. Yanking his lead. Shouting at him. He wants to take all the meanness back.

Jamie has made it as far as the check-in hall. But he hasn't checked in. He had taken a cab all the way to Heathrow, sitting, watching London through the window as its magnificence faded, becoming eventually the miserable outskirt rows of squat, pebbledash houses, low and grey, teenagers on the roadside in crispy-looking tracksuits, blowing dragon's breath from the cold.

All the way in the taxi as London was left behind, Jamie should have been feeling release – slackening fear, tightening joy, as the megalith city mile by mile disappeared. As all his ghouls disappeared. LA coming closer, LA; his house, his car, his life.

But in his head were thoughts of Buster, the dog. Of Mum, his mother. Memories of having inflicted deliberate pain. Deliberate. This is what he was now. Dad was right, he had worms in his head – in his heart – after all.

The logistics could take care of themselves. He'd do whatever needed doing on the phone. The hospice could recommend a funeral director, and he'd pay them to register the death or whatever else needed doing. Dad could go into the ground next to Mum.

*Don't cry now, Jamie. Don't cry.*

Jamie had paid the taxi. Got out with his suit carrier and a small extra bag of stuff he had accrued. Gone into the terminal.

Here he was, under the departures board.

Here he was.

Here he was and this is what he was:

Heartless.

Heartless.

His heart, where was it? Thrown back at number 24 Bolan Street like a petrol bomb, maybe. Buried in the sand of Malibu Beach, maybe. Up a tower, down a well. Guarded by a giant, kept in an eggshell. Surrounded by thorns, waiting to be kissed by a handsome princess. On a kite string. In a post box. Swimming in an ocean like a fish. Dead. Dead. Dead and cremated and scattered as ash on Ben fucking Nevis.

Under the departures screen. *Don't cry, Jamie.*

Is this what he was, now?

Heartless?

His heart left where?

When did he become this?

Jamie walks to the café at the end of the terminal building, he has not checked in yet. He will first go to the ticket issue desk and buy an upgrade to business class. He will not even attempt a freebie. He will buy it. And he will sit in his own big seat, legs long, all the way home. He will go to the ticket desk and buy his new, posh seat before checking in. And before going to the ticket desk, he will go to the café at the end of the terminal and buy a coffee. He thinks of Meryl. *Meryl Streep*. Somewhere in London. London churning and seething for so many bloody centuries. Too much. It was too much.

You just be brave, dear, said Meryl Streep, you just be brave.

And Jamie was brave: he was. He had been brave for years without knowing it, marching into battle alone, a boy, a child. He had defeated his Wall People, he had defeated his father, he had defeated all the things that had grasped on to his ankles in attempts to floor him. He had never asked for help, beyond that one time, with Dad. All Dad had done was taken the light bulb, and bravery had sweated out of Jamie in fear-form, as terrified yellow pee, he has wet the bed, again.

Bravery, bravery, Jamie was brave. He would not stay; and so he left.

He stands by the café, he does not join the queue. *I will have a large latte and a muffin!* Jamie wants to shout it. None of this skinny grande venti shit for him.

*I will have a large latte and a muffin.*

Jamie puts his free hand to the back of his head and his fingers begin to jab and tweak at his hair. He notices himself doing it this time. The back of his scalp must be a mess of scar-lines and aggravated tissue by now. He did it on screen once, can you believe it? On screen! When playing that stupid fucking emaciated artist, that he starved for, and went half crazy for – for what? For what turned out to be a piece of Hollywood schlock.

His head might fall off one day. Maybe right here, right now. Maybe fall off like a bowling ball and roll along the floor, hitting the skirting at the edge of the airport café, having picked up dust and hair and price tags and sugar packets and all sorts of gruesome crap on the way. Those little sugar-crusted sugar packets, discarded and wafted to the floor once the contents have been poured into a bad coffee.

Jamie wanted another chance, with Buster. He would take him hiking down Runyan Canyon, and let him talk to and sniff at the other dogs, and take him to breakfast afterwards, and let him sit on the sidewalk – the pavement? Not in LA, it's a sidewalk there – in the sun, while he, Jamie, read the paper. He'd get him a bowl of water. It wasn't about Beth, it was about the dog – the dog. Buster.

It was about himself – Jamie. *Don't cry, Jamie. Do not cry.*

It was about Mum. Who even then he should have known was ill – he could see it – he could see it! – the cancer cratering mercilessly into her face.

He should have seen it.

And then what? He would have been kinder? He would have not smoked the cigarettes and had a pudding without fuss? He would have turned up when she was sick? Turned up at the funeral? Bullshit. He would have spat with cruelty all the same, because that is who he was now.

What would have happened had he taken Mum's arm that afternoon? She would have stiffened in shock, that's what. And then she would have had it as a memory. When she died. That her son had taken her arm one afternoon. Her son from America.

He wanted another chance. He looked at the menu board, Modesto, Medio, Grandioso. Still he did not join the queue.

His head was loud. He wanted to sit down. He wanted a girl here, that he loved. To rest his head against.

Jamie turned away from the café, its menu board, its

340

queue, and walked. Past the check-in desks, A to E. Past the airline ticket desk. Under the departures board.

He went to the escalator, up into Arrivals. He hoicked his suit carrier further up his shoulder, even though it wasn't slipping.

He walked through the men with moustaches and name boards, out of the automatic revolving door, back into the cold. It was dark outside, now, winter dark, dark as the middle of the hardest night.

Jamie walked to the taxi rank, stood at the back of the file. It was moving fast. The flight would leave without him. No coffee, no aeroplane – airplane? No. Aeroplane here in London.

*Do not cry, Jamie. Jamie, don't cry, okay?*

Like Meryl Streep said, just be brave.

He *is* brave.

Brave and heartless.

# 6

Jamie sits on the low wall of the hospice car park. His bags are next to him, and his head is in one hand. In the other is a triangle of egg mayonnaise sandwich, from which he takes large, smooth bites.

It is cold to be eating sandwiches outside, but this is how Jamie wants to do it. He wants no one watching, he wants to eat alone, calmly from the bag of food that he has bought at the corner shop.

1 egg mayonnaise sandwich, in a plastic packet.

1 ham and mustard sandwich, in a plastic packet.

1 bag of honey roasted peanuts, in blue foil.

1 disgusting-delicious chocolate muffin, in printed cellophane.

1 bottle of mineral water, with a sports cap.

1 carton of pineapple juice, with a straw glued to its side.

As he has eaten each new food he has placed the

wrapping back in the plastic bag, so that it is now a lucky dip, a mixture of empty packets and full. The water grounds the bag at the bottom with its weight.

Food done, stomach hot with it, Jamie removes the water bottle from the bag and puts it on the wall next to him, and then ties the handles of the bag closed. Landfill.

He squeezes some of the water over his fingers, to rinse them. He rinses his mouth out and spits behind him, into the earth bed from which a hedge grows. He pushes two pellets of chewing gum into his mouth from a small pack.

He is sitting here, with no one to see him. He is sitting here alone. His stomach is hot and sickly, his skin and fingers are cold. Cold, cold, cold. Remember this cold in Los Angeles, where there is only really one season. Los Angeles, which is home. When back in Los Angeles, remember the cold of London, where Jamie was born. Whose accent Jamie carries round the world like a flag, but without pride. In LA, everyone's from somewhere else, and it doesn't matter. Another Englishman in the hood. Nobody cares. Peanut butter and jelly; America America; nobody cares.

Dad is inside the building behind him, and is probably dead.

Jamie left him over five hours ago, groping at the sheets and saying his name, and he's probably dead.

Jamie stands, and walks a few paces to the other wall,

which is higher than the little one he has sat on –
maybe eight feet high. The lighting here is dim. He
puts his damp hands against the wall, and then his
forehead, and gently, with no intention of hurting himself, bumps it against the bricks a few times. It is
enough.

He dusts the wall-grit that has stuck to his palms,
picks up his bags, including the plastic bag of waste
from his picnic, picks up the bottle of half-drunk water,
and walks around the car park to the hospice entrance.

The foyer is not too horribly lit, with floor lamps in corners and reading lamps on the reception desk. It is
quiet. The man behind the desk looks up and smiles
correctly at Jamie as he enters.

'Hi,' Jamie says, not quite walking up to the desk, just
dangling in the central well of the foyer, which is empty
but for him.

'Hello, sir. Can I help you?'

'No. I'm alright. I'm here to see my dad.'

'Could I ask you for his name?'

'Why?'

'It's after hours, sir. I'll need to check in the register,
and then get you to sign the visitors' book.'

'It's only ten o'clock.'

'Open visiting ends at nine. There's no problem, sir.
You can go up and visit your father no problem. You
just need to sign in.'

'Oh.'

Jamie walks up to the desk.

'James Hallow,' he says, 'is my dad's name. He's on the third floor.'

'Yup, and your name is?'

'Jamie. Hallow.'

'James and Jamie! Must get confusing.'

'Hm.' Jamie makes this short noise through his nose. He doesn't want to be nice. But he doesn't want to be rude either. This is not the man he wants to talk to. He wants to talk to someone else. 'Is Meryl here?'

'Meryl?' asks the man.

'Meryl, the volunteer. She was here earlier today.'

'Not that I know of,' says the man, which irritates Jamie and sees his brow and nose lift into disdain. *Not that I know of* is a fucking useless thing to say, for a man who is paid to sit behind a desk knowing of exactly that kind of thing.

'Is there anyone I can talk to,' says Jamie, 'about my father?'

The door to one of the lifts has opened, and two young women are walking out, obviously sisters, with the same dark hair. There is a fairer-haired man with them.

'Have you got your car here?' asks one of the girls. 'No, I took the tube straight from work,' says the man, as they walk behind Jamie towards the sliding door. Jamie notes that they don't need to sign out.

'God, it's such a relief getting out of here,' says the other girl as they exit.

The receptionist, if that's what he is, has cross-checked and now says, 'The sister in charge is Cathy, who'll be either on the second or third floor. I can buzz her, if you like?'

'No, that's alright. I'll just go up.'

After printing and signing and entering the time, Jamie goes to the lift. What he had wanted to ask, to whoever was the right person – the sister in charge, Meryl, a doctor if doctors existed and were taken seriously in this place – is whether Dad is dead or not. As the lift doors close it strikes him as a profoundly stupid and unaskable question, but it is what he had wanted to ask nonetheless.

He didn't want to be here, mechanically ascending floors, if his father was dead.

But, of course, if Dad *was* dead, they would have called. They had his number. And the *not that I know of* man downstairs would have said something, if Dad was dead. He wouldn't have accepted Jamie's signature and allowed him up, if Dad was dead.

So he must be alive.

Maybe he'd be alive for days to come – who the fuck knew? Not Jamie. That sunken body that looked to Jamie like a corpse already, could be alive for days. They had told him Dad was dying, but they had not said when it would happen.

Jamie is not a superstitious man. He never has been. The rituals he has witnessed in other people – an actor touching his earlobe in a certain way before going on stage, a friend knocking on wood, his father muttering the same gobbledegook prayer outside his bedroom door every night for years – he sees as ridiculous. Life doesn't work in serendipities, trotting itself meekly into place as if the world were decorated by numbers. Walking under a ladder will not bring bad luck, unless there's a builder up it with a wobbly can of paint. Bumping into a long-lost friend in an obscure place does not portend a host of orchestrating seraphim, only that the world is small and full of chance.

Finding presage in the paving stones, or one meaning in another, is akin to seeing people in the walls of your childhood house. It is nonsense. It is headache. It opens you up to slimy things. Believing in and acting on a jabberwocky destiny turns you to mush, to crap, to nothing worth anything. Kismet makes bad marriages, bad decisions, and bad futures. Life is – and to Jamie, that is what makes it bearable in the slightest – all chance.

And yet

Who knows what this means

But

Walking towards the door of his father's room, 414, Jamie feels once more, as he did at the airport, that there is some essential thing of his inside. It is why he turned from the terminal and came back here. It is something he doesn't understand.

It's not Dad. He's done with Dad – was done with Dad a long time ago. It's not a forgotten wallet, although that's sort of what it feels like – for fuck's sake, everything he needs, passport, keys, socks, even water he is carrying on his person at this moment like a camel. He doesn't know what what what, but he is here for something. He doesn't understand.

As he walks past other rooms, some with doors ajar and visitors inside, some dark and quiet, Jamie keeps remembering his mother's face, looking up at him from her biscuit when he told her he was leaving for Los Angeles. That face, that expression, is rotted now in a grave he has paid for but never visited. Because somewhere along the way he became a cunt. All indignation, all thorns, a dog-kicker.

Heartless. A heart neglected for so long that it grew legs and walked away.

And here is Dad's room. And here he is. Fuck, afraid.

If only Meryl would turn up and tap him on the shoulder with some silly sentence. Meryl who is *not* his mum, if she *were* his mum his heart would have stayed a serpent, without legs, unable to run. If she were his mum then his mum wouldn't be rotted with cancer in the muck of a suburban graveyard.

Heartless cunt. Dog-kicker.

Here at Dad's door.

It smells of fast food. Someone nearby is eating take-away. Jamie is not alone on the floor, that is the main thing. There are other visitors. Who also had to sign in the visitors' book, or who got here before the curfew.

And here he is, at Dad's door.

The door handle turns, and Jamie pushes into the room, with his suit carrier on one shoulder and a bag in one hand. He walks around the bed, putting his things down with a rustle by the far wall.

The overhead lights are on and the blinds are open, so the room is reflected in the large plate window. There is Jamie, in an overcoat, looking at his reflection and pulling his fingers through his hair. There is Dad, a shape covered in sheets on the bed behind. There is the room, its vase of flowers, its lightbulbs, its carpet, walls, salmony colours. There is no Margaret. She is neither reflected nor seen as Jamie moves to the window and twizzles the blind slats shut. He clears his throat.

'I'm just closing the blinds, Dad.'

He says it as if he had never left the room, as if he and his dad are domestic and easy – all is a-ok – bo diddly, baby – fine. The threatening tears and the fury and the self-disgust of the airport and the cab ride here do not register in Jamie's voice.

But before he turns away from the blinds and towards the room, Jamie blows out through his mouth, as if blowing hard on a candle. One hard breath out.

For a few seconds he shuts his eyes and takes refuge in the blackness of his eyelids.

Dad is alive. He is not dead in the bed. It is a relief that has Jamie's adrenalin gunning inside him, making his breath audible and his heart fast. His veins work to pump out the panic that had entered just now, when he came in and saw Dad lying so deadlike and still. In one respect, at least, this is not a childhood nightmare: Jamie is not alone in a strange room with a corpse. There are noises, quiet and rattly, coming from Dad's throat. His chest is moving in small lifts and drops.

Jamie isn't here for his father, we've already established that. He is here for himself. There is something of his in this room, and it is his heart. By coming back, he is unkicking the small kick he gave Buster, that stupid fucking dog. He is unsaying spite, and undoing carelessness. He is here to pick his heart up and put it back into its slot and do the right thing. Like he should have done with Mum – he should have taken her arm on the way to the pizza place, not for her happiness, but for his own. It would have made him the better person. It would have been the right thing to do. This is what Jamie tells himself.

He tells himself he is not here for his father.

His father is long gone. His father is nothing on this earth that could induce him to do anything. His father is nothing but a cheeseblock carcass. A dead old man.

Jamie stands by the side of the bed, looks down at

the hand that lies neatly on top of the sheet. It is knuckly and the skin looks thin, the veins are blue and run down the hand in humps. It has thrown enough punches in its life, this hand of Dad's. Not at Jamie – Dad in memory never hooked or uppercutted his son, only shoved, elbowed, squeezed, slapped, cowed. The punches got thrown at other big men, who Jamie never knew, other big men in bright red gloves. Jamie admits that there is something magnificent about the hand, still, frail and knobbly as it is. Hook, jab, uppercut. Dad's splintered hand. The veins are so big and blue there could be fish swimming down them.

'Dad,' says Jamie, 'I'm going to be here for a while. By the bed, alright?'

Of course Dad doesn't answer, he is down in the depths, caught in the seaweed, mermaids laughing at him. Jamie looks at his father's face. There are whitish flakes under the eyes, fluid that has dried up. It looks dirty.

He stands for a minute, in his coat, staring into the middle distance. Then he breathes in sharply through his nose and goes to the bathroom, that is full of pull-cords and unforgiving light, and toothbrushes – one new, one old – neatly on the sink top. Jamie pulls a handful of tissues from the box on the shelf. They are peachy-coloured and manufactured by a lesser, industrial brand. In some cupboard in this place will be a stack of them – two hundred boxes of cheap, peachy tissues for the blowing of drivelling, dying noses. Jamie dampens them under the tap, squeezes them, and returns to stand over his father. With a strong movement, he wipes underneath his father's left eye, and then his right. He repeats under the left, where there is still a flake of white.

'Fuck it.'

Jamie throws the used wad of tissue over his father into the bin, and turns around. He takes his coat off, drapes it on top of his pile of bags, and sits, legs crossed, into the armchair.

Touching Dad's face has unsettled Jamie. It is something he has not done before, through a shield of damp tissue or otherwise. He remembers being lifted up by Dad, like that time he was sick on the bathroom floor; he remembers the feel of Dad's violence; and he remembers those strangely lit happy moments, of Dad's arm resting nonchalantly on his own small shoulder. He suddenly remembers the feeling of Dad's hand in between his shoulder blades as they crossed the road together.

But there is no memory of Jamie ever himself initiating contact. There is no memory of reaching for Dad, ever.

Perhaps when he was a baby, he had reached out for his father's face? There's no way of knowing, now. Mum, who could have told him, is dead. And Dad . . . is what? Almost dead. With porridge for a brain. Silent.

Unable to swim up from his prehistoric, murky hollows and answer questions on childhood face-touching.

Soon it will be just Jamie, with all such answers to self-indulgent, pointless questions lost.

'Hi there,' says a voice in a half-whisper from the door.

Jamie looks up. It is a young woman, a nurse. Light brown and blue, and solid-looking. Pink-cheeked – one of those skin-tones that look perpetually blushing.

'He's asleep, is he?'

'Er, yeah, seems to be.'

'Oh, don't stand up, please. I'm Felicity, one of Mr Hallow's nurses.'

'Right,' says Jamie, he has stood up anyway, 'I'm Jamie. I'm his son.' He doesn't know what to do, a handshake doesn't seem right, so he stands, and puts his hand at the nape of his neck.

'Nice to meet you, Jamie,' says Flop, in a tone immediate and engaged. She looks him in the eye.

Jamie grabs uncomfortably on to the first thing. 'Are you Australian?' he asks.

'No, I'm from New Zealand, actually.'

'Oh, sorry.'

'It's alright.' She smiles. 'I'm used to it. Has your dad been asleep since you got here?'

'Yeah, I think so. I mean – yes.'

'And he hasn't shown any signs of being in pain?'

'In pain? No. I don't know.' Jamie's hand is twiddling

354

now. 'He hasn't moved at all. He's just been like that – lying there.'

Flop nods. 'Well,' she says, 'he's probably best left peacefully for the time being, then. I checked on him an hour ago, and he was fine, so I think we'll just leave him. But if he wakes up, or needs anything, or if *you* need anything, you know to just press that button there,' Flop gestures to a big orange button on a remote control on the bedside cabinet, 'or come straight out and get one of us.'

'What might he need?' Jamie says quickly, suddenly feeling that he is being hailed on by hard raining hail, suddenly feeling anxious.

'Hopefully he won't need anything. Please don't worry. I'm finishing up my shift now, but Claire'll be taking over looking after your dad, and she'll be around all night. It's just if your dad needs some pain relief. If he looks like he's in pain, just ask him. But really, Jamie, we're taking care of you tonight, so you don't need to worry. We'll be in and out, checking on your dad.'

'Will he wake up, then?'

Flop looks steadily at Jamie, but takes a breath. She shakes her head. 'I can't say for sure. I'm sorry. You just don't know. He may well stay sleeping, now. Or he may come to for a while. You just don't know.'

Jamie nods.

'Can I get you anything, Jamie? Would you like a cup

of tea? Or something to eat? The cafeteria's closed, but the visitors' kitchen is open all night and I'm sure there'll be something there.'

'No, I'm alright, thanks,' says Jamie. His chin is hanging close to his chest. There is a hard hail hailing on him, of pain relief and not waking up and an infinitely weird reality that he cannot fathom.

*No, I'm alright, thanks. No, I'm alright, thanks.*

It feels as if he has been saying no all day. No. No. No to everything. It's tiring, and hateful. No, no, no, he always says no. Stone-throwing no-ing.

'Actually, a cup of tea might be good. I don't even like tea,' he says, 'but I think I actually would like some now.' He looks at Felicity and smiles a shabby half-smile.

'I can get you something else, if you'd like? Coffee? Hot chocolate?'

'No, tea. Tea would be great.'

'Tea it is. I'll be right back. Milk and sugar?'

'Just milk, please, thanks.'

Felicity smiles, nods, looks at Jamie's unconscious father for a moment, and leaves for the kitchen.

And now here the tea sits beside him, he has put the mug on the floor next to the armchair. The tea steams tea tendrils upwards, and Jamie does not want to drink it yet. He just wants it on the floor beside him, warm. After Mum had drunk one of her millions of daily cups, the plastic tablecloth would have a hot, almost melty circle where the mug had sat, and Jamie would put his hand on it until the heat had gone.

Warm things made you feel less alone. Warm things like a mug of tea on the floor, a circle of heat on the tablecloth, a life in Los Angeles. Heat on your back as you drove, and the world was okay. A hot palm from Mum's mug, and the house felt benign. Steaming tea on the floor, and this room was less empty.

Dogs must do that, too. With warm tummies and muzzles they must make their owners feel happy.

But Jamie booted dogs away, shut them up in the TV room. Instead of a dog, he had tea. Felicity? Was that her name? The New Zealand nurse. She had brought Jamie this tea, and he was keeping it beside him like a companion. He pictures himself, with a joyless smile, despairing melodramatically over the cooling of his Good Friend The Tea, while remaining unmoved by his own father's death in the background.

With an angry, irrational urge Jamie wants to grab his father's hand – swimming with fish, blue and twisted, the only bit of Dad he can bear to look at for more than a minute. He wants to take it angrily, hold it angrily, without forgiveness have it in his own.

But he is frightened to.

*Be brave*, said Meryl, *be brave*.

But Meryl isn't here. Only the tea. Which Jamie picks up from beside him and grips tightly in his fingers.

'Dad?' says Jamie.

There is no answer. The breathing continues rhythmical and strained.

Jamie leans his head on to the back of the chair and looks at the ceiling. The mug is hot – too hot – in his hands. And the room is too brightly lit – too bright. He will get up and turn the main lights off. It's probably easier for Dad that way, also, with less light abrasive on his eyelids.

*Dad. Wake up.*

Jamie sits, his head back. He looks at the ceiling.

He has never understood his own heart; only that it feels like a slaughterhouse.

# 7

The room is dark, a decent shade of dark, and James Hallow can see her shape by the window. It is her shape because it carries her light, and her fearlessness. He will call out to her, as clear as a bell:

But no noise comes.

His throat is broken, someone has smashed it into pulp as he lay. It is full of glue. Someone has poured it full of glue.

Now what? What if she does not see him? What if she goes away and does not know he is calling to her?

He tries again, and this time a crippled sound emerges, a bubbly 'Ooo', which is forested at the back of his larynx.

With a strength that comes from nowhere – the beesips of protein drink long since used up – James pitches his arms into the air, to reach for her. They flail, and every time he throws them up, the sheer weight of them brings them back down hard – flop – on to the bed again. He holds them up and tries to hold them up, but they keep falling down. They are like caught fish, crazy and desperate.

'James,' says Margaret, all grace in the dimness, 'James, I see you.'

She takes two steps towards him.

But as she has spoken, so has Jamie. He has risen from the chair and he has said,

'Dad?'

Margaret stops. She looks at the son. He is looking down at his father, his fingertips touching the sheets.

'Dad?' he is saying.

Margaret has stopped as if in a net, caught by the knowledge that she must not go any further. It has been a burden to her always, knowing what is right and what is wrong like this. It has prevented her time and time again from running towards what she wants. Now, she wants to go to James, this man who is her friend. But the saints among us do not run towards their wants. They stay standing where they are.

So she is stopped in the centre of the room, knowing that it is wrong to go on, her heart smarting from the punch of this sudden goodbye.

James watches her. He has not yet noticed that Jamie is here beside him, the son he has been straining to conjure. All he sees is Margaret, suspended away from him. He continues to look at her.

For a moment he is confused. He looks at her and feels sure that she was coming towards him, coming to put her mineral-smooth hands on him. He knows he saw her approaching.

And yet she is no longer close. Yet she has stopped. Yet she is disappearing – he swears it – she is vanishing as if she had never come.

This confusion is threatening to a mind as worn and determined as James's. It is a pebble rattling in a thin glass. Without her he will sink back down, he is sure of it. His eyes start to close, and the seaweed once more begins to wrap itself around his feet.

But, a life raft, Jamie is here.

'Dad!' Jamie is saying, '*Dad*, I'm here.'

It is a gungy soup that surrounds James, but this persistent voice, belonging to the grown man that was once his small son, his Jamie, is enough.

James turns his head in the direction of the sound, and the seaweed is forced to loosen its grip; suddenly this moment has come.

He sees Jamie beside him, and hears him saying,

'Dad, I'm here.

'Dad, are you alright? Are you in any pain, Dad?'

Jamie speaks with a sense of alarm. Since the nurse put pain on the table, Jamie has been anxious over it. Unlikely as it sounds, it had not occurred to him that his father might be in pain at all, and the thought disturbs him.

But the old man just looks towards his son, and smiles.

He smiles.

It has been a losing battle, this life. James lost his brain to the sawdust floor forty years ago, and his heart and his self followed fastly after. But – it is a good way to die. With your son beside you.

When there is so much to say, but no gums or lips or tongue to say the so much with, all you can do is smile. It means you are happy.

'Dad, you know it's me, right? It's me. Jamie.'

He wants to add, 'your son', but even in this moment embarrassment claims its patch, and Jamie censors himself.

Dad is moving his head. Jamie cannot tell if it is a nod or a bob or a shake.

'Dad? It's me. Jamie.'

The facial ligaments are loose like laundry flapping, words won't come no matter how James manipulates his mouth.

'Dad?' says Jamie.

'Moo,' says James.

It is all he can manage.

Jamie does not rear back in disgust, or flare his features into a snigger. He only looks at his dad's face, that is pumping and chomping so hard to try to get something out.

'Dad? Are you in any pain, Dad? Do you need any pain medicine?'

'Mugh,' James is saying, 'Mugh,' and Jamie glances across to the big orange button on the nightstand. Maybe he should call the nurse.

He looks back at his father's face – and it *is* his father's face, he recognises it, despite the appearance of melting wax, the distended shapes, the monstrousness. It is the vastness of the nostrils that upsets Jamie the most, as if they have been eaten away. He doesn't understand it, how this can happen to a face – it is as if certain parts of it have already begun to decompose. He feels angry with his father for looking like this, for becoming this thing that curdles and squeezes at Jamie's diaphragm to see. Angry.

Before he can decide to call the nurse or not, a word arrows from James's mouth – he has done it! – the word he has been struggling for –

'Jamie,'

he says.

Jamie hears his name, muddily spoken as it is.

'Jamie,' says his father again.

He looks at his father, and his father is looking back at him.

'Yes, Dad.'

'Jamie.'

It is a perfect word. *Jamie*. It could be that the whole world is contained in that one name. Exhaled out, it hangs in the air like a drop of dew; exhaled back again, it recalls James to himself. This dewdrop word, born and born again each time James says it, contains within it everything.

Underneath his pyjama shirt James Hallow's heart is slowing down. His blood travels in dense, thick gusts. And Jamie does not know which one of them has done this – whether it was him or his father – but he sees that the index finger of his left hand is curled underneath two of Dad's.

Of course he cannot remove his finger, now that it is there.

'I won't call the nurse,' he says, 'I think we're fine,' and Dad's two fingers feel so heavy on top of his, they are nailing him to the spot, he is rigid with awareness of them.

Is it enough, the touch of a finger, when there has been so much else?

For James Hallow, it is enough.

*Jamie.*

*Jamie.*

With one of his son's fingers under his, as his heart crochets to a stop.

With the word *Jamie* as the whole world, and this lone, beloved finger as a flaming sword to turn every way, this life has been enough.

Whereas for his son? His son stands. His heart beats. Jamie will continue to stand like this, frozen by the embrace of his father's two fingers, until he is moved.

He will feel his father's dead fingers above his own, and he will not forgive.

If Jamie could walk from the room, down the corridor, into the lift, and out of the building – he would. If he could hail a taxi, blow from the cold, and go to Heathrow Airport – he would, he would. If he could upgrade to business class, smile at an air hostess, and settle into a flight home – he would have done so three hours ago. If he could take his finger out from underneath his father's – if only, he could, if only, he could.

But you can't choose these things. You can't choose who you love.

# ACKNOWLEDGEMENTS

Profound thanks to –

Georgia Garrett. Peter Straus. Jane Lawson, Rochelle Venables, Miriam Rosenbloom, and all at Doubleday.

Jane Lawson again. And again.

My father, Andrew – my unpaid editor, and, luckily for me, one of the world's greats.

My perfectly beautiful little Atticus, whose advent brought this all about.

RDWC. Without whom, there would be, not one word.